DISCARD

RUTHLESS STRANGER

MAFIA WARS - BOOK ONE

MAGGIE COLE

PULSE PRESS

DISCARD

This book is fiction. Any references to historical events, real people, or real places are used fictitiously. All names, characters, plots, and events are products of the author's imagination. Any resemblance to actual events or places or persons, living or dead, is entirely coincidental.

Copyright © 2020 by Maggie Cole

All rights reserved.

No part of this book may be reproduced in any form or by any electronic or mechanical means, including information storage and retrieval systems, without written permission from the author, except for the use of brief quotations in a book review.

PROLOGUE

Aspen Albright

"DON'T TURN AROUND," A DEEP VOICE MURMURS IN MY EAR, sending chills down my spine. His accent sounds like a mix of old-world Eastern European meets modern-day U.S., but I can't place exactly where it's from. I have to pay close attention to understand what he's saying, but it only makes my intrigue about him intensify.

The scent of scotch flares in my nostrils, mixing with bergamot and cardamom. A large hand wraps around me and slides along my stomach, creating a blaze of hot, nervous flutters zinging to my core.

I begin to turn my head, but his cheek holds mine in place. His stubble lightly scratches my skin, and I draw in a deep breath. "You don't seem to obey very well." Something about how he speaks tells me I better learn quickly.

Obey him? What does he mean?

"I'm sorry," I whisper. I'm not sure why I'm apologizing, and I shiver against his hard frame as the blinking lights of the city flash outside the window. The music from the surround sound is seductive. A woman sings, but it's in another language. The concoction of my overly due-to-get-laid loins, encouragement from my girlfriends to be "spontaneously reckless," and a slight buzz from the alcohol we've been drinking all day doesn't help me resist Mr. Stranger Danger's advances.

If his body didn't feel like I was melting into it, maybe it would help.

But why should I resist? I'm a freshly divorced, hasn't-gotten-laid-in-too-long-to-count woman on vacation.

What happens in Vegas, stays in Vegas, so I have nothing to worry about.

His pinky finger slips farther down my body, and he glides his other hand up my thigh, as if he owns me, tugging me closer to him. "Let me be clear about my rules. The blindfold will go on and stay there until after I leave. From this point forward, you give your full trust to me. Whatever I say goes." Everything about him is confident, with no room to argue.

My heart races faster, and anxiety fills my chest.

What am I doing?

This is so unlike me.

What if he's a crazy psychopath, and I end up sliced to pieces and left in the hotel room?

His hard erection presses against my spine. "Do you have any questions or objections?" The heat from his breath hits my ear and doesn't help me form any coherent thoughts.

I swallow hard. "Ummm..."

He flicks his tongue behind my lobe, and my lower body throbs.

I softly gasp and close my eyes, not able to construct any question, never mind speak it.

"You can still get out of this if you want," he murmurs and drops his hand lower, grazing my slit through my dress while nibbling on the curve of my neck.

I freeze. *Do I want to get out of this?*

His lips hit my ear again. "I require consent. Your friends said you want this. Is this true? Hmm?"

I open my mouth to speak, but nothing comes out. His thumb strums against me, as if I'm a guitar and he's a professional rock star who sells out arenas every night.

He could be. I know nothing about this man.

"Give me a yes," he demands in his sexy accent.

Somewhere inside me, the scaredy-cat, rule-following, usually prim and proper woman hides. The Vegas, carefree me takes a deep breath. "Yes."

"Good. Close your eyes and keep them shut. If you open them before I blindfold you, this ends. Understand?"

I nod, still not sure what I'm getting myself into.

"If you don't submit to me fully, there will be no warning. I will stop and leave. Have I made myself clear?" He drags his hand up my torso, slicing through my cleavage, then grasps my chin and pushes my head back on his shoulder, scraping his stubble against my cheek again.

A whimper escapes me. It's so tiny, I'm not positive it wasn't in my head.

"Answer me."

"Mmhmm." I can't get anything else out. His body is a torture chamber I want to volunteer for. It's warm. Every move he makes, his muscles contract, pulsing into my flesh.

His hand on my thigh inches to the inside. It's lightning straight to every nerve ending I have. He quietly grunts when I shudder then asks, "You've not done this before?"

I pull as much oxygen into my lungs as possible and hold it in. "What? Obey?"

He strokes my lips with a lonesome finger. "That and spend the night with a stranger."

My insides shake harder. "Correct." I hook my hands on his muscular thighs, trying to steady myself.

"You're nervous." He doesn't ask but states.

"I..."

He places his finger over my lips, and I hold my breath.

"Blindfold first." A cool satin goes over my eyes, and he secures it tightly around my head.

My eyes were already shut, but something about the finality of the blindfold makes my pulse spike more.

He repositions his body in front of mine. His frame towers over me, and I sharply inhale as his finger slides through my cleavage. "Do you know what I've wanted to do since I saw you from across the casino?"

"No," I whisper.

He doesn't answer me. His hand possessively holds the back of my head. The warmth of his breath hits my mouth as his lips buzz against mine. "Spend every second of the rest of the night making you unravel in ways you never have before."

My insides quiver as he unleashes the first bout of chaos through every atom of my being. His lips and tongue ignite a fire in me I didn't know existed, traveling across my jaw and neck, before he releases the strap of my dress and sucks on my breasts.

When he moves back up, I search for his lips, wanting to taste them. He never lets me. The entire night, I spend doing things I've never done before, but he never kisses me on the lips.

The next morning, I wake up. Sunshine bursts through the window. I turn to the other side of the bed, expecting to see him.

But he's gone. A cut silk tie, which must have been my blind-fold, lies on the pillow next to me. Every other trace he was ever with me is gone, except for the delicious scent of his skin still clinging on mine.

It was supposed to be this way. I knew and agreed to the terms. He kept his word and stuck to his end of the deal. But

I still notice the ache of disappointment he's gone. Part of me is giddy from everything we did and all the ways he made me feel. The other half wonders if it was better to have never known anything so excruciatingly pleasurable existed.

There isn't a bone in my body that isn't aware I'll never experience anyone like him ever again.

I let myself get lost in my trip down memory lane for a brief moment. Then I get up, shower, and go to put on my clothes from the night before. I figure I'll do the walk of shame out of the high-end suite and onto the sixth floor to the room I'm sharing with my girlfriends. Panic fills me when I can't find my panties, bra, or dress.

I open the closet, and a new, white, very expensive sundress is hanging there. It has a built-in bra, but there are no undergarments anywhere. A note is attached. It reads:

My Krasotka,

Your dress and bra will be delivered to your room after they are cleaned. I'm keeping your panties.

A scribbled letter resembling an M is at the bottom of the paper.

I gape at the note and dress for a minute then bite on my smile.

Pervert.

M. His name starts with an M. Or is it for his last name?

That's all I know of Mr. Stranger Danger. He could stand in

front of me, and I wouldn't know it's him. I have zero clue what he looks like, his real name, or anything else about him. The only thing I'm positive about is his voice, bergamot and cardamom scent, and the way his body formed perfectly against mine. Most of the things he said, I didn't even understand since he often spoke in another language. I'm not sure how he knows what room number is mine, but for the first time in my life, I'm not going to overanalyze it.

Krasotka. He kept saying it all night, as if it were his pet name for me. What does it mean?

I grab my phone and type it into the search bar. It's Russian.

Krasotka: Gorgeous, Beauty.

Besides all the mind-blowing O's he gave me, it hits me that I genuinely feel happy and alive again. I haven't felt anything but unwanted, sad, and ugly in a long time.

For some crazy reason, I'm glad he kept my panties.

1

Aspen

A Few Days Earlier

"CONGRATULATIONS. YOUR DIVORCE IS NOW FINAL." KORA beams and holds her vodka tonic in the air.

I groan. "You shouldn't look so happy."

Her brown eyes widen. She pushes her dark hair off her creamy skin and tucks the lock behind her ears. She sternly reprimands me. "Yes, I should. You're lucky I gave you my bestie treatment. I used every trick in the book to get this done quickly and without a long, drawn-out battle. Trust me on this."

Kora is Chicago's top divorce attorney. Usually, the uber-wealthy women hire her, but she didn't even charge me to end my twenty-year marriage to Peter. Not that I was rolling in money married to Peter, nor am I now. I should be, but most of our marriage, Peter spent using my salary to start one failed business after another. At least, he told me he was using the money for businesses.

I tried to be a supportive wife, always cheering him on and encouraging him to follow his dreams. But I was stupid. My friends often told me to get my head out of la-la land. They warned me to stop allowing him to use all the money I made and make him get a job. I thought they didn't understand and were harshly judging him. I was wrong and should have listened to them.

Peter came from an upper-class family, and when his dad died, he inherited a few million. I couldn't touch it. But the irony of Peter's father leaving it in a trust and out of my control is Peter didn't need me to dwindle it down. He went through it all in two years. Then he went back to spending every penny in our bank account.

But I didn't divorce him because of money. The breaking point came when I found out why he wasn't paying attention to me in our bed. And that reason was a twenty-something-year-old blonde he bought new boobs for...with my salary.

"You're lucky I got him to agree to only a tenth of alimony," Kora reminds me.

I should only be grateful, but it burns me I have to pay him anything. "The law is so screwed up. I worked my butt off for twenty years. He gets to do whatever he wants and live off me. As a reward for my work ethic and his laziness, I get to pay him for the next ten years or until he gets married again. Whoever created alimony sucks."

"Yep. But it's a sliver of what it could have been. Tell me you're happy." She holds her glass out, still waiting for me to clink it.

I cave, hit it, then take a long swallow of my martini. The chilled gin slides down my throat in a smooth burn. "I am grateful it's over and for you. Thank you."

Now, what am I going to do?

I'm thirty-eight, divorced, and have nothing to show for the last twenty years.

At least I still have my job.

Why did I get married at eighteen?

Peter Albright swept me off my feet. I met him shortly after I graduated high school. Within three months, we got married. He was twenty-five and seemed to have it all together. I didn't know he lived off his grandparents' trust fund, or that it would run out within our first year of marriage.

Instead of going away to college in California as planned, he convinced me to get a job with the city. He claimed I didn't need my degree since we were getting married, and it was more important we be together. So I gave up my scholarship and took an assistant position in the zoning department.

My bosses promoted me over the years, but I can't go any higher since I don't have my degree. I run circles around everyone I work with but don't get nearly the pay I should. Since Peter never had a job or brought money in, I never ventured outside of my department or went back to school.

"Is it over?" Hailee's voice quietly asks.

I spin. "Yes. Thanks to Kora."

Hailee hugs me, and her blonde hair falls in my face. She pulls back, and her blue eyes are full of sympathy. Out of all of us, she's the most sensitive. Since kindergarten, we've been joined at the hip.

"I'm okay," I assure her.

She smiles, nods, and sits in the booth next to Kora.

"Is Skylar coming?" Kora asks.

"No. She had to work late. But she said she's in."

"Good. I'll book it, then."

"Book what?" I inquire.

Excitement crosses Hailee's face. "It's a surprise."

My stomach drops. I don't like not knowing what's going to happen. Maybe it's from my marriage to Peter all these years. I always waited for the other shoe to drop. I didn't used to expect bad things to happen. But over the years, calls from debt collectors, overdrawn bank and credit accounts, and canceled plans added up. If I got through a day with nothing unexpected happening, I breathed in relief. Since I separated from Peter, I realized how much anxiety he created in my life.

He is no longer with me, but I carry the residual effects of twenty years. I still hold my breath when I attempt to pay for something even though my finances have been in my sole control for the last few months.

"Please tell me," I demand.

Kora shakes her head and smirks. "Nope. You will receive a list of items to pack via text."

"Pack? I don't have money to go anywhere that requires a suitcase."

"Yep. We know. But that is why you have three awesome friends."

My gut flips. "This isn't necessary. I'm not a charity case for you to all take on. Kora already gave me her services for free. I appreciate everything you all have done, but now we need to resume normalcy."

Kora snorts and does something on her phone. "Please. It's all booked. You're going."

Hailee claps and glows. "I can't wait. It's going to be amazing!"

Heat rises to my cheeks in anger.

They only want what is best for me. Don't get mad at them.

I count to five then say, "Can you please cancel whatever it is you just did? I'm not—"

"No. We can't. It's paid for and not refundable. Smile, say thank you, then drink up," Skylar butts in. "Move over."

I slide across my seat. "I thought you were working?"

"Decided I was finished for the night. Told Bowmen to do his own ordering."

"Wow. It's about time. What happened?" Skylar works for a high-end fashion designer. She always knows how to dress and takes risks the rest of us don't. Like right now, her hair is magenta. I could never pull it off, but she's a work of art. Everything she wears, whether makeup, hair, or clothes, is a statement.

"I don't want to talk about it. I need alcohol." She picks up my glass and takes a long drink.

"Help yourself," I tease.

She sighs and sets it down. "Sorry."

"You're fine."

She motions to the bartender to give us another round and points to my drink. She turns back to us. "Tomorrow can't come soon enough. What time do we need to be at the airport?"

"Airport?" I blurt out, my panic rising.

"Chill out. You're going to thank us," Kora insists.

Before I can argue any further, Skylar's hazel eyes harden. "Tell me you didn't end up paying that loser." She removes her eyeglasses and cleans them on her shirt.

"Sorry, can't." I take another sip.

"I got it down to a tenth," Kora says in an insulted tone and crosses her arms.

Skylar grunts. "Still too much."

Hailee rushes to Kora's defense. "It's not her fault. She did the best she could."

"Yes, she did," I agree.

"Chill. I'm not judging your skills. It just burns me he gets anything after all the years he mooched off Aspen."

"Can we discuss something else? I don't want to think about Peter anymore," I voice.

The server comes over with our drinks. I finish the last of my martini and hand her the empty glass. "Thanks."

"You need anything else, ladies?" she asks. Her smile is big, displaying her perfectly straight white teeth. Her pink T-shirt stretches over her pert breasts perfectly. She's only in her twenties and blonde, and everything about her reminds me of the boobs I bought for Peter's new girlfriend, who also wears a diamond ring courtesy of my salary. But I'm sure he'll never marry her since he'll lose my alimony.

Don't be a disgruntled woman. It's not the waitress's fault.

I force myself to smile. "We're good. Thank you."

She leaves, and I drink a few more mouthfuls of my martini.

"So, what time do we meet at the airport?" Skylar repeats.

"Six. Flight's at eight. Gives us time to get through security and have a mimosa breakfast," Kora replies.

My chest tightens. "Can we go back to me not being a charity case?"

"Can we stop this conversation now since we aren't changing our surprise for you?" Hailee responds with a hopeful smile.

"Ugh. You're all—"

"Amazing friends who you love to pieces?" She bats her eyelashes at me.

I snicker and give up. "There's no point in fighting this, is there?"

Skylar holds her glass out. "Nope. Cheers to your new life. To sunshine and new beginnings."

"Don't forget new men," Kora adds.

"Nope. A man is what got me into this mess. I'm staying away. The chastity belt is on forever."

Kora dramatically gasps. "Oh, please. Don't be a boring divorcée."

"I'm not joking."

Skylar tilts her head and stares at me.

"What?"

"You know, at some point you need to get back on the horse, right?"

"No, I don't."

"Mmmm, yeah, you do," she insists.

"I don't need it in my life. I'm enjoying my independence."

"So don't get serious. Saddle up and leave the stallion in the barn when you're done."

Hailee spits out her drink, and a drop of alcohol hits my cheek.

She covers her mouth, laughing. "Oh, jeez. Sorry! Skylar!"

"What?"

Kora bites her smile. "Skylar's right. It's time for service. You're past your mileage date."

I put my burning face in my hands. "You guys!"

"We need to find you a grade-A stud. Someone who won't get emotionally attached and will show you what real sex is like," Skylar says.

I nudge her with my elbow and pick my head up. "Stop. And I'm not a virgin. Peter wasn't bad in bed."

My three friends all gaze at me with eyebrows raised.

"Why are you looking at me like that?"

"When wasn't he bad in bed? When you were in your twenties, and he paid attention to you?" Kora asks.

"Gee, thanks for reminding me that I wasn't attractive to him anymore once I hit thirty."

"He's an ass," Kora quickly replies.

The others agree.

"Whatever. Peter is no longer my problem. Well, minus the alimony."

Kora groans. "Seriously, it's an unheard of deal I negotiated for you."

I pat her hand. "Sorry. I know it is. And I'm so grateful to you. But I'm done with him and all men. They are nothing but a drag on my finances and independence. There is nothing they can offer me I can't do myself."

Hailee smirks. "Nothing but sweaty muscular flesh and O's all night."

17

"I can get all the O's I need on my own, thank you very much."

"Not the same," Skylar chirps and drinks her martini.

Kora leans in. "Don't turn around now, but Mr. Bad Boy just walked in."

Skylar and I both twist in our seats.

A tall, rugged-looking guy with a five o'clock shadow, expensive black leather jacket, and cocky grin catches us checking him out. He wiggles his eyebrows at us, removes his jacket, and displays his perfectly fitted T-shirt over his sculpted chest. His left arm is covered in tattoos.

"I said not to look right now!" Kora reprimands us.

I turn back. "Too young. He's barely thirty."

"Does that matter?" Skylar asks.

"I wouldn't turn him down," Hailee claims.

"I'd drop to my knees and play cougar," Kora follows.

We all laugh. When we quiet, Hailee locks eyes with me.

"What?"

"So, you want a silver fox, then?"

My stomach flutters. "No. I don't want anyone."

She taps her fingers on her glass. "But if you had to choose between younger or older, you're picking a new daddy?"

I choke on my drink.

Skylar's eyes light up. "Ahh...now we're getting somewhere."

I shake my head. "Nope. I'm done with men."

I say it confidently, but a twinge of disappointment flares when it comes out of my mouth. But I know I need to stay as far away from men as possible. My experience is they are nothing but trouble.

I trusted Peter. For twenty years, I gave my heart to him. The risk of love isn't worth the pain of betrayal. And the ink on my divorce papers isn't even dry yet. The last thing I need is any man touching me.

"Being lonely is better than recreating what I just went through. If it's just me, all I have to do is fend for myself. Nothing can go wrong. But if it does, it's my fault and no one else's. So, while I appreciate your concern for my relation-ship status, there is nothing I need or want from a man." It comes out strong and sure, but my friends don't appear as if they believe me.

So I ignore their looks and change the subject. One thing I refuse to do is bend on my promise to myself. It's time to find out what makes me happy and discover my purpose in life. As Peter proved, a man isn't going to help me do either of those things.

2

Maksim Ivanov

THERE'S A JOLT AS THE PLANE LANDS, AND THE GUYS HOLLER IN celebration. My brother, Dmitri, is getting married. We chose Vegas for his bachelor party.

There are ten of us—my brothers, Boris and Sergey, and Dmitri's fiancée's brother, Chase. Our friends Killian, Steven, Noah, Xander, and Jamison round out our crew. It's around four in the afternoon, Vegas time. The drinks started when we got on the plane in Chicago, and the party atmosphere is only going to get more intense once we hit the Strip.

My phone vibrates, and I pull it out of my pocket. I internally groan. Jade, a woman I've had a long-term, on-again, off-again, who-knows-what-the-hell-we-are relationship with, texts me.

Jade: *Let's get together soon.*

She always does this.

I ignore her text. The last time we were together, I told her I'm over playing her games. For years, I've tried to be more with her, but she won't commit. During our last conversation, I put it on the line. I gave her an ultimatum, and she chose to end things. That was a few months ago. I haven't heard from her since.

It wasn't the first time I told her I wanted more from her. She always turns me down then comes strolling back into my life. But this time, I told her there would be no more chances. We'd done it too many times. Together. Not together. Back again. It's gotten exhausting, and I can't take it anymore.

To ease the blow, I've thrown myself into my work, accelerating the timeline on real estate projects my brothers and I have gotten involved in. In my younger days, I would have gone out on the town and found a woman to help me get over my battered ego and heart. But I've stayed away from all women, not wanting any of the drama that comes with dating or sometimes even just casual sex.

Living in Chicago, there's always plenty of opportunities to find someone new. Even though I'll be forty-six in a few months, the ability to have a different woman in my bed every night doesn't get any harder. When I was younger, I assumed it would be.

I was wrong. It seems the older I get, the more attractive I am to women. I thought when I was younger that time would make women run from me. But the older I get, the more attention they give me. Some of them even ask me out. Many of them stare at me, as if they can't help themselves. It's as if I could have any woman in the city—except Jade.

Ignore her. Do not fall back into her game.

I put my phone back in my pocket and grab my bag from the overhead bin. The other guys are all in front of me, and I duck so my head doesn't hit the ceiling and follow them onto the tarmac. Two black cars wait to take us to the Bellagio. My brothers and Killian go in one car. The other guys go in the second.

"Everything okay?" Dmitri asks when I sit next to him.

"Yes. Hand me a vodka."

Sergey already has the bottle and pours me a glass.

I take a swig, and the burn of the vodka travels down my throat and into my stomach. I grimace. "This is cheap vodka."

Killian grunts. "Did you not tell the company the Russians were coming when you ordered the cars?" He's full-bred Irish. His grandparents migrated to the U.S. when his parents were children. The O'Malley clan followed, and they soon were running Chicago. There's a mix of O'Malleys who take part in their crime family and those who have steered clear of it. Killian's immediate family has tried to avoid it but at times have gotten pulled in.

Killian's sister, Nora, and Boris are together and having a baby in a few months. For years, they had a secret affair and kept it from Killian. My brothers and I knew. We kept warning Boris to stay away from Nora for different reasons, but one of the biggest was his friendship with Killian. The two both box and have been joined at the hip since we were kids. And Nora was expected to marry an Irishman. When she and Boris finally admitted to Killian they were together and pregnant, I had to stop him from killing Boris—or at least trying. If the two released their wrath on each other, I'm not sure who would win. So I went with Boris when he went to tell Killian.

Plus, we had reasons Killian needed to get over it. There were threats against the O'Malleys and Ivanovs, and we needed to eliminate them together.

"Funny. I'm switching to scotch when we get to the hotel anyway." I set the glass in the holder.

The drive from the private airport to the Strip isn't long. We pull up to the Bellagio. The valet takes our bags, and the ten of us walk into the hotel.

Gold-plated tray ceilings match the colors on the floor and reception desk. An oversized gold horse is situated in the middle of the lobby, along with blue couches. Guests stand in a long line, waiting to check in. Others sit on the couches with cocktails in their hands, wearing lanyards and name tags you get when you go to a convention. Thick red ropes create an area for VIP check-in, but it, too, is crowded.

An employee stands near the entryway. She's young, probably in her mid-twenties, and could walk the runway.

So Vegas cliche.

She smiles big and holds a clipboard and pen. She looks up and addresses me. "Sir, are you VIP?"

"Yes."

"Can I get your names for your rooms? It will help expedite you past this line."

"I can do better than that." I remove the booking reservation from my pocket and hand it to her. Everyone is on it.

She glances at it. "This is great. Why don't you go to the bar or pool and we will text you when your rooms are ready? There is a large convention here, and I'm afraid everyone showed up at the same time. Can I use the number on this reservation?"

"Sure."

"I'm ready for drinks in the sun," Killian claims.

"You just want to check out the women," Dmitri says.

"You're still single for a few more weeks," Sergey smirks.

Dmitri slaps him on the head. "Don't get any stupid ideas."

Everyone except Killian, Sergey, and me are married or in relationships.

"You can still look."

Dmitri snorts. "Not interested."

We head to the pool and go straight to the bar. The sun is hot, and the pool water sparkles. Guests fill almost all the loungers. Some people are swimming. Pop music blares from the speakers. I order a scotch, ready to have something besides vodka.

We push several tables together and sit down. My phone vibrates again, and I sigh.

"What's wrong?" Dmitri asks.

I glance at my phone. "Jade."

Dmitri arches an eyebrow. "She hasn't been around lately. You off again?"

"No. We're done."

"But she wants to get together?"

I swipe my screen to read the message.

Jade: *Are you ignoring me?*

I set my phone on the table. "Yep. Same old Jade."

Dmitri gives me a disapproving look. "Are you really done this time?"

"Yep."

"Sorry, brother, I know you like her, but you can do better. I've always thought she's kind of a bitch," Sergey interjects.

I point at him and defensively say, "Watch your mouth."

He scoffs. "You're going to take her back, aren't you?"

"No. But you don't need to be disrespectful toward her." We may not be together, but I'm still not going to let anyone degrade her. Jade does have a hard exterior, but she hasn't had it easy. If anyone knows what a rough upbringing is like, it's my brothers and me. So I do give her more leeway than I probably should.

"Has it been nine or ten years you've been on and off with her?" Dmitri asks.

I groan. "Eleven. And it sounds so bad out loud, doesn't it?"

Dmitri holds his hands up. "I'm not judging, but maybe it's time to stop the insanity."

"The insanity?"

"You know. Doing the same thing over and over but expecting different results?"

I take a big drink of scotch and let it sit in my mouth for a few seconds before swallowing. "That's why I'm not returning her message."

Dmitri nods. "Good. Don't. Time to find someone new."

I don't respond. I'm not sure I'll ever find anyone besides Jade who grabs my attention the way she does. She's been the one I've wanted for so long. We've taken our breaks, but I never stopped craving her when we were on them. And no one else ever seemed to fill the spot in my heart I have for her.

But something has shifted in the last few months. There's a peace surrounding my feelings for her I haven't felt before. It's not always present, but every now and then, it hits me. I'll always care for and respect her, but I've finally come to accept we aren't going to be together. Something in me snapped when she let me go this time. All the years of waiting for her to love me back came to a head.

I can't make her love me. I've tried. She doesn't. I wonder if she's capable of loving anyone or if it's just me. Either way, I can't continue the toxic cycle we're in. There's enough destruction in my life, and I don't need it in my relationship with my woman, too.

My phone buzzes again, but this time, it's the front desk.

"Time to check in," I tell the guys.

We all rise to leave.

"I'll get the tab," I say.

They leave, and I wait to pay. Four women sit at a table off to the side. I try not to eavesdrop, but it's impossible. They've been drinking and are excitedly talking.

"So, you would be okay getting back on the stallion if a sexy stranger blindfolded you, you couldn't see his face or know his name, and there weren't any relationship consequences after?" one of the women asks.

A sexy voice fills my ears. It takes everything I have not to look at her. She laughs. "Yes. And he would be bossy and order me around all night. But that will never happen, so I guess I'm keeping my chastity belt on."

Another woman groans. "Remove the chastity belt. I command you!"

"Yeah, seriously. After everything Peter put you through, it's time."

"Ugh. Did you have to mention his name? I was having fun," the angel says.

The bartender hands me the bill, and I give him my credit card instead of cash so I can listen longer.

"Sorry. Forgot it was a jerk-free weekend. So, are you still against being a cougar?"

"You make me sound sixty. I'm still under forty," she reminds her friends.

"Yeah. And there are lots of hot men under forty."

"Please. If I'm removing the chastity belt, give me a man who knows what he's doing."

Her friend snorts. "There are plenty of men who are younger and know exactly what to do. You should reconsider."

"This is my fantasy, remember? Don't be pushing your bottle feeders on me."

I chuckle inside.

The bartender hands me the receipt and my card back. "Thanks."

"You, too." I sign, turn, and intentionally walk past the four women. I can't stop myself, and when I get to the door, I spin to see what the woman looks like. She's easy to spot since she's sitting next to a woman with magenta hair.

I don't have any expectations, but the blood pumps harder in my veins. She's naturally exotic and exquisite. I could be wrong, but I assume she's part Native American and part European. Her eyes match her thick, straight, dark hair. It flows past her shoulders. Long lashes, heart-shaped lips, and a perfectly straight nose adorn her oval face.

Her eyes lock on mine, and I freeze. Her cheeks blush, and her lips slowly twitch, but a man steps through the door and bumps into me, forcing my gaze from hers. It knocks me out of my trance.

"Sorry," he says.

"My fault." I tear my eyes away from her and go into the hotel. I check in to my suite, take a shower, and am still thinking about her after I'm dressed.

My phone rings, and my gut drops. I answer it. "Jade, we aren't doing this anymore."

"What are you doing tonight?" Her no-nonsense voice comes barreling through the line.

I close my eyes and sit on the bed. "Did you hear what I just said?"

"Maksim—"

My heart pounds harder. "We've both been clear about what we want. I'm not doing this anymore."

Her voice softens. "I miss you."

Don't fall for it again.

She always does this to me.

"Have you changed your mind? Are you ready to stop playing games?" I ask but already know the answer.

"Why does it have to be your way or no way?"

Here we go again.

"I'm done with your guilt trip. It won't work this time," I angrily spout.

"Guilt trip? That isn't really fair, now is it?"

"Yeah, I think it's spot-on about what you do."

"Maksim, I'm on my way over. Let's talk."

Jade's idea of talking is keeping me in bed until the next morning.

How many times have we had this exact conversation?

The outcome is never going to change. Enough is enough.

"Jade, I'm in Vegas. Even if I wasn't, you aren't welcome to pop in anymore. I already removed you from security."

She draws in a deep breath.

I stare at the ceiling. I'm lying, but it's something I need to address when I return to Chicago.

This is the right thing to do.

Pain fills her voice. "So that's it? You're going to push me out of your life, as everyone else has done to me?"

My heart drops. I hate when she goes into victim mode, but I also despise hurting her. I want to tell her it's her fault for pushing everyone away, but I refrain. "I'm sorry, Jade. I hope you find whatever it is that will make you happy. Let's not have this conversation again. I need to go. Goodbye." I hang up before she can say anything more or make me feel worse.

It needed to be done.

It's the same thing I told her the last time I saw her.

Part of me feels proud I stood my ground with her, but the other side wants to call her back and see if she's okay.

Don't do it.

I leave the room and meet my brothers in the casino. The guys are all around the bar. Boris is glued to the screens, reviewing the bets he made on the games. The rest of the guys are at a table watching the screens, too.

"Scotch?" Dmitri asks.

"Double."

He nods to the bartender and holds up two fingers. "You talked to Jade, didn't you?"

I grunt.

He studies my face. "Don't let her ruin your night."

"I'm not."

"Is this the first time you've talked to her since you broke it off?"

"Yep."

The bartender puts my scotch down, and I take a big swig.

Dmitri pats my back and points around the room. "Maybe you should take advantage of the atmosphere. Lots of beautiful women here."

"Not—" My mouth goes dry. I can't see her face. All I see are her crossed legs and the back of her body. But it's her. I know it's her. Plus, her magenta-haired friend is at the table.

Suddenly, the word interested can't seem to come out of my mouth.

Maybe I should take advantage of the atmosphere and information I learned while waiting to pay the bar bill earlier.

She wants a wild night with no drama. I've had no desire to touch anyone besides Jade. But the urge to give this woman, a total stranger, exactly what she wants ignites in my belly. It smolders within me for the next several hours until I can no longer hold myself back. I nurse several scotches. When I see her friend with the magenta hair get up to go to the bathroom with another one of her friends, I make my move and approach them.

I've never done anything like this. But it's Vegas, I tell myself. And what happens in Vegas, stays in Vegas. It's a perfect situation. No one gets hurt. Both of us have a fun night. We go our separate ways.

Like all the years I thought Jade would change her mind, I'm once again wrong. But this time, there are more consequences to my actions.

3

Aspen

LOUD MUSIC, THE DINGING OF SLOTS, AND FLASHING LIGHTS create the atmosphere. Everywhere you glance, people are drinking, gambling, or watching the big-screen televisions. Hailee and I are at our table, waiting for Kora and Skylar to return from the restroom.

"What about those guys?" Hailee points to a cocky group of guys in their thirties. Televisions cover the wall, and they are watching the games.

I shrug. "Hot and almost all have wedding bands."

She winces. "Whoops. Didn't look."

A younger, light-haired man appears out of nowhere and slides in the seat next to me. He slurs into my ear. "Can I buy you a drink?"

I jump.

His blue eyes are bloodshot, and he reeks of too much alcohol. His head sways, and he brings his face closer to mine.

"No, thanks.

He wiggles his eyebrows and puts an arm around me. "Come on. One drink."

"I'm good." I escape his grasp and scoot my chair closer to Hailee. She puts her hand over her mouth, laughing.

He points at Hailee and circles his finger. "How about you?"

She shakes her head. "All good. We were leaving anyway."

"Noooo." He pouts then a goofy grin forms. "The party is just starting, and I'm it!" He pounds on his chest.

We rise and link arms. Hailee waves. "Bye."

"You girls are no fun!" he calls after us.

"That's why I'm never going cougar," I claim. "Too much babysitting."

Hailee snorts and steers me toward a slot machine. "I never said take the inebriated ones who can't handle their liquor home." She sits at a machine, and I take the seat next to her.

She slides her card into it and pulls the lever instead of using the buttons. "It's so much more fun going old-school. I wish we could still use coins." She hands me her card. "Here. Play."

"I'm good." It was nice enough my friends brought me on this trip, but the last thing I'm going to do is spend their money gambling. And my budget is too tight to waste anything.

"There you are," Skylar's voice booms behind us.

I spin in my chair.

Hailee glances behind her then resumes playing her slot machine.

"You took long enough. We thought you got lost," I admit.

Skylar and Kora disappeared for over an hour. Hailee and I both finished off two martinis.

They exchange a smirk-filled glance. Then Skylar takes the chair on my right side and pulls it into the aisle so she's in front of me. "So..." She bites her lip, as if she's going to laugh.

Kora takes a chair next to Hailee and drags it next to Skylar. She sits, too, staring at me like she knows a dirty little secret.

My belly twitches with nervous flutters. "What are you two up to?"

They glance at each other right as Hailee pulls the lever again. The machine turns neon pink and flashes while dinging loudly.

"Oh my...holy!" Hailee cries out. The numbers continue skyrocketing up.

The four of us jump up and cheer, continuing to watch the slot machine numbers get higher and higher until it finally quiets.

"Twenty thousand dollars!" Hailee screams.

"How did you do that?" Skylar asks.

"I just...holy...twenty thousand dollars!" Hailee shouts.

We rotate between gaping at the machine and hugging Hailee.

"Twenty thousand dollars!" Hailee repeats, her eyes wide.

"This must be an all-around lucky night. Hopefully, the luck hits Kora and me, too," Skylar chirps, and her smile tells me my instincts are correct, and she's up to something naughty.

"What are you talking about? I didn't win anything," I claim suspiciously.

Kora slips her arm around my shoulder. "I'd say you hit the jackpot."

"What are you talking about?" I ask.

Kora glances at Skylar.

Hailee hits the button, and a ticket pops out of the machine. "I need to go to the cashier. There's no way I'm gambling this away!"

Kora's lips twitch. "We'll go with you after we escort Aspen to her suite."

I cross my arms. "My suite?"

Another look I can't decipher passes between Skylar and Kora.

Hailee gets over her shock. "What have you two been doing all this time?"

Kora tightens her arm and spins me. "Let's talk about it on the way upstairs."

"You're confusing me right now."

Skylar steps on the other side. "Just trust us. You'll thank us tomorrow."

"For what?"

"Umm...hello! I just won twenty grand!" Hailee declares and steps next to Skylar.

"We know. We're excited. Put your ticket in your pocket for a few minutes. We have to drop Aspen off."

What is she talking about?

I stop walking. "I'm seriously confused right now."

"You and me both. What's more important than cashing out my twenty G's?" Hailee asks.

Skylar smirks. "Come with us and find out."

"Ugh. Fine. I hate it when you two do this kind of stuff," Hailee whines.

"Do what?"

"Leave me out."

I raise my hand in the air. "I'm not in the knowledge zone, either."

We get to the elevator right when the doors open. Everyone steps out, and the four of us step in. Kora slides a key card and punches a button.

"We're on six," I say.

Skylar points to everyone but me. "We're on six. You're on thirty for the night."

My stomach flips. It's as if it's aware of what's to come. "What are you talking about?"

"Skylar, Kora, what is going on?" Hailee demands.

The elevator dings and comes to a stop. The doors open. Kora and Skylar each grab my hand and pull me out.

"You'll see," Kora replies.

Hailee continues to grumble, following us down the hall, and I don't say anything. I've had too many martinis to count, and I'm used to Skylar and Kora being secretive. They always seem to have something up their sleeves. Whatever they are doing will probably result in lots of laughs and some crazy memory.

Just go with it.

It's Vegas.

They wouldn't do anything to hurt you.

They lead us down the corridor. Light-brown carpet has chocolate-brown, sky-blue, and cream lines every few feet. Manly, rich-brown paneling lines the wall from the floor to my knees, and the rest is covered in creamish-gold wallpaper.

We stop in front of the only door I've seen.

"I know Hailee won big, but I think this is beyond your budget," I comment, knowing how the rooms on the top levels are expensive suites that the four of us together would never be able to afford.

"We aren't paying for it." Skylar's voice is full of sugar and sin.

My stomach flips again. *What are we doing here?* "Then who is?"

"Mystery man," Skylar practically sings.

"Who is that?"

"Now, it wouldn't be a mystery if we told you, would it?" Kora reprimands.

"Once again, I'm totally confused," I state.

Kora swipes the key to unlock the door, and we walk into the suite.

I freeze several steps in. "Wow." The Vegas skyline is lit up. It stretches and twinkles for miles. A fireplace is turned on in a cozy sitting area. Eggplant-colored accent pillows and curtains are set against soft, off-white furniture and walls. A sexy woman's voice singing pumps through hidden speakers, but it's in a different language, so I don't know what she's singing about.

"Quick, let's check it out." Kora loops her arm through mine and drags me farther in.

"I feel like we're in the Twilight Zone. Someone seriously needs to fill us in on what is going on," Hailee interjects.

"We will. Promise. Let's take a quick peek first," Skylar replies.

We walk through the suite in awe. There is a sunken bar, marble bathrooms, a steam shower, a formal dining room, solarium, whirlpool tub, and two king-size suites.

"This is bigger than my apartment!" Hailee exclaims.

"Why are we here?" I ask again.

Skylar leads me over to the bar. A round of drinks is waiting for us on the counter. There are two martinis, a vodka tonic, and a cosmopolitan.

"I'm getting creeped out now," Hailee mutters. They are the same drinks we had downstairs.

Skylar motions to the seats. "Sit, and we will explain."

Hailee raises her eyebrows at me, but we pull out the barstools and sit.

Kora holds up her drink to make a toast. Her eyes light up. "To fulfilling your fantasy."

Skylar's expression matches hers, and she holds her glass up next to Kora's. "And removing the chastity belt!"

Butterflies take off in my stomach. "What are you talking about?" I ask for what feels like the millionth time.

"Toast first," Kora says.

"Enough! What in the hell is happening here?" Hailee demands.

Kora takes a sip of her vodka tonic. "Skylar and I went to the bathroom and ran into a man in the hallway."

"A silver fox!" Skylar gleams. "Well, there're very few grays in his hair, but he does have some and he isn't younger."

"Yep. No courgarlishousness for you tonight," Kora sings.

My pulse increases. I blurt out, "So you decided to bring us to his suite? A stranger?"

"Calm down. Do you want to know why?" Kora asks.

"Please, fill us in." Hailee's annoyance fills the air.

"He's super-hot, has a sexy accent, is in his mid-forties, and is obviously rich," Skylar gushes.

"You sound like you bought him," Hailee blurts out.

Kora playfully backhands her on the shoulder. "Stop it. We did not buy him. But he won't take from Aspen. In fact, he's going to do everything she wants for the night."

"What? Did you prostitute me out?"

"No!" they both cry out at the same time.

"You want me to sleep with him? A stranger?"

"Yes," they say in unison once again.

I glance behind me. "Where is he?"

"He's not coming in until we leave. And you have to abide by the rules."

"Have you two gone crazy?" I take a mouthful of my gin concoction, wondering how my friends could ever be this insane or create this scenario.

Skylar stirs the cocktail straw in her cosmopolitan. "Nope. We are seizing the opportunity to help you get exactly what you want."

Hailee puts her forearm on the bar and turns in her chair. "And what exactly does she want?"

Kora accuses, "Were you not paying attention at the pool?"

Hailee tilts her head. "You're going to have to be more specific."

"Blindfolded by a stranger. No name. No face. No relationship issues. An older man who will command you in the bedroom and give you one night of multiple O's." Kora's eyes light up.

"Remove the chastity belt! I demand you do!" Skylar dramatically yells.

"Are you crazy?" I ask.

"Yep, they've lost the plot," Hailee agrees and drinks her martini.

Skylar sighs dramatically. "Let's look at this. You're in Vegas. There are no strings. He's going to give you exactly what you want. At any time, if you want him to stop, he will."

"So he claims. You don't know this guy. He could be a total psychopath." I point out the most important fact, but my insides also stir.

What if I could do it?

No, I can't. It's too crazy.

But is it?

"Skylar and I have vetted him for you. You should trust us. This is the one thing you need and also want. You'll never get a more perfect situation. We're miles from Chicago, he's smoking hot with a body to match, and he agreed to all our terms."

"Oh my God. You two..." Hailee shakes her head.

Skylar groans. "Don't sit on your high horse, Hailee. We're in Vegas. Crazier shit has happened here. Aspen needs to get back on the horse, and this is an awesome way to do it. The man is a Thoroughbred. Her entire fantasy can be fulfilled."

I drink a third of my martini, letting the cold liquid slide down my throat.

It's been so long since anyone has touched me.

Maybe I should do it.

Nope, it's crazy. It's not anything I would ever do.

Maybe that's the point. And it is Vegas.

"You'll never get another opportunity like this," Kora cuts in.

"Every divorcée needs to get back in the saddle at some point. Why not have your fantasy come true when you do? If anyone has earned a night full of mind-blowing O's, it's you," Skylar insists.

"But he could be a psychopath," I say again.

"He's not!" Kora exclaims.

"No. And he's totally your type. Trust us," Skylar urges.

Could I really do something like this?

Skylar twists a lock of her magenta hair around her finger. "He agreed to all your rules."

"My rules?"

"Yes. Your fantasy."

"How did you even get to the point of discussing this?" Hailee asks.

"He heard our conversation at the pool and approached Skylar and me." Kora says it as if it's totally normal.

Heat burns my cheeks. "What?"

"And this just gets better," Hailee mutters and finishes her drink.

I take another large mouthful of mine.

Is this seriously happening right now?

He heard me. How embarrassing.

Why am I mortified? He's willing to be a participant.

He could be crazy.

"Where is he?" I glance around the room again, but nothing has changed.

Kora points to the front door. "Waiting outside. When you're ready, we will leave, and he will come in."

The burning in my face intensifies. "You're serious?"

"Yes."

I put my hands over my face. "This is so embarrassing. He must think I'm totally desperate."

"Nope. He's actually got the hots for you," Skylar claims.

I look through my fingers. "What?"

"He's been watching you all night. He promised us he would abide by all your rules. Tomorrow, he'll leave before you take the blindfold off. He's going to give you the night you want. It'll be all about you."

44

My heart pounds harder. "I can't—"

"Why not? You're divorced. Your husband didn't pay any attention to you. This is your fantasy come true, and this guy is a grade-A stud. There is no doubt in either of our minds he knows what to do. He's not younger, he's several years older, and you'll never see him again. We're in Vegas, no one but your closest besties will know. What is stopping you except your fear right now?" Skylar raises her eyebrows.

She's right.

This is insane.

One night of feeling good.

I can give myself O's.

Not the same thing.

I don't have to ever see him again.

I couldn't do it.

I blurt out, "Hailee, go talk to him and see what he's like."

Hailee gapes at me. "Are you considering this?"

"No. Well... I don't know. Just...you go talk to him." Hailee has known me longer than anyone. Kora and Skylar are crazier than Hailee and me. If Hailee talks to him and tells me to do it, then maybe I'll consider it.

What am I doing?

Hailee rises. "I'm going to go talk to him, just because I'm curious about who this guy is, but this is completely insane, and you two have lost your minds." She points to Skylar and Kora. "When I get back, we're all leaving. Together."

But maybe I should do this.

Nope. I'm leaving with the three of them when she returns.

Hailee shakes her head at Skylar and Kora.

Kora rolls her eyes. "Don't be all judgy and screw this up for Aspen. Go meet him. You'll see."

My stomach pitches with nervousness and excitement. Blood pounds in my ears, and my thoughts spin a mile a minute about what the night could be like in both good and bad ways.

Hailee stomps off, the sound of the door opening and shutting echoes through the room, and my pulse increases further.

She's gone for at least fifteen minutes. During that time, Kora and Skylar continue to try to convince me why this is the perfect scenario and I should do it.

By the time Hailee returns, I've not committed to it, but the growing desire to do something wild and crazy for once in my life takes hold. All I've ever done is be responsible. Peter left me no room to be carefree in my twenties or thirties.

I'm going to be forty in a few years, and my life is one big boring event after another.

Hailee comes in. I expect her to grab me and tell me to leave with her. But she doesn't.

"You should do it. He's perfect for you." Her voice is so convincing it further breaks my resistance.

"What?" Part of me is jumping up and down, happy she said that, and the other half wants to run out the door, petrified of the entire situation.

"Told you!" Kora exclaims.

Skylar holds up her hand, and Kora slaps it.

I put my hands over my face. "Oh my God. Is this really happening?"

"Yes," they all say in unison.

"Go in the bedroom. Face the window. Don't turn around when he comes in or attempt to look at him. If you do, the fantasy is over. He'll leave. The rules are clear," Kora states and grabs my elbow and leads me to the bedroom.

I've never done anything so insane. But maybe it's time to do something for me for once.

I'll never see him after tonight. My friends are right. It's perfect. No strings, drama, or long-term ramifications to worry about. No one I have to take care of and support afterward.

I'm just going to let go and be in the moment.

I can't believe I'm doing this.

My friends all hug me with excitement in their faces and remind me not to turn around, whatever I do.

When they leave, I stare out the window, gazing across Vegas, feeling the sin and excitement of the city. My stomach flips in anticipation. When the knock hits my ears and the door opens, I take a deep breath and do everything in my power not to turn around.

4

Maksim

PATIENCE IS SOMETHING I'VE LEARNED TO ACQUIRE OVER TIME. But it doesn't stop the anticipation of the future event from stewing in my veins.

When this woman's third friend comes out, whom I've not spoken to before, I'm not totally surprised.

I still don't know the name of the woman inside. Her friends told me I wasn't allowed to know. Since she doesn't know mine, it's only fair.

While I'm sure the woman inside hasn't done this before, I haven't, either. I've been waiting with my pulse pounding, so I welcome the break. And after a long barrage of questioning from the third woman, warnings I better stick to the rules, and threats about what she'll do to me if I do anything but please her friend, she leaves.

Did I pass her test?

It's not long before the three friends come out. I get another stern lecture and a reminder of the rules then the girl with the magenta hair holds her hand out.

"Give me your wallet."

"Why?" I ask.

"It's going in my purse. When you leave tomorrow, I'll give it back to you. I won't open it, but if anything happens to our friend, this goes to the police."

All my credit cards, a few thousand dollars of cash, and identification are in my wallet. I hesitate for a moment.

The woman raises her eyebrows, challenging me to say no.

In some ways, I'm amused. I'm also happy they are doing something to try and protect their friend in case I was a complete psychopath.

I'm a dangerous man. If they knew how much, they would not let me near their friend.

I would never hurt her or any woman.

I'm still a violent man when required.

No matter how much I want to erase the sins of my past, I can't. And at times, new reasons to fall into the role I despise are so pressing, I can't escape it.

Maybe it's why I tried for years to get Jade to fall in love with me. She's got a tainted past, similar to my own. While she doesn't know anything about my secrets, I know what she's been through and done. I learned by accident.

If she loved me, I would tell her everything. But something always held me back from disclosing to her all that I am. Perhaps I've always known she would never give me her heart.

The woman inside waiting for me is a stranger. I have no information on her. But it's apparent she's everything good and wholesome. There's an innocence about her, almost a naivety. She's everything I always stay away from because my past and the person I am are too dark.

Everything about the anonymity of the evening allows me to do this. If not, I wouldn't go near her. She's a woman who would deserve a man not involved in any of the things I am. Anything that could taint her would be wrong.

But after tonight, I'll never see her again. We'll go our separate ways and have memories without the complications.

I hand my wallet to the magenta-haired woman. She drops it in her purse and says, "What is your cell number?"

I give it to her.

"I'm texting you. When you leave tomorrow, message me."

My phone vibrates in my pocket. "Okay."

After several more warnings, they finally leave, and I sigh in relief.

I've never worked so hard to get laid in my life.

This isn't about getting laid.

What is this about, then?

Pleasing her.

Forgetting Jade.

Disappearing into someone who is the opposite of everything I am. A woman I would normally stay away from at all costs.

I open the door and step in. I make my way through the suite and get to the bedroom door. I take a deep breath, knock three times as instructed, and turn the knob.

Her back faces me. She doesn't move, and my pulse quickens. Her yellow spaghetti-strap sundress is formfitting. It hugs the curve of her ass with perfection. I have an urge to run my teeth down her calves. Her four-inch black stilettos position her the perfect height against my body.

As I cross the room, my heart beats faster. She taps her fingers, nervously, at the sides of her thighs. A muted floral scent hits my nostrils, and I inhale it deeper. "Don't turn around," I remind her, sliding my hand around her and resting it on her stomach.

She almost turns to look at me, but I put my cheek against hers. *This is her fantasy. Make sure you give it to her.* "You don't seem to obey very well."

She draws in a deep breath.

"I'm sorry," she whispers then shudders against me.

The sound of her voice hits me, and the feeling I got at the pool when I heard it returns, only this time, it's even more intense. Everything about her is overwhelming my senses. My erection grows, and I drop my pinky finger over her sex, stroking her, then tug her closer to me with my other hand.

She sinks into me. Our bodies mold, leaving me with no questions about our sexual chemistry or how good we will be together.

Reinforce the rules. She wants us to be strangers and for me to be controlling. "Let me be clear about my rules. The blindfold will go on and stay there until after I leave. From this point forward, you give your full trust to me. Whatever I say goes."

Her chest rises and falls faster.

I stop myself from looking closer at her so I won't give her a glimpse of what I look like. I move my mouth to her ear. "Do you have any questions or objections?"

A soft gasp rolls out of her mouth. "Ummm..."

I flick my tongue behind her lobe, and her breathing gets louder.

"You can still get out of this if you want," I murmur and drop my hand lower, grazing her slit through her dress while nibbling on the curve of her neck. I pray she doesn't say she no longer wants this.

She freezes.

As much as I want her, I need to hear she doesn't want to back out. That as crazy as this is, she's a willing participant and doing this on her own accord, not because her friends set her up for it. "I require consent. Your friends said you want this. Is this true? Hmm?"

She opens her mouth, but nothing comes out.

"Give me a yes," I demand.

She takes a moment but confidently replies, "Yes."

Thank God.

If she'd told me no, I would have respected her wishes and walked out. But it would involve me tearing myself away. Being this close to her is an invitation to the holy grail. Having to step outside would be torture.

"Good. Close your eyes and keep them shut. If you open them before I blindfold you, this ends. Understand?"

She nods, and I restrain from turning her head and kissing her with no restrictions.

She wants me to control her.

"If you don't submit to me fully, there will be no warning. I will stop and leave. Have I made myself clear?" I drag my hand up her torso, slicing through her cleavage that rises and falls with her shortened breath. Then I grasp her chin and push her head back on my shoulder, scraping my cheek against hers.

A tiny whimper escapes her, and my dick pulses.

"Answer me," I demand.

"Mmhmm."

I smile at her consent and the fact I'm already affecting her like this. I haven't even done anything yet, and she's a cork ready to be popped.

I inch my hand along the inside of her thigh, slowly creeping toward her heat. She shudders. I grunt with satisfaction then ask a question I already know the answer to. "You've not done this before?"

She takes another nervous inhale. "What? Obey?"

I stroke her heart-shaped lips, enjoying how her warm breath seeps into my finger. "That and spent the night with a stranger."

"Correct." She hooks her hands on my thighs.

My cock twitches. Her hands are a buzz of energy, awakening every nerve ending in my body. I state, "You're nervous."

"I..."

I hold my finger over her lips. I can't handle not being in front of her anymore. "Blindfold first." I step back and pull out a silk tie I bought from the store downstairs. The sales clerk looked at me like I was crazy when I asked him for scissors and cut it. I wrap it around her head and tie it then move in front of her.

She's even more gorgeous in person. Her skin competes with the smoothness of the silk. I wish I could see her eyes, but these are the rules. She swallows hard and licks her full lips.

I want to kiss her. Really kiss her. But without her seeing me and able to know who she's kissing, it seems too intimate. So I restrict myself and set a new boundary. I can do everything with her, but I won't kiss her on the lips. Because I have this feeling, if I do, I won't be able to stop or ever get her out of my mind again. So it's to protect me more than her.

"Do you know what I've wanted to do since I saw you from across the casino?" I ask.

"No," she whispers.

I possessively hold the back of her head, and I touch her lips while speaking. "Spend every second of the rest of the night making you unravel in ways you never have before."

Yep, do not kiss her. She'll ruin me.

Instead, I kiss her everywhere except her lips. I focus on her jaw and neck then push the straps of her dress down to focus on her breasts, unclasping her strapless bra and tossing it on the floor.

In Russian, I say, "Who am I kidding? You're going to ruin me with or without your lips."

Her hands slide up my arms and into my hair, gripping me while she softly moans and tries to stabilize her body, but her legs are trembling.

I release her zipper all the way. Her dress slides down her body. I turn her to the glass. She's a magnificent piece of art with all of Vegas flashing around her.

Her earrings and one single-strand bracelet are the only pieces of jewelry she wears. They are simple and delicate but not authentic.

A woman like her should be adorned in jewels—real metals and gems, not fake costume pieces.

The only other items remaining on her are black lace panties and stilettos. I stand back, admiring her beautiful curves and tracing my finger over a mole near her belly button.

Her lower body squirms.

I remove my shirt and pants then step forward so my body touches her warm, pulsing skin.

She gasps, her mouth forms an O, then shuts.

I graze her ear as I say, "I've never seen anyone as beautiful as you."

Her pulse pounds in her neck, and I suck on it while her hot sex pushes against my hard-as-steel cock. I step even closer, so she can't move between me and the glass, and circle my hips so my erection slides back and forth against her panties.

"Ohhh," she moans.

"Do you feel how hard I am for you, my krasotka?"

"Yes," she barely gets out then swallows hard.

"I've been burning for you since I laid eyes on you."

"You have?" Her voice has doubt in it.

"Yes." I kiss her jaw, release her panties, and press my cock harder against her, sliding across her swollen clit.

She's already so wet for me.

"Oh God," she whimpers and clutches my shoulders.

I play with her nipple and suck on her pulse again, continuing to shimmy my shaft over her clit until she unravels, her arms tight around me and nails digging into my back.

In Russian, I murmur against her flushed cheek, "That's a good girl, my krasotka."

When my cock can't handle it anymore, I keep her pressed to the glass and trail my lips down her body, doting on every inch of her hot skin until I'm on my knees.

Her fingers lace into my hair, tugging it before I even touch her dripping sex. The scent of her arousal seeps into me, teasing my inner beast.

I run my hands up and down her thighs and kiss the outside of her pussy until a drop of her juice rolls down her thigh. The pads of her fingers twitch. She begs, "Please."

It's so quiet, I hardly hear it. And I want to listen to it again. So I don't give her what she wants.

"Oh...please." She pushes my head into her body harder.

I move my thumb over her marbled clit, sucking on her mound but not feasting on her how I'm dying to.

She moans like an animal in heat, competing with the woman singing Russian over the surround sound. Within seconds, her body erupts in tremors against the glass. Her chest caves over my head, and her breasts push into me.

The blood pumps harder in my veins. When she comes down, I finally allow myself to have the meal I've been craving since I saw her at the pool.

5

Aspen

FIRE BLAZES FROM MY TOES TO MY HEAD. MR. STRANGER Danger swiftly palms the back of my thighs and positions them over his shoulders. There's no room to move between him and the glass, and his mouth is a whirlwind of tormented pleasure.

Every move he makes seems calculated. Since he positioned me against the window, he's made me soar from his cock and thumb, which were both better than anything I could have done without him. But his mouth...oh my God.

Everything is dark from the blindfold. I'm not sure if it makes things more intense, or if it's because no one has touched me in so long, or if Mr. Stranger Danger is just phenomenal in his O game. But everything about him makes my body buzz with adrenaline. And the scent of him should be bottled up and sprayed in buildings. It's that intoxicating.

The stranger has already spent more time and paid more attention to me than Peter did in the last five years of our marriage. And I'm dying for this man's tongue, lips, and teeth to ravish me.

But he teases me further by scraping his stubble on my inner thigh then kissing both of them, saying something in whatever language he speaks.

I could ask him, but it turns me on more to not know anything about him.

And if what he did to me is a preview of the rest of the night, I'm going to owe my friends for life.

Tingles race through my legs and pulse into my loins, creating a throbbing sensation that makes my inner walls spasm. "Oh God, please," I beg him.

"Please what?" his deep voice asks with his sexy accent. His lips hit the inside of my leg before he lets out a deep, feral groan while licking a drop of my juice from the middle of my thigh, running his tongue as close to my sex as possible without touching it.

My flutters spin faster. I slide my hands over his broad shoulders and grip his thick hair. "Please."

"Tell me what you want me to do," he commands then flicks his tongue on the same spot but not where I want him.

"Yes...please...do that!"

He grunts. "Where?"

My proper self is gone. Desperation for him consumes me. If he wants to hear me speak dirty, then I will.

What word do I use?

"My pussy. Please."

He groans again then flicks his tongue across me. He's a cobra, and I'm his prey. He utilizes gracefulness and speed, controlling my body's every reaction. Right before I'm about to orgasm, he slows down.

"Oh God. Please. Don't stop."

Instead of giving me what I want, he becomes the King Cobra, nibbling on my clit with his teeth.

"Oh...fffff...oh...oh God!"

He grips my hips tighter and sucks me. A pattern of licking, sucking, and biting makes me break out in a sweat.

Dizziness, heat, and adrenaline ricochet in all my cells. Words fly out of me, fast and loud, competing with his deep groans, which make me believe he's enjoying it as much as I am. And that's new for me. Peter never expressed any form of enjoyment the few times a year he would go down on me.

The self-consciousness I've always felt during this act is nowhere to be found. It's as if the stranger has completely removed it. His hunger for me seems limitless. For the first time since forever, I feel wanted. But I don't remember it feeling this intense with Peter, even when we first got together.

My cries get louder, flowing out as I dig my nails into his head, holding him as close to me as possible while my hips circle fast, desperate for him to give me my release.

He unleashes a tidal wave of pleasure. As soon as the tide breaks, another one, more forceful than the last, crashes through me. He mumbles foreign words from time to time. I don't understand any of it, but his voice is full of power and lust.

I think I can't take anymore, but he continues to destroy every limit I have until I'm so limp, I'm hanging over his head, still shaking, the blackness of the night never changing.

He sets me down, but his body and the glass hold me up.

His torso is a wall of muscle, pumping hard with his warm blood and flexing against me. His soft chest hair is a contrast to the hard pecs beneath them, and when he stands next to me, it's next to my face when my stilettos are on.

How tall is he?

I slide my hands over his six-pack. *So this is what one feels like.* I continue around his back then slip them down to his ass, which is just as contoured as the rest of him.

Is he a fitness model?

Oh God. How is it possible I'm with him right now?

Within seconds, he scoops me up in his arms and takes me to the bed. He speaks in his other language but keeps saying the word, krasotka. It's the only one I hear repeatedly.

My insides still quiver, but I reach for him, needing to feel his flesh against mine.

His warm breath, full of my arousal, hits my ear. "Do you want me? Or have you had enough?"

Is that an actual question?

"I want you. Please." My raspy voice comes out in a plea.

His lips twitch. I feel it against my cheek.

I grasp his head, trying to find his lips, but he doesn't let me have them. I don't know why he isn't kissing me on the lips, but I don't ask him. It seems wrong to ask anything when I don't even know his name. If this is a boundary for him, then I'm not going to push. But I'm dying to know what it feels like to slide my tongue against his. Instead, I kiss him on the cheek, lowering my head until I'm in the curve of his neck.

He quietly grunts and runs his hands down the sides of my torso.

"Please let me have you," I mumble into his hot skin. The tip of his cock touches my entrance.

He pulls back. "Let me get a condom, krasotka."

It's a good thing one of us is being responsible.

All I can think about right now is how much I need him inside me.

He moves one arm away from me then takes my hand. "Put this on me," he commands then guides me to his swollen cock.

Is he enormous, or am I imagining it?

I do my best to roll the condom over him. When I think it's on, I ask, "Will you check I got it on okay?"

He pauses then kisses my forehead. "Yes. You did good, krasotka."

I let out a breath and nervously joke, "Score one for me!"

He chuckles. His laugh is deep and sexy, like everything else about him. "If we're keeping score, you've been on the board with points since I first touched you."

My ego soars, and I bite my smile. Everything about this night is my fantasy, but I want him to feel the same intensity of pleasure he is giving me. Part of me wants to rip the blindfold off and see what he looks like, but he made it clear if I did, he would leave, which is the last thing I want.

I put my hands on his face, tracing my thumbs over his lips, wondering again what it would be like to kiss him.

He dips down and sucks on my breast, sending a new heat straight to my core. I arch my back off the bed, moaning, then slide my hands to his ass and pull him over me. I blurt out, "Don't make me wait any longer."

I'm not sure who this woman is tonight, but the ability to give my trust to this stranger and let him freely do whatever he chooses is the opposite of my planned out, straight-and-narrow self. And I've never begged any man before. In some ways, I always felt awkward during sex. It was all about Peter mostly, and everything was over quickly. The stranger rushes nothing. He seems focused only on attending to my every need and desire.

He grabs both my shins and pushes my ankles toward my lower body. He dips his finger into my sex, gliding in and out a few times as his hot breath hits my knee, sending a trail of tingles down my thighs. He removes his digit and lurches over my frame.

Every sensation I could have erupts in me the moment his cock pushes into my body, sliding against my walls in a heavenly concoction of pleasure.

He mutters something in his foreign language, slowly moving his erection in and out of me, allowing me to take more of his length with every thrust.

"Yes...oh...," I breathe as heat annihilates my body.

He speaks more words I don't comprehend, and his hand takes both my wrists and pins them above my head against the headboard. His teeth lightly dig at my collarbone.

My flesh singes under him as his muscles ripple over me. I don't need to see his body to know it's a perfect ten. But I blurt out in a whisper, "I want to see you."

He freezes but then reminds me, "No, you don't. That isn't what you wanted." He strokes my cheek with the back of his fingers.

He's right.

"But—"

"I won't go back on my word. Just relax and feel, my krasotka."

"Okay." I nod then lose myself again to everything—the woman's voice wailing out a song, his intoxicating bergamot and cardamom scent, the feel of his hardened body pounding into mine, and his lips trailing on my neck. He touches something within me, and for the first time ever during sex, I climax, becoming unglued in a way I didn't know was possible.

"Oh my...oh...what...oh!" I scream out.

Our skin erupts in sweat. The sound of our fornication and sweet smell of sex is potent and, like everything else tonight, explodes into my senses.

He tightens his grip on my wrists, thrusting harder, and my body spasms around him, unable to stop.

"Krasotka," he growls then says something else in his native tongue.

When he unleashes the power of his body further on me, pushing me into another state of bliss, I think I might blackout when white stars erupt.

He collapses over me then releases my wrists while both of us are still breathing hard, and my insides continue to be a quivering mess.

I'm not sure what I expected, but the next thing he does surprises me.

He rolls over and pulls me into his arms, speaking his foreign tongue, stroking my hair, and kissing my head. The beat of his heart thumps in my ear. I reach up and stroke his cheek, still not able to see anything.

It's intimate and more than I ever got from Peter. It strikes me and chokes me up, making me happy the blindfold is still on.

The rest of the night, every time I wish the blindfold would come off, I remember this moment and don't ask or attempt to pull it off.

Not a minute passes where his focus on me waivers. When our breathing calms and hearts beat normal again, he says, "I want to take a bath with you."

My pulse quickens again. "Okay."

He kisses my head again. "Stay here. I'll come get you in a few minutes."

"All right."

He gets off the bed. I immediately miss his arms.

Something moves next to me.

He pats the bed. "Slide under the covers."

I move over, and he tucks the blanket over me, then leans back to my ear. "Don't fall asleep."

"If I do, just wake me up," I tease but also mean it.

"I'll be back." He kisses my cheek and leaves. He isn't gone long before he slides his arms under my body and carries me into the bathroom.

"Do you always carry your women around?"

He snorts. "Nope. Just you."

I try to hide my smile but can't. He sets me in the warm water, and I scooch forward. He gets in behind me and tugs me back against his chest. He asks, "How long are you in Vegas?"

"Two nights. My friends brought me here."

"Oh?"

Great. Why did I say that?

After a few minutes goes by, he says, "You're celebrating a breakup?"

My chest tightens. "How do you know that? Did my friends—"

"No. Just a hunch."

I release a breath and admit, "Divorce." Heat crawls up my face. I always feel a sense of embarrassment around my failed marriage. I shouldn't. Peter is the one who cheated. But the fact he chose another woman over me still hurts.

"Ah, I see." The stranger traces my jawbone. "You feel shame over this?"

I turn to look away, but there's nowhere to hide. My blind-fold hasn't moved. You would think it would allow me to camouflage my emotions, but strangely, it makes it more challenging. I quietly reveal, "He chose someone else."

"He cheated on you?"

I can only nod in answer.

The stranger puts his mouth on my ear. "He's a fool. And a coward."

I'm not sure why I care what Mr. Stranger Danger thinks about me or why his words mean so much. But I don't respond, and I think he misinterprets my silence.

"For what it's worth, I know what it's like for the person you want to love you, not to."

I turn to him, shocked that a powerful man such as he could ever be vulnerable enough to admit that or that it would be true. I still can't see him, but I feel his warm breath merging with mine. "You do?"

"Yes."

I lean closer to him, so close to his lips, but he turns, and I kiss his jaw.

He doesn't want me to kiss him because of her.

He's still in love with her.

A hint of jealousy flairs in my belly, but I remind myself this isn't a relationship nor is it ever going to be. I can't expect him to have any feelings for me, plus, we just met. Well, and I don't even know what he looks like.

I flip over, straddle him, then put my arms around his shoulders, stroking the back of his head. "How long are you in Vegas?"

"Same as you. Two nights."

"Why are you here?"

"It's my brother's bachelor party."

I tilt my head, biting my smile. "Is he going to be mad you ditched him for me?"

The stranger tucks a lock of my hair behind my ear. "No. There are ten of us. I'm sure I won't be missed."

"I would miss you," I blurt out then my cheeks turn to fire.

I turn away. "Sorry. I should be quiet. I'm super bad at this."

He pulls my chin back. "At what?"

"Conversing with men, apparently."

"I don't think so. I rather appreciate your honesty." He leans into my ear. "Plus, you're naked, sexy as hell, and sitting on me. You can say whatever you want right now, and I won't think anything but perverted thoughts."

I softly laugh. "How many brothers do you have?"

"Three. I'm the oldest."

"That's nice. Any sisters?"

"No. How about you?" he asks.

"Only child. All I have are my friends."

"You seem to be close."

"Yes. I would be lost without them."

He drags his finger over my breast then rolls my nipple. "I'm glad you have them."

I take a deep breath. "Are you close to your brothers?"

"Extremely."

"That's nice."

He slides his hand away from me then puts something against my lips. "Try this."

A chocolaty scent flares in my nose. I bite into the hard shell, and juice from a strawberry drips down my chin. The sweet and creamy flavors mix, melting in my mouth.

He leans forward and licks the juice off my face, and I think he might finally kiss me, but his lips only hover near mine.

"Are you a dangerous man?" I blurt out. I'm not sure why I ask or chose this moment to do so, but everything about him screams power and dominance. Yet, I also feel protected with him. As soon as it comes out of my mouth, my cheeks once again flare with embarrassment.

"Sorry, I—"

"Yes. I am. You can feel it?"

I'm surprised by his admission and question. I bite my lip and nod. My heart pounds faster.

"But you're not scared of me?"

"No." It flows out of my mouth before I can even process it, but it's true. I knew the minute he stepped next to me, he wasn't an ordinary man. "What makes you dangerous?"

I should shut my mouth.

What is the point of this?

He lowers his voice. His lips are still near mine, and he continues to stroke my cheek. "I'm not going to answer that. But I'll admit if we hadn't made this arrangement, I would have stayed away from you even though I wanted you."

My stomach flutters with a combination of nerves and excitement that he wanted me from afar. "Why would you have stayed away?"

His lips brush against mine. "You're too good to be drawn into any part of my world."

What is his world?

Neither of us moves, and the tension in the air increases. The longer we stay frozen, the harder it gets to fill my lungs with air. I curse myself over and over for asking him. After tonight, I'll never see him again and don't even know what he looks like.

But my desire for him doesn't waver. It grows, burning hotter until every ounce of my blood pounds in my veins.

He finally breaks the silence, saying things I don't understand, while his erection grows under me. Then he moves me so fast, I don't realize it's happening until we're out of the water and I'm straddling him on the ledge of the tub with my heart beating faster.

He quickly slips a condom on and yanks my knees past his hip bones.

I moan, sinking on him, taking every inch of his glorious cock as it stretches and fills me. I wrap my arms around him, using his shoulders as leverage, and get as close to him as I can.

His large palms squeeze my ass, guiding my circling hips. "Krasotka," he growls.

I still don't know what it means. But I like that he calls me it. It makes me think I'm special to him. I shouldn't want to be. He just admitted to me he's a dangerous man. I'm not sure what he's done for him to define himself as one.

All I know of him is how he's treated me tonight and made me feel right now at this moment. The only experience I have with him is intense pleasure and kindness.

He thrusts me faster on him as our chests beat into one another.

Pleasure pools everywhere, with every slide of his body against mine.

"I love how you make me feel," I whisper, barely audible.

"So good, krasotka," he agrees in his deep, gravelly voice, which only makes me happier. His arms tighten around me. His lips speak more words I don't understand, near my ear.

We erupt together, our cries echoing against the marble, labored breath, and bodies trembling.

It's a good thing I won't see him after tonight. Our chemistry is too hot. The potent attraction I feel toward him isn't something I would be able to turn off. And the fact he revealed he's dangerous and I'm still in his arms is exactly why it's good I won't have contact with him ever again. Because if I had to tear myself away from him tonight, I wouldn't be able to.

6

Maksim

SHE TEMPTED ME BY ASKING TO REMOVE HER BLINDFOLD. I almost let her. And all night, I've restrained myself from pulling it off her.

I made a deal with her. It's a promise. I'll destroy everything for her if I do.

"Let's go have a drink," I tell her. I pull the robe off the towel heater and put it around her then wrap one around my body. The silk of her blindfold looks like it's not as tight as before. After a quick debate, I do the right thing. "Turn around."

She doesn't ask why and spins.

"Keep your eyes shut. I should tighten this." I untie the silk.

She reaches behind her and grips my thighs. "Have you done this before?"

"Slept with a stranger?"

"Mmhmm."

"Yes."

She stays quiet but holds her breath and bites her lip.

The need to make her understand she is special digs into my soul. This may be a once in a lifetime moment for both of us, but it doesn't reduce her magnificence or the memories of her I'll have etched in my brain forever.

I reposition the silk over her eyes, tie it, then lean into her ear. "I've never done anything like this with any other woman before. And I'm not a liar, so I won't be one to you. I don't remember all the one-night stands I've had, but you, my krasotka, I will never forget."

She releases her breath.

I take her hand. "Come. Have a drink with me." I lead her out to the bar and motion for the butler to make our drinks and stay quiet. He has a room inside the bar area of the suite. As soon as he makes them, I nod for him to go back into his room. I hand my krasotka her martini and take my scotch and lead her to the sitting area.

When we get to the room, I set our drinks on the table. I choose the chaise lounge and pull her onto my lap. I hold the glass to her lips, and she takes a sip.

"How do you know what I drink?" she asks.

"I watched you all night."

Her lips twitch. In a teasing tone, she asks, "Should I be scared of your obsession?"

"If we lived in the same city, yes. I wouldn't be able to stay away from you. I'd be forced to pursue you."

Her smile grows.

I take a drink of my scotch. It slides down my throat in a slow burn. I stare at her juicy lips, wanting to kiss her but refraining.

I'll never get her out of my head if I kiss her.

She's stunning perfection in her blindfold. Everything she feels I see in her expression. There's no way for her to hide. But I wish I could see her eyes. I only stared directly into them briefly at the pool. In the casino, I watched her, intentionally staying back. And she never faced me.

The black of the silk matches her hair. Her flawless skin is smoother than I imagined. I trace below the silk, and she inhales slowly.

She wants me to remove it again.

Every time she thinks it, I see it. But she's only asked once. She reaches toward me and puts her hand on my cheek.

I close my eyes for a moment, inhaling her muted floral scent. I assumed it was perfume, but we just bathed, so it must be her skin.

"What color are your eyes?" she asks.

"Isn't this against the rules?"

She avoids my question and tilts her head. "Are they dark?"

"No."

She takes her other hand and holds both sides of my cheeks. Her thumb grazes over my nose then lips. "I've never been without my sight before."

"You don't have strangers blindfold you for hours all the time?" I tease.

"Nope. I'm pretty boring."

"Nothing about you is anything but exquisite," I tell her and mean it.

She snorts. "You're good for my ego."

"I don't lie, remember?"

She traces my forehead and eyebrows. "How old are you?"

"Not young enough to make you a cougar."

She softly laughs, and her face blushes. "You heard everything at the pool, didn't you?"

"Not sure if I heard it all, but I think I got the important parts." I hold her drink to her lips again.

She takes a sip and repeats, "So, how old are you?"

"I'll be forty-six in a few months. What about you?"

"How old do you think I am?"

"Not anywhere near my age."

"Is that your way of avoiding guessing?"

I chuckle. "Yes. So tell me."

"I'm thirty-eight."

"How long were you married?" I'm not sure why I ask her. I don't even know her name or where she lives, but something in me wants to know the details about her life.

Her face falls, and she pulls her hands off my cheeks. "Twenty years."

How is that possible?

"You got married at eighteen?"

She turns toward the fire, but I still see the pain in her expression. "Yes."

I stroke her hair.

She doesn't move, and her face doesn't change.

"When did you finalize your divorce?"

She quietly replies, "A few days ago."

I pull her closer to me and lean into her ear. "So, I'm your rebound, huh?" I say it to tease her and don't expect the sting I feel when it comes out.

It's a good thing we have these rules, or I would be in major trouble with this woman.

She tilts her head then quietly asks, "And I'm yours?"

I instantly regret pointing out what I am to her. Since I'm not a liar, I can't deny it. "Yes. I suppose so."

She bites her lip and slowly nods.

I slide the shoulder of her robe down and kiss her smooth skin. "I think we have better things to do than talk. Don't you?"

She laces her fingers in my hair. Her chest rises and falls faster. I dip lower, sucking on her breast until her nipple puckers.

Every moan and whimper is music to my ears. How any man could marry her, find someone else, then let her go blows my mind.

I push her robe off her. "Straddle me."

She obeys.

I put her hands on the back of the chaise lounge. "Don't let go. And I want you to ride my face." I flick my tongue behind her ear.

She gasps.

I slide down and grip her hips. The moment her sex is over my face, I growl, "Ride me."

She hesitates for a moment, as if she isn't sure what to do. I tug her lower on my mouth, and she cries out, shuddering.

I set the pace, but she quickly takes over, circling her lower body into me and moaning like a wild animal.

I smack her ass.

"Oh!" she screams.

I rub her cheek and flick her clit until she comes, squeezing her thighs on my face.

When she's past her high point, I smack her ass again and suck her until she's screaming.

"Ride me," I bark out.

She takes control, setting a new speed, and orgasms so many times, I lose count.

When my cock is on fire and dripping to be in her, I slide out from under her. I grab a condom in the pocket of her robe. I splay my hand on her spine while pushing her down so she's hanging over the back of the chaise. I don't wait to enter her, spreading her legs to the edges of the cushion and thrusting inside her in one stroke.

"Yes!" she screams when I enter her.

In Russian, I let all my dirty thoughts fly. I tell her how much I love being inside her. How the taste of her sex is better than any dessert I've ever had, and her tight pussy might as well be the kingdom of heaven for my cock. How her ex-husband is a pathetic loser for ever letting her go or looking at another woman, much less touching one. And I tell her I wish tonight weren't all we had. If I were a different man and she didn't have these terms, how I would make her mine.

Once it begins, her body never stops shaking. I tug her hair as she spasms on my cock so hard, I forcefully detonate inside her, then collapse over her, breathing hard into her neck.

I flip around and tug her into me, stroking her back. We both try to catch our breath. And I have to hold myself back again from kissing her.

All night, we talk, laugh, and have sex. When the morning light shines through the window, I hold her until she falls asleep.

The dress I ordered from the downstairs boutique arrives. I saw it when I bought the silk tie, and once I saw her dress size, I texted the sales associate. I put her other dirty clothes, minus her panties, in the dry cleaning bag and add her room number to it. I only know it because I texted her friend to find out.

So many thoughts go through my head when it's time to leave her. I hesitate and almost wake her up to ask her if she wants me to remove her blindfold so she can see who I am.

But I'm a man of my word.

So I write a note and leave it with the dress. I kiss her forehead and she doesn't stir. Very carefully, I remove her blindfold and put it on the pillow. Then I stick her panties in my pocket and walk away from her.

She just gave me the best night of my life, and my pulse beats hard with regret that I'll never see her again.

7

Aspen

I SLEPT MOST OF THE DAY, WHICH I SUPPOSE ISN'T OUT OF THE ordinary for Vegas. When I open my eyes, a dim light is on in the room. Hailee, Skylar, and Kora sit on the bed with matching smirks on their faces.

"What?" I innocently ask but know exactly what they are doing.

"Spill it," Hailee says.

I can't hide my smile and put my hands over my face then peek through my fingers.

"I knew it!" Skylar high-fives Kora. "He's a total stud in the bedroom, isn't he?"

Heat instantly fills my face, and I try to hide in the pillow, but there's no getting out of it. I boast, "Grade-A."

81

Shrieks fill the room.

Kora removes my hands from my face. "Was it O, O, O, all night long?"

I nod and can't get the grin off my face.

"And did he tell you his name?" Hailee asks.

My face falls. "No. He stuck to the rules."

"Why do you look upset?"

"I'm not. He did everything he agreed to," I quickly reply, but part of me wishes I knew his name. And where he lived and how to get ahold of him.

He's dangerous. He even said you should stay away from him.

It was a one-night deal. Appreciate it for what it was and move forward.

Kora leans toward me. "We need deets."

I slip out of bed. "It was a great night. *He* was great. End of the story. I'm going to take a shower. Where are we going tonight?"

"That's it? You're not going to give us more than that?"

I shake my head. "Nope. And the chastity belt is back on, so don't get any crazy ideas tonight."

Not that anyone will ever measure up to him.

I race to the bathroom, to avoid any further questions, and lock the door. I lean against it and close my eyes. All I see is black, but I can still feel and smell him. I hear his Russian accent and deep voice. My core stirs with flutters, but then reality comes rearing its ugly head, and disappointment fills me.

He's gone. It's as if the entire thing was a dream and he's just an apparition. I shouldn't feel like this. It wasn't part of the deal. Plus, I'm in Vegas. Nothing permanent happens here. The ink is hardly dry on my divorce papers, and the last thing I should contemplate is anything long term with any man.

But he's so different.

Doesn't matter. He's gone, off-limits and dangerous.

What about him puts him in that category?

Although I felt his danger, and he admitted it, I can't imagine him ever doing anything harmful to me or anyone else.

I don't really know him.

Stop all these thoughts. Be happy you had a good time in O land, and forget about him.

I get in the shower and let the hot water beat on my back until it turns cold. When I get out, I dry my hair, put on my makeup, then step out in my towel.

I have a suitcase of clothes, but there's only one thing I want to wear.

I take his gift—the white dress he bought me—and put it on. Since he didn't seem to want me to wear panties with it, I don't put any on. It's another thing I would never normally do, but something about last night makes me feel a bit more carefree.

I slide into a pair of gold stilettos I brought and stroll back into the bedroom. Everyone is sitting around in their evening wear.

"Holy...where did you get that dress?" Hailee asks.

"Is that from downstairs? I swear I looked at that last night, but it was over three grand," Kora interjects.

Three thousand dollars? My stomach flips. I knew it was expensive but...

"Well? Where did you get it?" Skylar pushes.

"He left it for me."

"Mystery man?"

"Yes."

Kora whistles, and Hailee and Skylar gape at me.

"You must be one hot lay!" Kora teases.

My cheeks flush. "Stop it."

They all laugh, and after a bit more teasing, we leave for the evening.

We go to dinner at Caesars Palace and then a show. I feel guilty because everything costs a lot, and my friends are paying for all of it, but I can't seem to pay attention to anything. I keep scouring the room at the restaurant, wondering if he could be there. Any man with salt-and-pepper hair, I look at closer. There are many, but most of their bodies would never match to Mr. Stranger Danger, so it eliminates them quickly.

When we get to the show, instead of losing myself in the production, I'm lost in my memories of the night before. I desperately am trying to hold on to how he felt, smelled, and sounded.

After the show, we go to several hot spots on the strip. The drinks never stop flowing. I lose track of where we are. We end up in a more intimate bar. It has red, seductive lighting. Dancers wearing skimpy lingerie perform on a small stage and sometimes the bar.

Lots of men are here, and we soon have a crowd around us. Several hit on me, but I'm not interested. No one comes close to measuring up to Mr. Stranger Danger. I don't need to talk to them for more than a few seconds to know this. My friends, however, are quite cozy, and each has seemed to pair up with someone.

After several drinks, I rise. "I'll be back. I'm going to the restroom."

They all nod and go back to their flirtatious behavior. I step around the corner and down the dark hallway and go inside the bathroom. I do my thing and leave.

I take two steps out the door, and a hand goes over my mouth.

I panic at first, as he pulls me back and spins me into the corner of the wall, but then his scent fills my nostrils. My body molds to his, and he says with his deep accent in my ear, "It's me, krasotka."

I shudder from the pure force of his energy and stare at the red glow on the wall.

His hand slips to my chin, and he puts his cheek next to mine.

I close my eyes. *Is he really here? Am I imagining this?*

"I'm sorry to scare you."

I nod. "It's okay."

"I couldn't pull myself away when I saw you. I've been waiting to figure out how to talk to you."

My flutters go crazy.

I lean into his body further. "Did you know I was here?"

"No. I tried to keep my word. All day, I avoided coming to your room to see you."

"You did?"

"Yes, krasotka."

Happiness is a rocket shooting through me. He is still calling me his krasotka. He wanted to see me again.

"I've been searching everywhere I go for you," I admit.

He sighs. The beat of his heart thumps against my shoulder. His erection grows and digs into my spine. "You look more beautiful in this dress than I imagined."

I smile. "I didn't thank you for it. It was very generous. I don't think I've ever worn anything so...um...well, expensive."

"That's a shame. You deserve the best."

I release a breath I didn't know I was holding and grip the sides of his thighs.

He quietly groans, and it stirs everything carnal in my belly not already ignited.

"I need to give you something," he says.

"What?"

"Something I regret not giving you last night."

"You gave me everything," I blurt out. And he did. He breathed life into me again.

"No. I didn't."

"I don't understand."

He strokes my lips with his finger. "I bought another tie today. I felt crazy doing it. But I have it with me. Can I put it on you for a moment?"

"Maybe I should turn around, and we shouldn't use the tie."

"No. I gave you my word. And those terms allowed us to be together. Nothing's changed about me. You're still a woman I wouldn't pursue if we didn't have our arrangement."

I try to convince him. "I don't think—"

He puts three fingers over my lips. "Krasotka, can I blindfold you? Please?"

"Okay."

The seductive music fills my ears. My insides quiver at being back in his arms. He puts the silk around my eyes, ties it, then turns me. He moves me so my back touches the wall, and his hands cup my cheeks. His lips brush against mine as he speaks. "I'm going to regret this. I already know I will. You'll torment me, but it drove me insane all night last night.

And I'm sorry you can't see me when I do this. I know it's not fair, but I'm going to be a selfish bastard right now."

"How?" I ask, pushing my lips into his, my heart pounding so hard, I'm sure he can hear it. The faint taste of his mouth is a gateway drug to addiction. Every desire I had to kiss him last night is a hundred times more potent now.

He doesn't answer me. He only steps closer so there is no room to move or way to escape his hard, warm flesh. His thumbs stroke my cheeks, and his fingers slide into my hair, around the silk. He possessively tilts my head, and nothing else exists, except his lips, tongue, and teeth.

Dominance, desire, and danger are in his kiss. It all rips through my soul, tearing any shred of resistance to be his. But I can't be his. I already know this. We're miles from where we both reside. I still don't know his name, and I'm pretty sure he isn't going to tell me. He's dangerous and has already told me he'd never let me into his world, and I shouldn't want any part of it or him. But every inch of me wants to live in this kiss.

The night before, he made me come alive and feel things I never had. Tonight, his kisses show me that I was wrong about us. Last night was a sliver of how good we are together. Our hunger wasn't fully unleashed. It was a mere piece of what we now feed each other.

We kiss. And kiss. And kiss some more, until he finally pulls back and murmurs in my ear, "I want another night."

I nod, trying to catch my breath.

"Same rules."

"We don't have to—"

"No. It's better this way. I haven't changed who I am. If you tell me who you are, I will try to find you after we leave. I will have to make you mine. It is not in your best interest."

I grasp his cheeks, only seeing blackness, inhaling his berg-amot and cardamom scent. I shouldn't have anything else to do with him. I'm already deeper into this than I should be. My heart is going to hurt when I go home.

And I don't understand how he could do anything terrible or what makes him so evil. But instead of doing what my gut tells me I should, I step right into the lair.

"Then, let's have each other tonight."

He kisses me again, takes my hand, and slides a key card into it. "I hoped you would agree."

How could I not?

"Sixteenth floor. It's the only room they had left. Room twenty-eight. I'm going to turn you and remove your blind-fold. I'll go into the bathroom. When you hear the door shut, leave. Stand at the window when you get in the room. I'll put your blindfold back on when I get there."

I try one more time. "I really think we can forget the blindfold."

His voice darkens. "Same rules. If you can't follow them, I will leave. I don't want to, but I will."

My pulse beats harder.

"My krasotka, do you understand and agree?"

I move my hands up his chest and back to his face. "Kiss me again and seal the deal."

His lips twitch against mine before he removes any barrier I have to ever stay away from him. His fingers glide over my hip and ass. "Where are your panties?"

I try not to smile. "I didn't think you wanted me to wear them in this dress."

He groans then sends my quivering insides into more turmoil by kissing me again. "I need you alone. I'm going into the bathroom now."

And when I hear the door shut, I don't even stop to tell my friends where I'm going. I hightail it out of the bar to the room he reserved. I send my friends a quick text then turn off my phone. I stand at the window and wait, knowing any indulgence with him is setting myself up for heartache but unable to stop my path of destruction.

8

Maksim

THE SUN RISES, AND ALTHOUGH I PULLED THE DRAPES SHUT TO shield the light, slivers of it peek through. I've never hated the sun so much. I have to leave my krasotka. It is the last time I will ever see her. We are both leaving Vegas and going our separate ways.

In a different world, I would convince her to come back to Chicago with me. The blindfold would come off, and there would be no more secrecy about who we are. And I would do everything in my power to make her fall in love with me.

But my reality is cruel. She doesn't come from the same cloth I do. The man I have to be at times has ramifications. And they aren't anything I would ever subject her to.

Before I leave her, the order I placed arrives. It's a pair of organic yoga pants, a tank top, and a cashmere wrap. I figured she could wear it home and maybe sleep on the plane. I'm sure she'll be tired since we were up all night.

Before she fell asleep in my arms, she whispered, "Tell me your name. Show me your face. Please."

I didn't answer her. I only kissed her, as hungry as ever, then tugged her tighter to me. "Go to sleep, my krasotka."

She didn't speak for a moment. "You won't be here when I wake up, will you?"

I swallowed down the emotions creeping up. "No. It's for the best."

She circled her fingers in my chest hair while her lip shook against my pecs. Wet warmth trickled around the silk and onto my skin.

I stroked and kissed her head a thousand times until I was sure she was asleep. But now the sun is coming up, and it's only fair I go. I've already stayed too long. And I struggle with my final words to her but put them in a note:

My Krasotka,

I wish things were different...that I was different. Don't ever let any man not appreciate every beautiful part of you. I'll never forget you or our time together.

M

P.S. Call the driver on the card. He will take you back to your hotel and the airport when you're ready to fly home.

. . .

I PUT THE DRIVER'S CARD NEXT TO THE LETTER. THEN I CLASP a thin bracelet around her wrist. The jewelry piece is simple, not flashy, which she seems to prefer, but she can wear it with any color since it has all three metals—rose gold, yellow gold, and platinum. Tiny diamonds rest where the metal curves. I bought it yesterday. I saw it and held on to it in case I ran into her. If I hadn't, I would have sent it to her room. But I carried the dainty item with me, and it's as if I knew deep down I would see her again.

This time, I don't remove her blindfold. I only untie the silk. I'm too scared she will wake up. The previous morning, I would have been able to handle it better. Today, I would break away from my resolve to keep her safe and away from the dangerous world I can never shake. She is too innocent and pure to be a part of it.

I stare at my krasotka one last time. Her perfect lips that ruined me more than I could have ever anticipated, I crave to kiss again. But I can't. Her dark hair, as silky as her blindfold, I want to run my fingers through one more time. But I don't dare. And the way her chest rises and falls so peacefully makes my body ache.

It's time to go. If she wakes up, it's going to be worse for both of us.

I tear myself away from her and creep out of the room. I text Dmitri that I'll meet him at the private airport. I'm not in the mood to be around anyone just yet. And I don't want to answer any questions about where I went the previous two nights. The guys tried to grill me yesterday, but I didn't tell them anything and quickly changed the subject.

It takes minutes to arrive at the hotel. I go straight to my room, pack my bag, and meet the guys on the plane. As soon as I get in, the flight attendant shuts the door.

Most of the guys are still intoxicated and continue drinking. I put on a joyful face and participate in all the banter going on, trying to forget about my krasotka, but the hollow ache in my belly only grows.

When we arrive in Chicago, I get in Dmitri's car, splitting off from my other brothers and the guys.

"You want to tell me what's going on?" he asks as soon as the door shuts.

"Nothing."

His green eyes turn to slits. "Don't lie to me. You disappeared two nights in a row. You've been extra quiet the entire trip."

I sigh. I'm not a liar. I'm a lot of things I despise, but lying or telling the truth is something I control. "I met a woman. Vegas is over. That's it."

He stays quiet then says, "You saw her both nights?"

"Yes."

"Who is she?"

I shrug. "I don't know anything about her. Not even her name."

A deep line forms between his eyebrows. "How is that possible?"

I give him the short version of our arrangement, and for the first time in a long time, my brother is speechless.

He finally asks, "She never asked you what your name was or to see your face?"

"No, she did. I told her I wouldn't break my word to her, and it was for the best."

"Why?"

I glance out the window at the buildings we pass. Snow lightly falls, dusting the ground. I wonder where my krasotka is and if she, too, is seeing snow. "I would have had to make her mine."

Dmitri lowers his voice. "I see. And why would that be a bad thing?"

I turn to him and meet his gaze. "I don't need to explain to you the man I am. You know what I've done and the things still looming over us. Anytime we think there is an end, it's always a beginning. And now that Boris's blood mixes with the Irish..." I close my eyes, wishing all the pieces of my darkness would vanish. I open my eyes and sternly say, "There is nothing in my world I want to subject her to."

"I felt the same way with Anna. But Anna had a choice. She didn't want me to throw us away. The part of our world that is evil is only a sliver of our life. And one day, we will be free of it. You deserve to be happy, Maksim. And Boris needs to stay away from the O'Malley's battles."

"His baby will be half O'Malley. It's not that simple, and you know it."

Dmitri shakes his head. "We need to keep reiterating to Boris there's been enough bloodshed. Killian, too."

The driver pulls off the expressway, and we stop at the light.

"I don't get it," Dmitri says.

"Get what?"

"All these years, you've been with plenty of women. You loved Jade, but you didn't worry about her."

Jade. This is the longest I've ever gone without thinking about her.

My krasotka made me totally forget about her.

"Jade is cut from our cloth. You know this." The only person who knows Jade's history is Dmitri. He was with me the night Jade had a meltdown about her past. Her father was beating her mother, and she shot him. Her brothers helped her dice her father up and dispose of the body. Her one brother fell into drugs and was threatening to talk to the police if Jade didn't keep paying for his habit. When she called his bluff, he came over high as a kite and almost killed her. She escaped and ran to my place. She didn't know Dmitri was in my house when she was sobbing hysterically with blood all over her.

Dmitri crosses his arms. "She is. But Anna's not. I don't think you should believe you have to settle for someone like Jade if there is another woman who will make you happy."

Have I been settling for Jade?

I didn't protect my brothers or mother from this life. I don't need to introduce anyone else to it.

"This woman I met doesn't deserve any part of our fucked-up shit," I mutter and turn back to the window. "Anyway, it doesn't matter. She's gone."

The car stops in front of my building.

"Maksim—"

"Let's drop it, okay?"

Dmitri sighs. "Sure."

"I'll talk to you tomorrow."

"Okay." He pats me on the back, and I get out.

The driver opens the trunk and hands me my bag. I go into my building, and my gut drops.

Not today.

Jade sits on the couch in the lobby. Her thigh-high black boots hide the legs I've licked too many times to count. Her miniskirt is short enough to reveal enough skin to usually drive me crazy.

She knows I love her in those boots.

This isn't happening.

"Maksim," she says and rises. Her jet black, edgy, chin-length bob is perfectly smooth. Her beautiful Asian skin is flawless as silk. And her hardened, I-don't-take-anyone's-shit expression that I used to admire suddenly seems overbearing and incredibly cold.

Maybe it's the warmth of being with my krasotka for the last two nights, but it doesn't rile my blood the way it normally does.

"What are you doing here?"

"I've been waiting for you."

"Jade, I'm not doing this today. I've had hardly any sleep in the last two days, and I don't have the energy."

She steps forward, puts her hand on my arm, and tilts her head up. Her eyes turn from cold to lukewarm. It's an expression she only reserves for me. No one else ever sees any softer side of her. "I haven't slept a lot, either. Let me come up with you. I'll run a bath and then we can take a nap. We can talk later when you're refreshed. I promise."

My jaw twitches. There's still a small part of me that wonders if we can be something more. But I don't know if it's possible anymore. Not because of Jade but because of me. This weekend was too intense. I experienced the opposite of everything Jade and I were. And I'm not sure if I want to go back. Even if I can't have my krasotka, I just don't know if I have any feelings left for Jade.

"I can't. Not today."

I've never resisted Jade before. She's always had some sort of power over me. And something flashes in her eyes. I'm not sure what to make of it, but I've seen similar eyes before in men when they realize they are about to lose.

Her eyes glisten. "I screwed up. Don't throw me away, please."

My chest tightens. "I need to rest, Jade. I can't think right now. Go home. We'll talk later."

She steps closer and reaches up, grasping my cheeks. "Can we have dinner this week and talk?"

I don't respond right away. Her hands feel like cold cement on my face. The zinging warmth of my krasotka's touch is all I can think about.

Jade desperately begs, "Please, Maksim."

I cave. "All right. Later in the week."

She smiles, pulls my head down, and stands on her tippy-toes. She attempts to kiss me, but I turn so she hits my cheek.

Her eyes get that look again, and it pains me. I don't want to hurt her. But I'm not sure if we can ever be again.

Do I even want her anymore?

It's a question I never thought I would contemplate. I've just always seen myself with her. But now, all I crave is a life with my krasotka. I'm an almost forty-six-year-old man. I'm not naive. My krasotka and I will never be. But I'm not sure where that leaves Jade and me.

9

Aspen

A STRONG ODOR OF GARLIC AND BUTTER SEEPS THROUGH THE thin walls and into my apartment, flaring in my nostrils. My neighbors cook almost every night. It usually comforts me, especially since Peter moved out, and I've been all alone, but nothing can fill the void that keeps growing.

I don't understand it. It's been a few weeks since Vegas. But every day, the ache expands. I hate I don't know his name or where he lives. I dream of his face, but it's just a mere outline of what I assume he looks like from my hands feeling his chiseled features. Every time I look at the bracelet on my wrist, I choke up. But I can't bear to remove it.

At night, I lay my head on my pillow, and his scent and voice fill my mind. I pretend his arms are around me.

How could I have been with Peter for twenty years, but I didn't feel a quarter of this longing for him?

It was only for two nights. I need to get a grip.

It doesn't matter how much I tell myself to get over him. My obsession with him doesn't dim. I even take the cashmere wrap he left me in the hotel room to work almost every day. It's a beautiful natural color and goes with nearly everything, but I wear it because it makes me feel like he's with me. And I realize I'm probably losing my marbles. He's a stranger. Gone and never coming back. I wish I could appreciate what we had and move on. But he haunts me.

I try to keep myself busy. I go to yoga after work every day. I went out with the girls last weekend on both nights and volunteered at the children's hospital the rest of the time. A family came in who spoke Russian. I kept looking around, hoping he would magically appear.

For all I know, he lives in Russia. There is nothing I know about him, except he's dangerous. And I read the two letters he left me over and over, as if they will give me some hint as to who he is and where he could be.

No one knows I'm dying inside. I've not told my friends anything. They would tell me to hop on another stallion and ride him until Mr. Stranger Danger was out of my system. But I know no one could help me forget him. Any other man will only be a disappointment. I'm sure of it.

I stick my yoga mat in the closet, take a shower, and put on my pajamas. Thick snowflakes are falling, and the cold hits my warm skin when I stand by the window.

It's Thursday night. The neon bar sign across the street blinks, but two of the letters are burnt out. It's been that way for a year now, but they don't fix it. The street is empty of pedestrians, which isn't unusual since the neighborhood isn't the greatest.

This is my life.

I need to stop feeling sorry for myself.

The buzzer goes off and jolts me out of my thoughts. I don't know who would be coming over this late. It's after nine.

I press the button. "Hello."

"Aspen, let me up."

"Peter, what are you doing here?"

"It's freezing out here. Can you let me up?"

I sigh and release the lock. I put my robe on then open my front door and wait for him to arrive.

He opens the stairwell door, slightly out of breath. Snow covers his Chicago Cubs hat. His blue eyes peer at me, and my stomach clenches. I've always loved his eyes. They are what caught my attention when I was eighteen and crossing the street. His eyes have never changed, and every time he told me about a new business venture or something he wanted to do, they lit up with excitement. And I always fell for those eyes.

"They still haven't fixed the elevator?" he asks, and his blues turn to surprise.

"Nope."

"You should move down a few floors, then." He gives me his teasing smile I used to be so attracted to. Now I want to smack him.

I fold my arms across my chest. "What do you want, Peter?"

His face falls. "Can I come in? We need to talk."

"About what?"

"Do you want the neighbors to hear?"

He's right. And these walls are already thin.

I shake my head, open the door farther, walk to the couch, and sit down.

Peter plops down, practically on my lap.

"Do you mind?" I elbow him.

He moves an inch away then turns. "How've you been?"

My anger builds. I slowly repeat, "What do you want, Peter?"

He turns so his knee is on the couch, and his arm is on the back. "We made a mistake."

I gape at him. "We?" It comes out harsher than I expect.

His eyes widen.

Yep. I'm no longer your "yes girl."

He reaches for a strand of my hair and twirls it around his finger.

I smack his hand, and it yanks my hair. "Ow!"

He holds his hands up. "Sorry."

"What do you want, Peter?" I repeat, sterner this time.

He grabs my hand.

I'm too confused over what is going on and don't tear it away for a moment.

"I miss you."

I pull my hand back. "You miss me?"

"Yes."

"Why? Does your fiancée need a tummy tuck?"

His lips twitch.

"You think this is funny?"

He reaches for my cheek, but I duck away from it.

"Don't touch me."

"Aspen, I know you're angry. I made a huge mistake. Let's work through it. I don't want to throw twenty years away."

The ticking of my wall clock and pounding of my blood between my ears are the only things I hear. "We're divorced. You already threw it away."

"We don't have to be."

My insides quiver and heart races. "Excuse me?"

His face turns more serious. Regret fills it. At least, I think it's genuine, but that's the problem. Looking back, what was real about anything he told me during our marriage?

He slides his arm around me, and there is nowhere to go. "I'll make it up to you, I promise. Just give me another chance. I love you. I want to come home."

When I first learned he betrayed me, I would have given anything for him to tell me he loved me and still wanted me. But it's too late. I've seen what a relationship between two people should feel like. And while I wasn't in a relationship with Mr. Stranger Danger, at least he wanted me. Every touch and kiss ignited my soul. And his actions only involved my best interests. Everything he did showed me what I want from a man.

I'll probably never find anything like what was between us for those two days, but I'll be damned if I'm going back to someone who never put me first.

"Get out."

"Aspen—"

"Get out!" I scream, which is the first time I've ever raised my voice at Peter. Even when I found out he cheated, I was too busy crying to yell.

Peter's shocked look only increases the rage I feel.

I rise and point to the door. "This is my house. You're not welcome here anymore. Get out."

Peter rises and steps toward me. His frame towers over mine, and he grabs my arm and squeezes it hard. "Why are you acting like this? All couples go through things. This was ours. Let's move forward."

His grasp digs into my arm. "Let go. You're hurting me."

MAGGIE COLE

He doesn't release me. "Listen to me. I made a mistake. It's over. We need to move forward. I'm willing to leave her, move back in, and be your husband again."

I shake my arm but can't escape him. My insides shake. "Let go!"

He glances at my arm and pulls his hand back.

I go to the door and open it. "Get out. Don't come back. We're through."

He steps in front of me again so his body is touching mine. He softens his voice. It's what he always does whenever he wants something. I used to fall for it, but now it disgusts me. "Think about it. I know you still love me."

I don't respond, just blink back tears and turn my head toward the hallway.

I don't love him. And everything about his visit only slaps me in the face about how stupid I was to waste twenty years of my life on him—all of my twenties and most of my thirties. I'll never get those years back.

He kisses me on my forehead and leaves. I slam the door and lock it then turn out the lights and crawl into my bed.

I hate this bed. He used to sleep in it with me. But I don't have money to buy another one.

I toss and turn all night, sometimes crying. I mourn the years I'll never get back. I grieve that I didn't make Mr. Stranger Danger tell me his name and where he lived. I try to stop myself from falling into the pit of loneliness.

The next morning, I do the only thing that gives me some comfort. I fix myself up as nice as possible. I put on the tank top Mr. Stranger Danger gave me then put on the cashmere wrap he gave me. I ignore the bruises on my arm from Peter's grip.

It's never happened before. Peter's never laid a hand on me. I'm not sure why he squeezed my biceps so hard last night. But his fingers left marks.

I still don't know what to make of his visit, other than the assumption his new girlfriend or fiancée or whatever she is to him, isn't bringing home the bacon.

I put on an arctic-blue pencil skirt then shove my feet in my camel-colored knee-high boots. I stare at my bracelet for several minutes.

Pull it together. It's time to go to work.

I take the L-train since I can't afford a cab or even an Uber. By the time I get to work, I'm feeling normal again. I go through security, and when I get to my office, my boss knocks on the door.

"Hi," I say.

"Morning. Did you get the memo?"

"About...?"

He sighs then nervously runs his hand through his dirty-blond hair. He sits, and his face turns red, which makes his freckles pop out more.

"Fred, what's wrong?"

"The mayor sent a memo."

"And?"

"There's a zoning issue with a project in Oak Park."

"Did you tell him wrong department? We handle Oak Lawn." I smirk.

Fred's face falls further. "That's what the memo was about."

My pulse increases. "I'm not following."

"The mayor is combining the Oak Park and Oak Lawn territories. He's shredding us down to one team."

My gut flips. "I need my job."

Fred nods. "Yes. Me, too. The good news is we're the chosen ones."

I release a breath. "Good. I mean, sorry for everyone else, but..."

"We have a meeting in ten minutes. Some bigwig investors have a project in Oak Park, and they've been held up by a parcel of land Lorenzo Rossi owns. Well, owned before someone killed him."

A bad feeling fills me. "Rossi, as in the crime family?"

"Yes. Anyway, the lot reverted back to the city since Rossi didn't clean the land in time like he agreed to. So the bigwigs are coming in to buy it."

I tap my fingers on my desk. "What does this have to do with us? We aren't sales, either."

"No. But they signed five minutes ago, and there are zoning issues. The mayor said we need to figure it out."

I lean closer to Fred and lower my voice. "What do you mean, figure it out? What's wrong with it?"

Fred pulls at his hair. "Before Rossi died, he rezoned the land for industrial."

"What was it?"

"Residential and retail commercial."

"Why would he do that?"

"You're asking the wrong person. But the mayor said we need to do whatever it takes to figure this out, and quickly."

"That's not an easy fix."

"I know. And once we figure that out, these investors have several other projects the mayor said have priority."

"Why are they getting special treatment?"

Fred holds up his hands. "I'm the messenger. But does it matter?"

"No, I guess not."

"Okay. Well, ready to do double the work for no pay increase?"

I groan.

Fred forces a smile. "Carmen has all the files in the conference room. Ready to go undo some crazy mob crap?"

I rise. "Lead the way. Maybe it'll be exciting for once."

Fred grunts. "Don't count on it."

"Do I have time to grab a coffee at the cafe?"

"Yep. Can you get me a double espresso?"

"On it."

I rush downstairs, get a coffee and Fred's espresso, then go into the conference room. When I step inside the room, I freeze.

A man, at least eight inches taller than me, stands in an expensive suit talking to Fred. The material stretches over his body like a glove, as if it were custom made. He has wavy salt-and-pepper hair. The delicious scent of bergamot and cardamom flares in my nostrils. In a thick, Russian accent, he says, "How long is it going to take to rezone this parcel?"

"It needs to have board approval," Fred replies.

I must be going crazy.

It can't be him.

My loins tell me otherwise. It's his voice and scent.

"Ah, there she is. Let me introduce you to Aspen. She's the expert you want to talk to. Any loopholes to get this passed sooner, she'll find. Aspen, this is Maksim Ivanov."

Maksim spins, and the look in his eyes tells me I'm not crazy. It is him. And I recognize him. I saw him standing in the doorway at the pool in Vegas. And all the pieces of the outline I had in my mind get filled in. He could be the poster child of tall, dark, and handsome.

His eyes are the brightest blue I've ever seen, making Peter's seem dull in comparison. I knew they were light because he admitted it to me. But seeing them takes my breath away. Even though they are stunning, dominance and danger lurks in them. But his desire for me is also evident. He's not forgotten me, and I see it. His low-cut beard is barely there, as if he might shave it some days and might not on others.

I spill the coffees over both of us. The hot liquid soaks my wrap and skirt. It slides down his shirt and pants.

"Oh God," I whisper, shaking. "I'm sorry."

He recovers quickly. "It's okay. Let's get cleaned up in the bathroom. Show me where it is, please." He leads me out of the room, practically holding me up. My knees are weak. Every step I take seems like I'm climbing a mountain. And when he pulls me into the bathroom, he locks it, spins me so I'm against the door, and pushes his hands in my hair.

"Your name is Aspen?"

I try not to cry, but a tear escapes. I can only nod.

He wipes my tear with his thumb. "You live in Chicago?"

I barely manage to reply, "Yes."

He hesitates then says, "You know who I am?"

"Yes. And I've missed you."

Maksim

SHE'S MISSED ME.

I'm not the only one thinking about us.

This isn't good. She can't be in my world.

Her eyes are full of tears. There's so much emotion spinning in them, and it includes desire and pain. And I'm not blind. I see it's all for me. But I've never had a woman look at me how she is.

Don't be selfish. Do the right thing for her.

I shouldn't do it. I should dry her off, walk her back to the conference room, and figure out a way to never see her again.

But I can't.

I lower my lips to her and say, "I've missed you, too, my krasotka."

Her tears fall, and I can't wipe them away fast enough. So I give up and kiss her, slowly at first, trying to savor every piece of her and us, but not able to control my insatiable hunger for her.

Her tongue rolls against mine, igniting the fire I thought died when I left Vegas. But it didn't. It's as hot and uncontrollable as before. And every breath she gives me, I take, unable to stop kissing her until someone knocks on the door.

"Just a minute," I bark.

"Oh, sorry. I'll go to the other one," a woman's mousey voice replies.

I return to kissing Aspen.

She even has a sexy name.

I've been obsessing over what her name could be. I stopped myself several times from texting her magenta-haired friend or tracing the number. I still don't know their names, either. I thought they were from California since her phone number had a San Francisco area code.

There's another knock on the door.

"Just a minute," I repeat.

Aspen bites on a smile. I trace it with my thumb.

"You live in Chicago?" she cautiously asks.

"Yes."

She takes a deep breath, and we lock eyes.

My heart pounds in my chest. "I've not lied to you. I am the man I claimed to be in Vegas. It's not the safest situation for you to be with me."

She bites her lip and furrows her brows. "Tell me why."

I stroke the smooth skin on her cheek, not breaking our gaze.

It's too much for her to know. In eleven years, I never told Jade.

She's nothing like Jade.

She finally asks, "Do I not get a choice?"

The blood between my ears pounds so loud I'm sure she can hear. I know everything about this woman's body. I'm limited to details on her life and who she is. But I've never had such an urge to trust someone.

Tell her she doesn't get any choice in the matter and end it. It's best for her.

She's not going to want any part of me if she knows who I really am anyway.

Instead of telling her what I should, I sternly reply, "You don't know what you're asking."

Pain crosses her eyes. She whispers, "So is this it?"

Tell her yes. It's better this way.

Against every voice in my head telling me to put her first, I selfishly choose me. Everything feels right when I'm with her. And every moment away from her has been torture. No matter what I do, the ache for her has only grown over the last few weeks. All I've done is obsess about her, wondering if she is okay, where she's at, and what she's doing. And I've slowly been dying inside, remembering every moment of what it felt like being with her and thinking I would never see or touch her again. "I have an idea."

Hope fills her expression. "I'm listening."

Don't do it.

"Why don't we have dinner at my place and I'll fill you in?"

Her lips twitch. "Yes."

"But, you won't want anything to do with me when you know what I'm capable of." It's the truth and better if she's prepared for it.

She swallows hard then pulls my face back to hers. "You won't ever hurt me." It's a statement and not a question, but I still answer.

"No. Never."

She kisses me. It's sweet, needy, and full of everything she gave me in Vegas. It doesn't leave out any of her desire and only serves to drive my greed for her deeper.

Someone else knocks.

"Still busy," I yell.

She caresses my cheek. "We should get cleaned up. I'm sorry about your suit."

"You can throw coffee on me any day," I tease.

She glances down and touches her wrap then winces. "I love this. It's ruined now."

I lean into her ear. "I know what store it came from. I'll buy you another one."

She shakes her head. "You don't have to—"

I consume her lips again and then mumble, "You're not supposed to argue with me, remember?"

She softly laughs.

"I missed your laugh, krasotka."

"You did?"

I cup her cheek. "Yes. Everything about you, I missed. And you're just as beautiful as you were in Vegas."

She wraps her arms around my shoulders and snuggles into my chest, inhaling deeply.

I kiss her head. "Come on, let's clean up, then you can tell me how you're going to help me with this parcel."

I lead her to the counter. I wipe my pants with towels, and she takes off her wrap to do the same. Something on her arm catches my eye in the mirror.

I spin her into me.

Her eyes widen in surprise. "What's wrong?"

"What happened to your arm?"

She closes her eyes and exhales. "Nothing."

"I won't lie to you. I expect the same honesty in return," I say in a low voice, trying to control my anger. "These are finger marks."

She gazes up, meeting my eyes. "It wasn't intentional. It's never happened before."

Stay calm so you don't scare her.

"What hasn't?"

"Peter came over last night."

"Your ex-husband?" Jealousy flares in my bones. I hate that another man got to spend twenty years with her. He's a stupid man for ever looking at anyone else when he had her, but I still despise she shared her bed with him for all those years.

"Yes."

"Why?"

Annoyance flashes in her face. "He said he made a mistake and wants me back. He wants to move back in."

My pulse quickens, and my chest tightens. Twenty years will make many people do a lot of things. "Please tell me you aren't letting him?"

"No. Of course not. I'm done."

I breathe in relief. But then I get angry again. "How did your arm get bruised?"

"He just grabbed it. He didn't mean to. It was the only time anything like that has ever happened in twenty years. I don't think he realized how hard he was gripping me."

I stare at her arm, trying to stay calm but feeling the beast in me awaken. It's the one that surfaces before I kill. And I do everything I can to restrain him.

She reaches for my cheek. "Maksim."

It's the first time she's said my name. It rolls out of her mouth with sugar attached. I'm reminded again at how innocent and wholesome she is.

She pins her gaze on me. Her dark-brown eyes tug on my heart. "It was an accident. I promise you."

She may think it was, but he was holding her too tight for a reason.

"How long has he been harassing you?"

She shakes her head. "He's not. It's the only time he's contacted me."

I hesitate, but her eyes plead with me to believe her. And I don't doubt her, but I don't trust him, either. "If he contacts you again, I want to know."

Her lips twitch until she has a full-on grin. "Does this mean I'm going to be seeing more of you after tonight?"

I palm her ass and tug her against my erection and cradle her head with my other hand. I kiss her neck then murmur in her ear, "There's nothing I want more than you. But we're going to talk tonight. What I tell you, you shouldn't take lightly, my krasotka."

She inhales deeply. "Okay."

There's another knock on the door.

I kiss her one last time then escort her back to the conference room, not touching her and missing her body already.

When we get into the room, I pull the chair out next to mine and motion for her to sit. I refrain from doing or saying anything that isn't professional with her.

The next hour, she runs circles around her colleagues. She listens, asks questions, and comes up with possible solutions. She points out pitfalls the board may use to deny our request, then she discusses how to get around them.

I'm not sure why anyone else is even in the room. She's running the show. The rest of them sit back and say nothing.

I look at the business cards in front of me.

How is she only a permit technician?

The other titles on the cards are Permit Specialist, Code Enforcement Officer, and Senior Planner. All are higher on the totem pole. She shouldn't even be in this meeting based on her title.

The more she shows her brilliance, and the others sit back and twiddle their thumbs when she presents hurdles, the angrier I become.

She's being taken advantage of here. They are surely getting way more pay, and she's getting the short end of the stick.

When the meeting is over, I hand her my card, not bothering to give it to any of the others. I only address her. "My cell phone is on here. Please call or text with any updates."

She smiles, and my heart skips another beat.

I don't want to leave her, but I go through the motions, doing my best to keep it professional so I don't embarrass her in front of her coworkers.

As soon as the elevator opens on the first floor, my cell vibrates. I pull it out.

Unknown: *It's Aspen. We didn't talk about the details for tonight.*

I walk quickly to my car before I add her as a contact and reply.

Me: *Send me your address. I'll pick you up at seven if that works?*

Aspen: *Yes.*

Dots appear as if she's typing then they go away.

Me: *Ask me whatever you want, my Krasotka.*

A moment passes before she responds.

Aspen: *Should I bring an overnight bag?*

My adrenaline surges, but I remind myself of who I am.

Me: *Yes. But if you decide to leave after I tell you things, I won't stop you.*

She only texts back her address.

Uneasiness erupts inside me. The neighborhood she lives in is rough. It's no place for a woman like her.

I text her again.

Me: *What time do you get out of work?*

Aspen: *Five.*

Me: *My driver will wait for you outside to take you to your place.*

Aspen: *That isn't necessary.*

Me: *There isn't any point arguing about this.*

She doesn't respond.

The car stops at a light. I roll the divider window down. "Adrian, look at me for a moment."

He obeys, and I snap a picture of him and text it to Aspen.

Me: *This is my driver, Adrian.*

"Missing my good looks when you aren't with me?" Adrian jokes.

I snort. Adrian is my cousin. He's also my top bodyguard. Things are low-level risk right now, so when things are calm, he drives for me. "Funny. You'll go back where we were and pick up a woman named Aspen at five. You'll take her to her apartment and escort her into her place. Wait outside her door until I pick her up at seven."

"Got it."

"If you see anyone approach her, you protect her at all costs."

"Yes, sir."

She may have said her ex is harmless, but I saw her bruises. And no one is going to touch or harass her, whether she becomes mine or not.

Now I know she's in the city, everything I assumed is correct. I'm not going to be able to stay away from her unless she tells me she no longer wants me. It'll be painful, but I'll have to respect it. And she's never again going to be unprotected.

Anyone who tries to harm her will experience my wrath. Mercy won't be part of it.

11

Aspen

THE DAY DRAGS BY AFTER MAKSIM LEAVES, BUT MY FLUTTERS never calm. Part of me is nervous about what he's going to tell me. Another part of me screams it doesn't matter. He's a good man. I can't imagine him as anything else. Whatever he's done can't be so bad I need to stay away from him.

He bought a piece of land Lorenzo Rossi, the son of the Italian mob boss, owned.

That doesn't mean anything.

Doesn't it?

I try to push the thought out of my head, but it nags at me.

What if there's a connection?

My knowledge of the mafia is limited. I don't watch movies or TV shows about it. I haven't studied it. But from time to time, coworkers will make comments about the construction unions being owned by them. And Giovanni, Lorenzo's father, was imprisoned in the last year for something to do with embezzling the union pension fund. The governor was involved, too. After his arrest, he was murdered. Rumor had it, Giovanni ordered the hit.

I want to spend my day researching everything I can about Maksim, but the combining of two departments has me handling one fire after another. And I don't think I've ever been so busy but also felt like the day was going so slow.

When five hits, instead of staying how I usually would, I leave. Nothing is going to stop me from my date with Maksim.

I get into the lobby. As soon as I step out of the elevator, Adrian steps away from the wall. "Aspen?"

His Russian accent is thicker than Maksim's. His sandy-blond hair and blue eyes remind me of Peter's, but that is where the similarities end. He's built like a brick house, and although his looks could charm any woman, his eyes have a warning in them not to mess with him.

"Are you a bodyguard or driver?" I tease, but it comes out nervously.

His jaw clenches. He assesses me for a moment. "I am whatever I need to be in the moment. And I have strict orders to protect you."

Flutters take off. Anxiety over what I'm getting myself into, but also an appreciation that Maksim cares so much about my safety, overwhelms me. I put my hand on my stomach to steady it. I've never needed any sort of protection. This seems over the top, but I can't lie to myself. A part of me is enjoying that for once in my life, someone is looking out for me.

Adrian's gaze drops to my gut. "Ma'am, are you okay?"

I force a smile and remove my hand from my stomach. "Yes. I'm ready if you are."

He puts his hand on the middle of my back. It's nothing but protective. He continues to glance around while beelining to the car. When I get inside, there's a dozen, long-stemmed, red roses on the seat.

I pick them up and inhale them. I've never gotten roses before. Even when Peter and I dated, he never gave me flowers. He claimed flowers only died, so why spend the money. But it's not like he gave me anything in their place.

I don't need to be showered with gifts, but it's nice to be spoiled for once. And it's another gesture Maksim has made that adds up to more than Peter did for me in twenty years of marriage.

His thoughtful actions make me wonder again how there could be anything so horrible about Maksim that I would need to stay away from him.

There isn't. He's overreacting about something.

But I know he's dangerous. I can always feel it.

My phone rings, and my flutters change to happiness. I answer it. "Maksim."

His Russian accent makes me listen closer so I can understand him through the phone. "Have you changed your mind about tonight, my krasotka?"

Panic fills me. "No. Have you?"

He grunts. "It would not be possible. I told you if I knew where you were, I would not be able to resist you."

I smile. "Good."

"I did not ask. Are you allergic to anything, or is there anything you don't eat?"

I rest my cheek against the seat and stare out the window at the passing Chicago skyline. "My father fed me too much fried bologna as a child. I'm not a fan."

He chuckles. "I won't ever feed you bologna, then. Anything else?"

"Nope. That's it. What about you?"

"My mother cooked lots of porridge when I was a boy. I'm okay if I never eat it ever again."

"I'll keep it porridge-free when I cook for you, then."

"Ahh, you cook?" I can feel the smile in his voice even though we're on the phone.

"I dabble."

"What else do you dip your toes into?"

"Not a lot. I'm boring, remember?"

"I'm not buying that."

There's a moment of silence. I glance at the flowers.

"Maksim?"

"Yeah."

"Thanks for the roses. I've...umm...it's the first time I've ever gotten them...well, any flowers, really."

"Fool," he mutters.

My pulse increases. "Sorry. Umm…"

"No. Not you. Your ex."

I take a nervous breath.

"I have to go, my krasotka. I will pick you up at seven."

"Okay. Thank you for sending Adrian to take me home."

"You're welcome."

The city turns from nice to more rundown the closer we get to my neighborhood. Snow falls so thick, a white blanket begins to form. When we finally get to my apartment, Adrian pulls next to the curb and parks. He gets out and opens my door.

"Thank you. Have a great night," I chirp.

He grunts, protectively places his hand on my middle back again, and moves me toward the front door.

"What are you doing?"

"Escorting you to your apartment."

I stop. "What?"

Adrian arrogantly arches his eyebrows. "Is this the part you argue with me?"

"What?" I repeat.

"I've been given strict instructions. There is no point fighting me on this. I have a job to do. Can we avoid the drama?"

"Drama?"

He nods, and his lips twitch.

"Is this normal?" I ask and wipe the snow off my eyelashes.

"What do you mean?"

"Does Maksim provide a bodyguard for all the women he dates?"

"I don't discuss my employer's business with anyone. And I suggest we go inside since this snow is wet and coming down harder."

I stop questioning him and move into the small lobby, consisting of the broken elevator and door to the stairwell.

Adrian pushes the button for the elevator.

"It's out of order. Hope you haven't gotten your workout in yet," I tease.

He snorts and opens the stairwell door. "What floor are you on?"

"Ten."

He nods. "That's doable. It could be worse. Let's go." He takes my purse and roses from me.

"Hey. What are you doing?"

"Maksim will not be happy if you carry these things up ten flights. Do not argue. You'll just be wasting your breath again."

I groan. "This is a bit extreme, don't you think?"

He shrugs. "Not if you're a gentleman." He motions for me to go through the door.

I step into the stairwell and mutter, "I guess chivalry isn't dead."

"Not with the Ivanovs or anyone in their employ," he replies.

We walk the ten flights of stairs rather quickly. I'm used to it, but when we get to the top, I tease Adrian, "That was impressive. Guess you're used to cardio."

"I run ten miles a day."

"Ten miles," I shriek.

He chuckles and opens the door. "Yep."

I step out and freeze.

Oh, crap. Not now.

Peter is sitting outside my door. His arms hug his shins, and his face is in his knees.

I quicken my stride. I stop in front of him. "What are you doing here?"

He jumps up. "Waiting for you. We need to talk."

"We did last night. There's nothing left to say. It's over. *We're* over. Don't keep coming here."

"We aren't over. Stop being stubborn."

"I'm not!"

Peter reaches for my face, but Adrian grabs his arm and bends it behind his back. He growls, "Don't touch her."

Peter's eyes widen in fear and surprise. "What the—"

Adrian pushes me back with his other hand and steps between Peter and me. "I believe Aspen told you not to come back. The next time I see you here, you're leaving in a body bag."

"Don't threaten me," Peter blurts out.

Adrian spins him into a headlock and keeps his arm pinned.

"Argh," Peter wails.

"Adrian," I cry out, scared he's going to break Peter's arm or kill him.

Adrian doesn't back down, and Peter continues to whimper. His face grows red as he winces.

"Adrian!"

Adrian leans into Peter's ear and says something so low I can't hear it.

Peter chokes and nods, and Adrian finally releases him. He sternly counts down from ten.

Peter gives me a quick, angry glance, then scurries into the stairwell.

I spin to Adrian. "Was that necessary?"

His face hardens. "Yes."

"No, it wasn't," I insist. I don't like Peter coming around, but I also don't condone violence.

The blues in Adrian's eyes pool together in cold confidence. "You're under Maksim's protection. Anyone who comes near you and doesn't listen when you tell them to leave you alone will be considered a threat."

What am I getting into with Maksim?

This is how he handles things?

He has warned me from day one about who he is. Have I not been listening?

I break my gaze with Adrian and pick my purse and the roses off the floor where he dropped them. I fish my keys out and open the door to my apartment. I don't say goodbye or thank you. I'm still too shaken up and upset over what he did. But most of all, I'm scared.

I lock and deadbolt the door behind me. Adrian won't hurt me or force his way in, I'm sure of it. But I have an urge to put a security blanket over myself and never come out.

I sit on my bed and question everything about Maksim and me.

Why am I pushing to be with someone who leads me down a dangerous path?

I try to convince myself to text Maksim and tell him I've changed my mind, and we shouldn't pursue anything between us. But I can't. I stare at the notes on my nightstand, feeling all the aches of not having him in my life for the last few weeks.

I rise and go through the motions of getting ready. I take a shower and shave. I put all my effort into doing my hair and makeup. I put on a pair of black leather pants, a form-fitting, black top, and my four-inch ankle boots.

I sit on my couch, nervously tapping my fingers on my leg, not sure if I should go or not.

Men's mumbled voices and Russian accents leak through my front door. I peek through the peephole and am shocked to find Adrian still outside.

Has he been here the entire time?

Maksim sounds and looks angry.

I open the door, and their conversation halts. Maksim looks at me. His eyes light up, but then his expression falls. He swiftly steps inside, shuts the door, and pulls me into his arms, palming my head.

I melt into him. It makes any decision no longer a choice. I can't debate about what's the right or wrong thing for me to do. All I can do is inhale bergamot and cardamom and listen to his heartbeat.

"My krasotka, you are not all right."

I'm not sure how to reply. I slide my arms around him, not wanting to be anywhere, except in his embrace.

Several minutes pass, and I wonder if his heart or mine races faster.

He slowly tilts my head up. His blue eyes swirl with darkness. "I will not allow any man to harass or harm you. Whether you come with me or not, you are under my protection now and in the future. This will not change, and I will not lie about it."

I swallow the lump in my throat. "Peter is harmless." It comes out less confident than I want it to, but part of me doesn't understand Peter's latest obsession with coming to my apartment, either.

"He's already left bruises on you. His desperation will only grow. I know about these things."

"How?"

Maksim's jaw clenches. "It doesn't matter how. I do. And I won't allow him to bother you in any way."

I stay quiet, a mix of thoughts confusing me. Part of me does want his protection. But it also feels selfish to want anyone to get hurt because of me.

Anguish fills Maksim's eyes. "Have I lost you before I've told you the entire truth of who I am?"

My reaction isn't calculated. It's quick and without thought. I reach up and cup his cheeks. Before I can stop the words, they rush out. "I already know I can't lose you."

Relief fills his face. He kisses me, stirring every bit of life I have left, deepening my craving to be his forever. When he pulls back, he doesn't say anything. He takes my coat off the stand, holds it open, and I slip into it. He leads me down the stairs and outside the building where a snow-covered Adrian is waiting.

We get into the car. Maksim slides me onto his lap, and our lips and tongues duel in a blaze of need. The entire ride to his penthouse, we stay lip locked. I forget about everything, except him and how he makes me feel.

Maksim

AFTER I LEFT MY MEETING WITH ASPEN, I CLEARED MY DAY and researched anything I could find out about her ex-husband. Besides being a fool, from what I could tell, he's nothing but a trust fund baby who couldn't do anything worthwhile with the money. He's had no job and one failed business after another in the twenty years they were married. Then he went through his family's fortune. Aspen's worked the entire time since she graduated high school, supporting him.

All he's done is mooch off her—lazy sack of shit.

The more I dug, the deeper my disgust grew. His current girlfriend, the one he cheated on Aspen with, is getting her master's in business. But her social media account just changed in status from *in a relationship* to *single*.

He wants Aspen back so she can support him again.

Over my dead body.

I spent two hours in the gym, trying to blow off steam, before leaving to pick Aspen up. I didn't want to be with her feeling the anger pooling in my veins.

After I showered and dressed, I saw the message from Adrian telling me what happened outside her apartment. The two hours I spent cooling my rage was for nothing. I stewed the entire way to her place.

As I drove farther into her neighborhood, my disgust for her ex only grew.

He inherited enough money. Aspen shouldn't be living in this dangerous of an area. But all he did was make her work her ass off and take advantage of her.

I walked into her building when someone came out. The elevator was broke, further tugging at my emotions, and I climbed the ten flights, taking several steps at a time. I only got a few sentences into my discussion with Adrian before Aspen opened the door.

She stole my breath, like she always does, but it was clear she was upset over what happened. We seemed to get past it by some miracle, and she still came with me to my place, but now my stomach is flipping. I can't shake the feeling I'm going to lose her. It's the same gut-wrenching feeling I had when I left her in Vegas.

I'm making her a martini. She's standing at the window with her back to me, peering out into the Chicago night. It reminds me of how she stood at the windows in Vegas, waiting for me to blindfold her.

I pour the liquid in a glass and carry it over to her. I step behind her, wrap my arm around her, and put my cheek on hers.

She shudders against my body and closes her eyes. Her one hand reaches for my thigh. Her other one wraps around mine, which holds the stem of the drink.

"You okay, my krasotka?"

She nods, opens her eyes, and turns her face to mine. "Maybe it's better if I don't know."

A lump grows in my throat. I want to agree with her suggestion. "You already had one man in your life who was a coward. I won't be the second. You deserve to know what kind of man I am."

She turns back to the window. She quietly replies, "If I hadn't met you in Vegas, and we didn't have our arrangement, what would you have thought when you met me today?"

I release her, put her drink on the side table, then take her hand. "Come." I lead her to the couch and pull her onto my lap.

She tilts her head then strokes a lock of my hair off my forehead. Her touch is lightning to my veins. I want to take her directly to my bedroom, but I know it's the coward's way out.

"If I hadn't already met you, I would have told myself to keep it professional and not cross any lines. It would have driven me crazy. And I would have left the meeting in awe at your intelligence and knowledge, just like I did today."

Her lips twitch.

"You're being taken advantage of by your colleagues, my krasotka."

Her face falls, turning slightly red, and something else fills it. If I'm not mistaken, it's shame.

"I've hit a nerve?"

She focuses on my chest and outlines the V of my neckline, stopping at the button. "I don't have a degree. I can't advance any higher than my current position."

"That's ridiculous. You're more qualified to deal with zoning issues than anyone else who was in that room."

Her face hardens. "It doesn't matter. I don't have the educational requirements."

I snort. "You're more qualified than anyone I've worked with in your building."

She avoids my eyes, circling my chest hair. "Can we change the subject?"

I tilt her chin so she can't avoid me. "You're brilliant, my krasotka."

She stays quiet.

"Should I return to talking about how I'd be going crazy, making myself stay away from you?" I tease.

She smiles and traces my lips. "The first night we met, I was dying for you to kiss me."

"I'm sorry. I knew it would make it harder for me to forget about you."

"But you did the next night."

"Yes. Either way, I was going to be tormented by not knowing what it was like or having the knowledge."

She bites her lip.

"What is it? You don't ever have to worry about asking me something."

She inhales slowly. "It wasn't about her?"

"Who?"

"The woman you told me about."

I forgot I told her about Jade. And I see in her eyes the real question she wants to ask.

I sternly say, "No. She had nothing to do with me not kissing you. And I'm not in love with her anymore. We are over, and both know it. We finished before Vegas."

Her breath releases as slowly as she took it in. "When were you with her last?"

I assume she's asking me when I last slept with her. "Months before I met you."

"So you're free, then? The only annoying ex is mine?"

"Yes. And yours won't be harassing you anymore."

She furrows her eyebrows. "Please don't hurt him. I don't want anyone injured over me. I don't like violence."

And here's how I'm going to lose her.

"He's been warned. Nothing happens to him if he stays away. If he attempts to harm you, there will be consequences. I cannot guarantee you his safety. That is up to him."

"Maksim, I spent twenty years with him. He was my husband. I don't want him injured."

My jealousy betrays me. I blurt out, "You still love him."

"No. I told you I don't. But that doesn't mean I wish ill things upon him."

My jaw twitches, and I turn toward the window.

She straddles me and grasps my cheeks. Her brown eyes are a mix of emotions. I'm not sure what to make of them. "This woman you used to love. You wish her harm?"

"Of course not!" I growl.

"It's the same thing."

"She's not leaving me bruised and sitting outside my door after being told to not come back."

"I told you what happened."

"And he was back today."

The truth hangs in the air. But I hate causing her to worry. As much as I'm jealous he got to have her for twenty years, I don't want this to be the thing that breaks us.

"You have my word. As long as he doesn't attempt to harm you and stops harassing you, he will not feel my wrath."

She opens her mouth to speak then shuts it.

"You want to know what my wrath means?" I slide my hand inside her shirt so it's over her heart. "Your heart is racing. Are you scared of me, my krasotka?"

She shakes her head. "No. I'm scared of what you are going to tell me you are capable of."

I caress her skin with my thumb and keep my hand over her heart. I lower my voice. "What do you think I am capable of? Hmm?"

She closes her eyes, as if in pain, and it shatters me. I shouldn't be putting her through any of this. Since I picked her up, I've seen the shift in her expression. She got a tiny glimpse into my reality, and it may be making her rethink being with me.

I lower my hand so it's under her bra cup, pressing her nipple between my fingers, continuing to graze my thumb across her chest. I shouldn't touch her when we discuss this, but I'm a man with an obsession, and she's it.

She swallows hard and pins me with her gaze. She chooses her words carefully. "I get the impression you are a man who will stop at nothing to protect what is yours."

I nod. "You are correct. And you are mine to protect now. The moment I saw you, something awakened in me. I will kill for you if I ever have to, whether you chose to stay with me or not."

Her eyes glisten. She quietly asks, "And you have killed before?"

My stomach flips.

I'm going to lose her.

She doesn't deserve to be lied to.

"Yes. Enough times I have lost track of how many men have taken their last breath before me."

Her heart thumps harder against my hand. She draws in a deep breath and blinks hard, but several tears fall.

Any reasoning left tells me to remove my hand from her blouse, kiss her one final time, then send her home forever. But I don't. The speed of my fingers never changes. And I take my other hand and slide it down her pants, cup her ass, and pull her closer to me.

"Why do you kill?" Her lips are inches from mine, torturing me.

"You ask a loaded question. There are things I'll never be able to disclose to you. But I have connections to the Russian mafia. Our family, in some ways, is merging with the Irish one. I don't want any of this, but this is my reality."

Her lips quiver. "You're part of the Russian mafia?"

I sternly say, "No."

"I... I don't understand."

I've often wondered how I would tell a woman about my past. There have never been any clear-cut answers. Tonight is no different. But this isn't in my head. This is now life, and the woman in front of me isn't someone I want to lose. But I don't see how I will ever hold on to her after our conversation is over.

"Maksim...please. Tell me."

I already trust her, but I still ask, "Anything I tell you, you give me your word it stays between us? No matter what you choose to do after you know everything?"

She surprises me by running her hand in my hair and leaning forward to kiss me sweetly. "You have my promise."

It only fuels my need for her more. "I haven't ever told anyone this."

"Not even her?"

To break up the tension, I tease, "You seem to be worried about my ex-relationship."

"You still loved her when we were in Vegas." Jealousy fills her eyes.

So I'm not the only one envious about past relationships.

Did I still love Jade? Had I not already been over her?

I can't say for sure when I lost my feelings for Jade, but anything I felt for her didn't dwindle away when I met Aspen. It exploded into a thousand pieces, never to be put back together again.

But I can't confirm nor deny Aspen's statement, so I don't do either. "I've told no one, not even her."

"Why are you telling me? You wouldn't have had to."

I slide my hand out of her shirt and cradle her head. "If I let you believe I was someone else, and you found out my truth, would you stay with me?"

"I..." She starts to shake her head then stops. "I don't know. I'm having a hard time figuring out how to let you go now."

It stabs at my heart but also gives me hope. She should be running from me. I just told her I'm a murderer and not just a onetime killer but a serial one.

"I don't want secrets and lies between us, Aspen. Do you?"

"No. Of course not."

"Okay. Then why don't I tell you the things I can so there are no misconceptions about who I am or what I'm capable of."

She nods.

I muster the courage and start. "When I was ten, my parents fled from Russia. My brother, Dmitri, was eight. Boris was three. Sergey wasn't even born yet. In some ways, things were harder here than in Russia. They didn't speak English. The jobs they took paid barely anything, and both my mother and father worked three to four jobs at a time, trying to feed the six of us."

"That must have been tough."

"Dmitri only remembers a little bit about the good times in Russia. I remember the most. But I was also a child and didn't go through what my parents did. But we went from thriving to barely surviving. And there were many others in our community who were in the same boat. But then there were the ones who preyed on poor families who were trying to make it day-to-day."

Compassion fills her eyes.

I keep talking because if I stop, I'm not sure if I'll get through it. My chest tightens, and my insides shake—all the guilt and anguish I carry from my family situation surfaces.

"When I was sixteen, my father got sick. We had no insurance. Dmitri and I tried to find jobs to help, but my mother insisted we stay in school. My father made us promise to get our education. And then he died."

The memory of my father slowly changing from the strong man I grew up with to skin and bones makes my gut churn faster.

Aspen strokes my cheek. "I'm sorry for your loss."

I glance out to the lit-up Chicago skyline. "I quit school to work. My mother and I fought, and she reminded me of my promise to my father to stay in school. But we couldn't live on her income alone, and she knew it. So, I went to work. But several weeks later, my mother came home and slapped cash on the table and informed us she got hired full time to be a secretary for my father's good friend. He was a Russian man with several businesses. My mother insisted I return to school."

"Did you?"

I turn back to Aspen. "Yes. And when I graduated, my mother had the money for me to go to community college. She said my father would be proud, and the best way to help our family was for me to keep getting my education. I still wanted to work full time to help her, but she insisted she was making enough. So I found part-time work and went to classes. Dmitri did the same, and everything seemed like it was working out for us."

I focus on the flickering fire, trying to calm the rage building in my chest. After all these years, I still want revenge. We haven't gotten it yet, but I want it. If I had the chance, I would take every ounce of wrath in me and show Zamir Petrov the beast he made me become.

I turn back to the window, staring into the night sky. "I finished college. Dmitri was in his last year when Boris found out who my mother's real employer was."

Aspen strokes my cheek. "Who did she work for?"

"The Russian mob boss, Zamir Petrov."

Aspen gasps. It's quiet, but I still hear it. I slide my hand back in her blouse over her heart. I don't know why I do, but something in me needs to feel the beat of her life against mine.

"So, your mom is in the mafia? And that makes you part of it?" Aspen asks, and I hear the confusion in her voice.

"No." I swallow the lump in my throat. "My mother killed herself after what happened. And we aren't in the mafia."

Aspen's heart races faster. She covers her mouth in horror.

I roll her nipple in my fingers, as if it'll calm her heart or mine. "There was a debt to pay. Everything we had, Zamir claimed was due to him. Our education, food in our bellies, and clothes on our backs."

Sympathy crosses her face. "You said your brother, Boris, found out?"

"Yes. He interrupted a meeting with Zamir and my mother. Zamir explained to Boris how he owned us. My mother claimed it wasn't true and not part of their deal. She insisted only she was indebted to him. But we all were. And he was ready for us to pay off our growing debt. Four boys were more valuable to him than one mother could ever be."

She inches her body closer to me so there is no room between us. She strokes the side of my head. "What did you have to do?"

I close my eyes, unable to look at her any longer.

She unfastens two buttons on my shirt and slides her hand inside, holding my heart as well. She puts her cheek on mine and whispers in my ear, "Tell me."

I keep my eyes shut, inhaling her muted floral scent. For years, I've tried to not think about what my brothers and I became. I pushed away any thought about my mother, help-less in Zamir's possession, watching us morph from innocent boys into monsters. "Zamir took my mother. He instructed my brothers, even Sergey, who was only twelve, to meet him in a warehouse to get her back. If we didn't come, he said he would put her in his whorehouse before killing her."

My krasotka inhales sharply and holds her breath.

I continue. Flashbacks of that night fly at me with intense speed. "When we got to the warehouse, plastic covered the walls and floor. Six metal chairs lined up perfectly straight with six warm bodies in them; five men and one woman, tied to the seats, with gags in their mouths. The woman was my mother. Zamir's thugs held knives to our throats while he explained how we would get our mother back."

Dizziness overpowers me, and my skin becomes clammy. I didn't realize the effect of telling my story out loud would have on me. My chest constricts. "I need some air."

I move Aspen off me and step out to my balcony. The snow is falling, and the frigid air feels good against my hot skin. I put my hands on the snow-covered railing and draw in a few cold breaths, looking out into the blinking lights of the city.

My krasotka's arms circle around my waist.

"It's too cold out here. I need a minute. Then I'll come back inside."

She only tightens her hold around me. Her cheek rests against my back, and she says, "Tell me what you had to do to get your mother back."

Snow continues to fall, and I barely feel the flakes sliding down my face. "We had a choice. Leave or earn our mother back. We chose our mother. And that night, we were all given a man to torture and split to shreds with a knife. They made us into killers that night. Zamir's thug tortured one man, and we all had to replicate what he did to the man we were assigned to. Our mother watched each of her children do the unthinkable, including Sergey, who wasn't even thirteen." The bile in my stomach rises and I swallow it back down.

"Maksim," my krasotka says several times until I finally realize she released me and is standing next to me with her back to the city.

She dips under my arm so she's between the wall and me. Snow covers her head and eyelashes, and her lip trembles.

"We need to go in. It's too cold out here."

She holds my cheeks. "No. I want to know the rest."

"Zamir didn't give our mother back to us. He made each of my brothers and me do ten jobs while my mother watched, tied to the chair and gagged. She eventually stopped crying, and Zamir made it clear that he still owned us after we got her back."

A moment passes and my krasotka asks, "What does that mean? You said you aren't in the mafia, but it sounds like you are."

"For several years, we tortured and killed men for Zamir. He would call, and we had to show up. Then Boris got into betting. We didn't know about it. When he was twenty-two, he went to Vegas and won over fifteen million dollars. When he came back, he bought all our freedom for ten million dollars. Anyone with the Ivanov name was never to be touched again. Boris gave me the rest of his money, and we started buying properties. But Zamir still owns Boris. Once a year, he calls on him, and whatever he wants him to do, he does. Until Boris or Zamir dies, the agreement will not cease. And it will always tie our family to the mob. No matter how legitimate our businesses are, we are still part of it. There is no escape. And Zamir is always looking for a way to pull us all back in."

Aspen shakes, and I'm not sure if it's only from the cold and snow or the realization of who I am and what I'm capable of.

"We need to go inside." I pull her in and shut the balcony door.

The truth is out. Every ounce of self-hatred and disgust I have for myself surfaces. And my fear I'll never see her again fills every cell in my body.

She steps forward and splays her hands on my chest. Her eyes glisten, full of pain, and she quietly says, "Maksim."

It's too much for her.

I don't just murder men. I torture them. Of course it's too much.

I tried to prepare myself for this, but my heart sinks. I take a deep breath and stroke her cheek. "It's okay, my krasotka. I don't blame you. Let me call Adrian to pull the car to the front. I'll take you home."

13

Aspen

GUILT EATS HIM. PAIN SLICES THROUGH HIS SOUL. SELF-loathing emanates off his muscular frame.

It tears me to shreds. My heart hurts from all he's been through. I struggle to breathe, thinking about what that monster made him do and the hold he still has over him and his brothers.

The strongest man I've ever met stands in front of me. And he's broken. I don't know how he survived it all. But I see how he blames himself for his brothers' involvement and even his mother's death.

I'm overwhelmed by it all. I wouldn't have anticipated how he became dangerous. In any hypothetical world, I would make it black and white.

He's a killer.

He tortures men before he steals their last breath.

He will do it again if he sees fit.

But I can't seem to hold him to my usual moral standards. All I see is how destroyed he is by who he is and his lack of ability to control his family situation.

And it hurts. So much more than I could have ever comprehended. The anguish on his face is a blade dicing up my heart. I try to find the words, but all I can get out is, "Maksim."

He bravely takes a deep breath and strokes my cheek. A new pain sears through his expression, but his voice remains steady and strong. "It's okay, my krasotka. I don't blame you. Let me call Adrian to pull the car to the front. I'll take you home." He pulls back, walking into the kitchen and away from me.

What? No.

I gape in shock for a moment then follow him.

He picks up his phone, but I step behind him and throw my arms around his waist.

He freezes. "Krasotka."

"Shh." I don't know what else to say. I can't get my thoughts in order quickly enough. All I know is I don't want to go home and be anywhere he isn't. His truth hasn't changed how I feel about him. It's not created the loathing for him he warned me it would. It only makes him more human.

For the first time since we've met, I understand that it's not just me who needs him. He needs me, too. I thought his hunger for me was just our chemical attraction. But this sexy, dominating, powerful man needs something no one has given him.

He needs love...from me.

His hand slowly slides over mine, but he still stays planted, breathing harder.

Instinct takes over. I dip my hand to his belt and release it and his pants, stroking his erection as it hardens under my touch.

He quietly groans, gripping my hand that is still on his waist. "Aspen—"

"You told me the truth. I am still here, wanting—no, *needing* you. I didn't ask you to take me home. There's not one part of me that is running from you. If you want my truth, I'll give it to you, too."

He spins, and his pants fall. His fingers slide through my hair and tilt my head. He brings his lips inches from mine. The intensity of his eyes pins me. "What is your truth?"

"Since I woke up in Vegas without you, I've been falling apart. You brought me to life, and without you, I'm wilting away again."

He blinks hard, steps closer, and traces my cheekbones.

"No matter what I did, I couldn't escape you. But I also didn't want to. I tried to hold on to any memory I could while the hole in my heart kept expanding until it started suffocating me."

He nods, as if he, too, experienced the same ache, but says, "I still don't want you near any darkness, my krasotka."

"It's darker without you," I whisper and admit what I've been trying to avoid over the last few weeks without him.

He closes his eyes, and I panic he's going to open them and tell me I can't be with him.

I stand on my tiptoes and draw his lips to mine. Desperation to be his, not only tonight but in the future, drives every flick of my tongue crashing against his.

He picks me up and sets me on the counter, pulling off my pants while never leaving my lips. Not that I would let him. I'm gripping his head, as if my life depended on it. But in some ways, maybe it does. Everything only feels right when I'm with him.

He enters me, and I cry out his name, clinging to him and pretzeling my legs around his hips. I meet the speed of his thrusts, matching each delicious one as he pounds his length and girth into me.

"Maksim. Oh God!"

"I've missed you, my krasotka. Every second. It wasn't only you suffering."

"Yes." I nod then pull his face back to mine, panting into his mouth.

The cold quartz does nothing to cool my scorching skin. Within seconds, we break out in a sweat. I fumble to remove his shirt, wanting to see the magnificence of what I could previously only feel. I yank it too hard. The buttons go flying.

He grunts and takes his two hands, puts them on the neck of my shirt, and rips it in half.

I laugh but not for long.

He expertly unhooks my bra, shimmies one of my sleeves off me, along with the strap, then leaves it hanging from my other arm. I lean forward and kiss his torso, but he dips down and sucks my breasts while slowing his thrusts to an excruciatingly pleasurable speed.

"Oh God," I moan, digging my nails into his shoulders. Every feeling I had with him in Vegas reignites, but this time, I can see him. And nothing is more beautiful or sexy than his face.

He wraps his arms around my back and palms my head, murmuring something in Russian in my ear while speeding up his thrusts.

He unravels me. An uncontrollable trembling starts in my core and consumes every inch of my body. Heat and adrenaline burst in all my cells. And his murmurs become growls as he pounds harder into me until I'm a rag doll in his arms, unable to do anything but make animalistic sounds I've never heard before.

When he pumps his hot seed into me, he cries out my name, and I see stars.

We collapse against each other. Clothes torn. Flesh pumping with blood. Skin covered in sweat.

We don't move or talk. The sound of our heavy breathing and beating hearts seems to echo in the room. When he finally pulls his head back, he pushes his forehead to mine and closes his eyes.

I shut mine, too. More time passes. We breathe together. When our air intake is back to normal, he pulls out of me.

"Shit," he mumbles.

My eyes fly open. "What?"

Guilt fills his eyes. "I'm sorry. I didn't think about a condom."

I caress his cheek. "I can't have kids. And I'm clean."

Shock fills his face.

I look away, feeling my pulse creep up again.

He gently moves my face toward his. "Krasotka?"

I bite my lip and focus on the ceiling, avoiding him. "I had a hysterectomy a few years ago."

He strokes my cheek. "And you're okay now?"

"Yes."

He hesitates then asks, "But you wanted children and didn't have them before you had the operation?"

My chest tightens. "Yes. I never felt stable enough to have kids. I could hardly keep our bills paid with just Peter and me. Then one day, I had no choice in the matter," I admit in a low voice, feeling the reoccurring sting that always creeps up whenever I think about the fact I don't have kids.

I'm not sure what I expect Maksim to do with this information or why I answer him so freely. But he pulls me into his chest and kisses my head. He doesn't say anything but strokes my hair.

I let him comfort me until I'm no longer choked up. I finally pull out of his embrace. "I'm assuming you're clean?"

"Yes. You don't have anything to worry about."

I brush the hair off his forehead. "Good. Guess we don't need to use condoms anymore."

His lips twitch. He glances at my ripped clothes then his. His eyes twinkle. "Might be better not to worry about."

We both start laughing, and he picks me up and carries me into his bedroom. We spend the rest of the night entangled with each other. When morning comes, I wake up in his arms, and nothing has ever felt better.

14

Maksim

SNOW FALLS AT A RAPID PACE. SUNLIGHT STREAMS THROUGH the window. Everything warm and good lies in my arms.

I stroke my krasotka's cheek, unsure how she's still here after all I told her. I was convinced she wouldn't want any part of me. All night, she proved me wrong.

I need to protect her.

It's not fair I'm subjecting her to my world.

Her eyes flutter open. She smiles. "Hi."

I dip down and kiss her lips. All the fire from the previous night ignites. She devours me with her kisses, as if I am her oxygen and she needs extra air to breathe.

I could kiss her forever.

She slides her warm flesh along mine and between kisses, asks, "What time is it?"

I slide my tongue in her mouth again, kneading her ass cheek and stroking her spine. "It's not six yet."

She groans. "I don't want to go to work."

"That's good then. It's a blizzard out there. I'm pretty sure your office will be closed." I grab the back of her knees and pull them to my hips so the tip of my cock hits her hot sex.

A soft whimper comes out of her, and she slides on my erection. "Maksim?" she whispers then greedily sticks her tongue back in my mouth.

"Hmmm?" I fist a handful of her hair at the back of her head and trail my lips down her neck.

"I don't have any clothes. I forgot to pack an overnight bag."

My lips twitch against her skin. "I'm going to keep you naked all day. You don't need any."

"Mmmm." She sighs and lazily circles her hips on me.

I slide my finger to her clit, circling it at the slow speed she's riding me, enjoying every noise of pleasure she makes and the way her eyes flutter and roll.

The time I spent with her in Vegas was a potent concoction of mystery and physical need. I loved every moment I was with her. But now I get to be the object of her affection. Every look she gives me sends more blood pounding through my veins. And knowing I told her my truth and she still wants me makes everything more powerful.

She rides me faster. "Oh, please...oh...Maksim..." Her eyes shut, and she grinds against my hand then pins me with her needy gaze.

I flick my fingers against her swollen clit and suck on her breast, tracing the edge of her nipple with my tongue

"Maksim...oh...ple...oh!" she cries out. Her eyes roll, and her mouth forms an O. The walls of her pussy spasm hard on my shaft.

I grasp her hip with my hand, moving her faster and meeting her thrusts with my desperate desire.

Her body is an earthquake, moving higher and higher on the Richter scale until she can't hold herself up anymore. She collapses against my chest but continues crying out and shimmying at the same speed on my cock.

Heat annihilates me, and my toes curl. "Krasotka," I growl, violently releasing inside her.

Our chests push against each other. Breathing hard, she tilts her head up. The brown in her eyes lightens. She sweetly says, "Good morning."

My cheeks hurt from smiling so wide. "Good morning."

She bites her lip.

I stroke her cheekbone. "Are you hungry?"

She shakes her head. "Still full from our midnight snack."

"You didn't have anything of substance." We never had our dinner. In the middle of the night, her stomach growled. We ate ice cream naked, feeding each other and licking it off the other's body at times.

She shrugs. "So, I don't have to go to work today?"

I grab my cell off the nightstand and pull information up on the internet. "All city buildings are closed."

"And you aren't sick of me yet?"

I kiss her. "I'll never get tired of you, my krasotka."

Nervousness enters her eyes. "How do you know?"

I tuck a lock of her hair behind her ear. "I'm a decisive man. I know what I want. And it only involves you."

She blushes. It's faint, sexy, and humble.

I kiss her again then pull back. "You know what I want to do?"

"No."

"Take you on our first date tonight."

She cocks an eyebrow. "Last night wasn't a date?"

"No."

She sits up. "Okay. Where are you taking me?"

"To one of my restaurants."

"You own restaurants?"

"Yes. My brothers and I own several. Just as investors though. I don't get involved in the day-to-day operations of anything unless it's our real estate."

She nods, looks out the window, then brushes my hair off my forehead. "I haven't said thank you."

"For what?"

She holds her wrist in front of my face. "My bracelet."

"Do you like it?"

Surprise fills her expression. "I love it. Why wouldn't I?"

"I just want to make sure it's your style. I don't want you to feel like you have to wear anything you don't enjoy."

A line forms between her eyebrows. "How could any woman not love this?"

I peck her on the lips. "I'm glad you like it." I get out of bed. "I'm making you breakfast. You need something besides sugar."

She kneels on the bed. "Okay. You win. I'll eat. However, I have a vital question."

I put my arms around her. "What?"

She plays with my chest hair. "Can I borrow a shirt, or were you serious about keeping me naked all day?"

I chuckle. "I'm always serious about discussions surrounding you being naked."

She holds my chin and smirks. "You're cooking unclothed, then?"

I pat her ass. "Button-down or T-shirt?"

"Mmm..." She ponders it for a moment.

"You're cute when you think hard."

She gasps. "I think hard all the time!"

I kiss her. "Yep, I know. I told you how smart you are. What kind of shirt do you want?"

"Button-down. Then we can rip it later if needed."

"Rip away," I tease, kiss her again, cop another feel, then go into my closet. I select a white dress shirt and hand it to her.

"I'll meet you in the kitchen. I'm going to the bathroom first," she says.

I throw on a pair of boxer shorts and leave the bedroom. Happiness is making me giddy. I don't remember ever feeling like this.

I open the fridge, pull out eggs, bacon, and some fruit. My phone rings.

I answer it in Russian. "Boris. What's going on?" A feeling of dread fills me. It's too early for him to be calling me. My brothers and I usually work out together around this time, but the blizzard would have all of us back in bed.

"The four of us need to talk."

The pit in my stomach grows. "Why?"

"Not over the phone."

I sigh. "What time do you want to meet?"

"As soon as the weather clears enough for our drivers."

I step to the window and glance down at the roads. There is no sign of life anywhere, which is unheard of in Chicago, even at this time of the morning. A white blanket covers everything. Snow is still falling. It's not as heavy as before, but it still adds to the problem. "It's going to be a few hours. Let's plan on my place at noon and change it if needed."

My penthouse is in the middle of my brothers', so we usually meet here for convenience.

"I'll call the others," Boris confirms.

"Boris."

"Yeah?"

"Are you okay?" It's rare for Boris to call a meeting. Something has to be going on with Zamir or possibly something with the O'Malleys that somehow affects us. As the oldest, I've always hated myself for not protecting my brothers, and especially Boris, who still has to deal with Zamir once a year.

His answer is short, and although confident, I'm not convinced. Boris is a trained killer but also a boxer. He's a fighter on every level and not the type of person who would ever admit any form of weakness. "I will be. See you later."

The line goes silent. I cross my arms, surveying the city, and try to calm my racing heart. There's a big problem. Boris wouldn't be calling the meeting if there wasn't.

Is it an issue with Zamir or the O'Malleys?

Maybe I'm overreacting, and it has to do with one of our real estate deals.

Fat chance.

My gut flips, and Aspen comes up behind me and slides her arms around my waist. "Maksim, what's wrong?"

I rub her arms and spin. I force a smile. "Nothing. I need to meet with my brothers later today. They are coming here around noon unless the roads aren't clear."

She furrows her brows. Her soft hand reaches up, and she cups my cheek. "Is this how it will be?"

"What do you mean?"

"When something is wrong, you will try to hide it from me?"

I freeze, holding my breath, not sure how to answer her.

Minutes pass in silence, and the worry in her face grows. But I also see hurt. Her next statement isn't accusing or harsh. She says it so softly, I have to listen closely. "I thought we weren't going to lie to each other?"

I close my eyes. She still holds my cheek. It's a reminder that as quick as she can tear her hand away, she can go at any time, and I'd lose her.

I'm in a new territory. Aspen knows who I am and what I'm capable of, but I can't start telling her every time there is a threat or issue to deal with. It's not safe.

I finally admit, "Something is going on. But I don't know what it is. When I find out, I'm not sure if I will ever tell you. The things that pop up from time to time, I'm not going to go into detail and discuss with you. Not because I don't trust you but because it's too dangerous. And I don't want to lie to you, either."

She takes a deep breath and steps closer. Her free hand grasps the other side of my cheek. She caresses my face with her thumbs. "Then how are we going to handle these situations so you don't lie to me? I don't want to be back in a dishonest relationship."

"I don't want to do that to you, either," I blurt out.

She nods. "Good. Okay. Then let's figure this out so we don't end up broken before we begin."

The thought of hurting her or not being with her almost kills my soul. Us breaking cannot ever happen.

"What would make you happy? When these things come up, and I can't give you the details, what do you want me to say?"

She thinks for a moment. "Exactly what you just said. Something is going on, but I can't go into details."

Surprised, I ask, "That's it?"

"Yes. You aren't lying then. I don't need to know all your business. As long as you are faithful and truthful to me, I will respect your privacy on these issues."

"My krasotka, I would never be unfaithful to you." I pin her with my gaze, trying to make her see how serious I am about my fidelity toward her.

"Good. I don't want to be a fool again."

"He's the fool," I reiterate to her. It burns me that she feels any shame for her ex cheating on her.

She releases my cheeks and steps back. "Okay, I think you owe me some breakfast."

She turns to walk away, and I spin her back into me.

"Hey."

"Hmmm?" She arches an eyebrow.

"I'm sorry. I wasn't trying to lie to you."

She smiles. "I know. You're forgiven. Now go cook for me."

"When did you become bossy?" I tease.

She smirks. "I've got the hots for this sexy Russian guy. He's good at giving orders, so I've been paying attention to him. I think he's rubbing off on me."

M

Aspen

MAKSIM WHISTLES, AND I JUMP. IT'S LOW AND SEXY, BUT I didn't know he entered the room.

I spin, and he steps forward, wrapping his arms around me. "You only get more beautiful, my krasotka."

I barely have any makeup on. I had mascara, some lip gloss, and eyeliner in my purse. The designer jeans and off-the-shoulder sweater Maksim had delivered earlier probably costs more than my weekly wage. The value of the dress and stilettos he bought for me to wear on our date tonight I won't even estimate.

My insides flutter, and I blush. I shouldn't. The man has seen me in every position possible. My sweat has merged with his too many times to count. I've begged him desperately both blindfolded and with my eyes open. He still sends my adrenaline racing whenever he looks at me or compliments me.

His lips twitch. The cocky expression on his face tells me he knows my insides are Jell-O right now. He dips to my ear, and his lips brush against my skin. "Which of your friends are you going to lunch with?" His tongue flicks my lobe.

Since he's meeting his brothers and the city is barely open, I figured the girls weren't working. I was right, so we decided to have a late lunch. There's a new restaurant we haven't been to, and when I mentioned I was calling to see if they were open, Maksim smiled.

"It's one of my restaurants. I'll find out for you."

I tried not to gape. I knew Maksim was successful and wealthy, but he seems to have a pulse everywhere around the city.

He confirmed they were open and said he informed the hostess I was coming with guests. At the time, Kora confirmed, but I hadn't heard back from Hailee or Skylar.

"All of them."

"Who's who?" His breath against my neck sends tingles racing through my spine.

I pull back, amused. "They didn't tell you their names?"

"No. We kept it secret. They had my wallet the first night. Your magenta-haired friend took it and said she wouldn't open it unless I did something bad to you."

I bite on my lip. "You gave her your wallet?"

"And my phone number. I thought you were from California since her area code is from there."

I could have contacted him over the last few weeks.

None of my friends told me they had his cell.

I didn't tell any of them I wanted to get ahold of him.

"She went to fashion school there then came back to Chicago. She's had the same number since college."

"Ah. That explains it."

I tilt my head. "Your area code isn't a Chicago one, either."

He shakes his head. "No. It's a New York one. I left my phone in a hotel room on a business trip. My cousin, Tolik, lives there and gave me a new one. They wouldn't give me my old number when I got back to Chicago, so I didn't see the point of switching area codes."

"What would you have done if she had a Chicago area code?"

His jaw clenches. "I would have left."

And we wouldn't be together right now.

He blurts out, "And then you would have haunted me. Everywhere I went in Chicago, I would be looking over my shoulder to see if you were there. The truth is, before I ever touched you, I fell for you, my krasotka."

I reach up and stroke the side of his head and admit, "If I had known she had your number, I would have called you."

"You would have?"

"Mmhmm. But don't ask me what I would have said."

He softly chuckles, pecks me on the lips, and says, "Adrian will take you to lunch and escort you inside. You won't even know he's there."

My chest tightens. "Is he going to follow me everywhere I go?"

His face falls, and he adamantly replies, "Yes."

There is no room to argue in his response, but I still say, "I don't think that's necessary. I'm sure Peter learned his lesson yesterday."

Maksim's eyes darken. His voice grows colder. "I won't take any chances with you, Aspen. Not with your ex-husband or anyone else. There are too many things going on in my world for me to be careless with your safety. I understand this isn't ideal or what you envisioned, but I won't let you go anywhere unprotected."

I'm not sure how I feel about this. On the one hand, it's nice to be protected. On another, it seems extreme, like a part of my freedom is being taken away.

Maksim's face hardens further, and I cringe inside. "We crossed the line we shouldn't have, and if you want to end this—"

"Why would you say something so horrible?"

His face softens. "It's not what I want. I am selfish and want you as mine. However, being with me has consequences. This is one of them. If you cannot incorporate my protection into your life, then we can never be. And I will still have someone watching over you from afar. It won't be as safe, but I will not ever let you be vulnerable to harm."

I swallow the lump in my throat.

Every decision in life has pluses and minuses. He is the pro. Giving up my ability to roam freely without a bodyguard is the con.

Do I want to be his, or do I want my freedom not to be escorted everywhere by a bodyguard?

It's not even a question. The longing I felt for him over the last few weeks and the emptiness that consumed me before I met him floods my soul.

He is confident as always, but I don't miss the nervousness in his eyes that I won't choose him.

I pull his lips to mine. "Then, I guess Adrian is my new bestie."

He breathes in relief. "Krasotka, I'll make it up to you. I'll—"

"Shh." I kiss him, trying to show him I only want him. No matter what, I choose him and want us.

The doorbell breaks our kiss.

"That will be my brothers."

"Okay. I'm going to go. What time is our date?"

He smiles. "Whatever time you want."

My stomach flips with a hint of anxiety. It shouldn't. He's made it clear he wants me with him. "So, I should get ready here and bring some things over?"

"Pack several suitcases if you wish." He winks, and my flutters take off.

"Maksim," a deep voice with a Russian accent calls out.

"Be out in a minute." Maksim moves me toward the door. "Come meet my brothers."

My nerves take off again. When we enter the main room, the view of the ice covering Lake Michigan is as cold as the tone of his brothers' voices. They speak Russian, and it sounds aggressive.

Maksim interrupts their conversation. "Take a breather for a moment."

They spin. The youngest brother cockily glances between Maksim and me. The one next to him looks at me once then raises his eyebrows at Maksim. His third brother has a shaved head and smiles at me.

It's like being in a tunnel of alpha-male testosterone. The Ivanov brothers all resemble each other to a degree. If I had a Mr. Potato Head, I would need duplicate parts of their features to mix and match. And even if Maksim didn't tell me their story the night before, I would feel their danger. They are intimidating, and I'm sure many people would second-guess whether they were safe men or not, but I don't feel anything but protected around them.

Maksim tugs me closer to him. "This is Aspen." He gestures to each brother in turn, introducing them. "This is Sergey, Boris, and Dmitri."

Dmitri steps forward. "Nice to meet you." He pulls me into an embrace and kisses my cheek. The others follow suit.

Adrian steps into the room.

"Give me a moment," Maksim says to them and leads me to the elevator corridor. He picks my jacket up and holds it out for me.

I slide into it.

He spins me, gives me a deep kiss, then says, "You still haven't told me your friends' names."

"Oh. Skylar has the magenta hair. Kora is the one you met with her. Hailee is the blonde."

"Tell Skylar, Kora, and Hailee I look forward to seeing them again."

"You think I'm telling them about you?"

His face falls.

"I'm teasing," I blurt out.

He kisses me again and playfully pats my ass. "I'll see you tonight." He calls out, "Adrian."

Adrian comes into the room. We leave, and he escorts me through the lobby and outside to the car. A driver is standing by the backseat door. He's ripped like Adrian and has a menacing glare on his face.

"I'm confused."

"By what?" Adrian asks.

"Aren't you the driver?"

"From this point on, I'm solely your bodyguard."

My gut flips. This seems a bit overboard. *Peter isn't a threat.*

You're dating a man who has ties to the mafia.

I've not had a lot of time to process what Maksim revealed to me. Every decision I've made regarding us has been swift and without analysis. My heart has led me. My typical straight-and-narrow, black-and-white self is nowhere.

Have I changed?

Am I becoming someone else now that Peter is gone?

The man I'm with tortures and kills other men.

The thought should frighten me.

It doesn't. The only thing I want to do is fall back into the warm embrace of his arms.

The driver opens the door, and I slide inside the vehicle. Adrian gets in the front seat.

The car is warm and comfortable. I'm used to the L-train and sometimes an Uber or cab if I'm splitting it with my girl-friends. I can't deny I appreciate the amenity or any other luxuries Maksim bestows upon me. And while I think he is going overboard with the bodyguard situation, I don't hate it. His commitment to protecting me when he's not with me makes me feel even more special to him.

I gaze out the window. A white blanket covers every possible surface. The roads were cleared earlier, but a light dusting covers them. Snow continues to fall in tiny flurries, or maybe it's the wind gusting off Lake Michigan blowing it around. The typical bustle of the city is gone, with hardly any pedestrians anywhere.

Chicago is beautiful and stark naked all at once. It hits me how similar I feel. Maksim has eliminated any ugliness I feel about myself in my heart or mind. But I also feel stripped of everything I know or previously believed.

Have my morals changed? Or do the circumstances of how someone becomes who they are override their sins? Does this make it so they aren't evil?

Nothing about Maksim feels devilish. He told me Satan is in him, but I don't believe it. I can't get past the layer of love he shows me to see anything terrible within him even though I've always felt the danger.

I'm pulled out of my internal debate when the vehicle pulls up to the restaurant's curb and parks. Adrian opens the door and reaches in to help me out.

I take his hand, and he escorts me inside. Kora, Skylar, and Hailee are already at the table, and they all gape at Adrian.

Even though I'm with Maksim, I can't deny Adrian's good looks.

"Ladies." His Russian accent comes out thick. He nods while arrogantly pursing his lips as they ogle him.

"And you are?" Kora asks.

"Sorry. This is Adrian," I jump in.

Why did I not think about what I would tell them about Adrian?

"Where did you two meet?" Hailee smirks.

"Umm..."

"Grab an extra chair. Sorry, we didn't know there would be five of us," Skylar tells Adrian.

"He's not staying...well, at least not at our table."

Confusion fills their faces.

"Okay, thanks. I'll see you when I'm finished," I tell Adrian.

He grunts in an amused tone, checks my friends out one more time, and strolls to the front of the restaurant.

The girls watch him walk away, and I sit. "You can wipe your drool now."

"You better spill it!" Skylar exclaims. "And if you're not with him, is he single?"

I shrug. "No idea."

"Well, find out!"

Hailee clears her throat. "Who is he?"

"Ummm...he's my bodyguard."

"What? Why do you need one of those?" Kora shrieks.

"Shh." I glance around the restaurant, but it's empty, except for us.

The three of them wait for me to continue.

Where do I start?

My pulse increases. "You know the guy I met in Vegas?"

"Mr. Tall, Dark, and Mysterious?" Hailee asks.

"Yes. He lives here."

A waitress with a brown ponytail approaches us. "Ladies. I'm Stacy." She sets champagne glasses on the table. A man behind her puts down an ice bucket stand complete with champagne. He opens a bottle of Cristal.

"We didn't order that."

Stacy smiles, displaying her perfectly straight white teeth. "Mr. Ivanov did."

"Mr. Ivanov?" Skylar raises her eyebrows.

"Thank you." I watch the champagne fizz to the top of my glass as Stacy pours it, trying not to squirm as my friends all look at me in question.

"Do you have any questions on the menu?" she asks after she fills all four glasses.

"No. I think we're going to need a few minutes," Kora replies, still giving me her what-the-heck-is-going-on expression.

"Sure. Take your time. As you can see, no one is going to need your table anytime soon," Stacy jokes and leaves.

"I thought you didn't know who he is?" Skylar asks as soon as Stacy takes five steps.

"You've been seeing him since we got back and never told us?" Kora accuses.

"No. He has a zoning issue going on, and we were in the same meeting yesterday." I take a long sip of champagne.

Hailee leans forward and disapprovingly asks, "He broke the deal and told you who he was?"

I take another sip, and the buzz of the champagne goes directly to my head. "No. I spilled coffee on him. I knew it was him."

"How?"

"His voice and scent."

Kora's face lights up. "What did you tell your coworkers?"

"Nothing. He whisked me off to the bathroom."

"Did you do it at work?" Skylar blurts out, and her mouth hangs open in excitement.

"No! And keep it down."

"But tell me there was a hot make-out session?"

My face burns.

My friends all screech.

"Shh," I reprimand them again.

Kora moves her chair closer to me. She lowers her voice. "So why do you have Mr. Please Bend Me Over following you around? And I hope he's staring at me and not you."

I glance across the room. Adrian stands against the wall with his arms crossed. The fabric of his shirt strains against his biceps. His blue eyes intently gaze at our table.

"He's dirty bad-boy hot," Skylar comments and takes a long sip of water.

Hailee points at Kora and Skylar. "You two need to hold on to your wet panties for a minute. Aspen, why do you need a bodyguard?"

"Ummm...well..." I drink more of my champagne to stall, still not sure what to say. I can't tell them what Maksim told me, nor do I want to. It's between him and me, and it's no one else's business.

"Aspen! Tell us!" Hailee frets.

"Adrian is also a driver at times. Maksim had him drive me home from work yesterday, and when Adrian dropped me off, Peter was there again."

"Again?" Kora raises her eyebrows. "Why would he be at your place? Your divorce is final and filed."

"Yeah," I say slowly. "He wants to move back in and be married again."

"Eew. Do *not* go back with him," Skylar orders.

"I'm not."

"What about Ms. Boob Job?" Kora asks.

I shrug. "Don't know, don't care."

"Is Peter threatening you?" Hailee asks.

"No...yes... I don't know. He grabbed my arm and left a few bruises on me—"

"Oh my God! Are you okay?" Hailee puts her hand over mine.

"Yes. It wasn't intentional. But Maksim saw the marks. Then when Peter was at my place again last night...well... Maksim's just extra cautious, so that's why he has Adrian with me." It's a half-truth. At some point, I'll need a new excuse as to why I still have a bodyguard, but I'm not prepared to explain anything else.

"Aww. That's sweet," Hailee coos.

"You should press charges against that ass." Kora shakes her head in anger.

"It wasn't like that. Peter has never hurt me before. I honestly think he didn't realize what he was doing."

"Not cool," Skylar mutters and drinks her champagne.

"Can we get back to Mr. O-O-O? And does he have any brothers?" Hailee asks.

My face heats up again. "Dmitri, Boris, and Sergey."

"One for each of us. Yes!" Kora does a victory pump in the air.

"Ummm...not exactly. Dmitri is getting married, and Boris's girlfriend is having a baby."

"I get dibs on Sergey," Kora says.

"You don't even know what he looks like," I tell her.

"Does he look and act like Mr. O-O-O?"

"Kind of. He's younger."

"I'm good with cougar land and open to a new cub."

"He's thirty-three."

"Bring him to mama."

"I'm not sure if he's single."

"First job when you see Mr. O-O-O is to find out the deets on his brother."

"I'm good with claiming the testosterone package in the corner." Skylar turns to Adrian and takes a sip of her champagne while eyeing him up.

"Can you be any more obvious?" I ask while laughing.

Skylar turns back, puts her glass down, then rests her forearms on the table. "So what does Mr. O-O-O do for a living?"

My stomach flips. "Can you all stop calling him Mr. O-O-O?"

Kora dramatically gasps. "Don't tell me he was a sex god in Vegas but can't get it up in Chicago!"

"What? No!"

She laughs. "I'm just teasing. Fill us in. What should we call him?" In a deep voice, she says, "Mr. Ivanov."

I elbow her. "Stop it."

"Aww, you really like him." Hailee's eyes shine.

I spend the rest of the lunch gushing about Maksim and avoiding anything about our secrets. When it's time to go, Adrian escorts me to the car, up to my apartment, then carries my suitcase down the ten flights of stairs.

When I get back into Maksim's penthouse, he pulls me to him and kisses me as if he hasn't seen me in forever.

I don't ask anything about what is going on between him and his brothers. He doesn't ask me how my lunch was. The only things that come out of our mouths for hours are the sounds of pleasure.

When I'm getting ready for our date, I wonder how a man who treats me so well and has quickly made me his number one priority could ever have any evil within him.

And that's the thing about love. It's blinding.

16

Maksim

ASPEN LEAVES FOR HER LUNCH. I GO BACK TO MY BROTHERS. They all smirk at me.

"When did you meet Aspen?" Sergey asks.

"In Vegas."

"She's why you disappeared both nights?"

"Yes."

Dmitri's lips twitch. "How did you find her?"

"By luck. She works for the zoning office."

Boris asks, "Did you get anywhere with the meeting yesterday?"

I sigh. "I learned a lot. The mayor merged departments. Aspen is the one running the show in there...not that she's

181

getting paid for it." The rage I feel over how much she's being taken advantage of stirs.

"What do you mean?" Dmitri asks.

"She knows more than anyone else who works there, but they won't promote her because she doesn't have a degree."

"That's such bullshit."

"Yep. Anyway, she created a list of things I need to do. I'll work with her to get it done."

Sergey grunts. "I'm sure you'll work nice and close."

I smack him on the back of the head.

"Ow!"

"Don't be disrespectful to my woman."

"Chill out."

I turn to Boris. "I don't think you came here to talk about zoning issues."

"I wish."

"What's going on?"

Boris's face hardens. "Giovanni Rossi's men found the evidence we planted. He's declared war."

My stomach pitches, and a knot grows in my throat. Giovanni Rossi is Lorenzo's father. He's in prison but still runs the Italian mob in Chicago and across the U.S. My brothers and I, plus Killian O'Malley, killed Lorenzo and his top three thugs. The O'Malleys believed Lorenzo murdered Killian and Nora's brother, Sean. That didn't sit too well with

Killian or Boris, but he also tried to screw my brothers and me with the land deal. He sent a package with an arm in it to my house. But the final straw was when he crossed the line that a mob family rarely does. He threatened our women. He set fire to Nora's bar then got the city to shut it down. And then he tried to have another "gift" delivered to Dmitri's soon-to-be wife, Anna.

His father, Giovanni, is old-school and smarter than him. He knows not to cross the line with women and children. It's an unspoken rule between mob families that men are the only ones you go after. But Lorenzo was cocky. His father would be smart enough to know not to mess with an Ivanov or our women, but Lorenzo wasn't.

So we put our cousin, Obrecht, who is a tracker, on him. We took Lorenzo and his top three thugs out at a strip joint in Gary, Indiana. But we had to pin it on someone so Giovanni wouldn't assume it was the O'Malleys or us.

Boris insisted we set up Zamir to take him down once and for all. For years, we've wanted to destroy him and be completely free. We could never find a way. Zamir is the most ruthless mafia king in the world. Both Dmitri and I were hesitant about planting evidence on Zamir. We knew it would lead to a full-out war.

If Zamir wipes out the Rossi family, it gives him more power, and the Russian community is at greater risk. But the Italian mafia isn't one we want to gain more control, either. Things have been unstable the past few years between the O'Malleys and Rossi family. Little by little, the Rossis have murdered the O'Malleys, greatly diminishing their power. Now that Boris's baby will have both O'Malley and Ivanov blood, we can't ignore the danger on either side.

So Boris decided it was best to let Giovanni and Zamir's families kill each other off. The only problem is, we are going to have to watch the balance of power and possibly intercede. If one side starts winning, the Ivanovs and O'Malleys need to quietly take more top guys out on either side to keep it in balance. The ultimate goal is to reduce the power of the Rossi and Petrov families to restore peace and safety.

It was a huge risk to set up Zamir, but Sergey and Boris were both insistent. Boris finally pulled his card and made the decision. Since he still pays for all our "debt" to Zamir once a year, plus his woman and future child were attacked, we couldn't go against his wishes.

"It took them long enough to find it," Sergey points out.

Boris and Killian kidnapped one of Zamir's guys. They spent the night torturing him until he finally confessed what they wanted him to into a recorder, which was that Zamir set up the hit on Lorenzo.

It wasn't true, but Boris can make a priest turn into Judas if needed. Zamir took to him and gave him extra training in torture when he was only sixteen. And sometimes I wonder if Boris is more dangerous than Zamir. When Boris tortures or kills, a sense of peace washes over him. It's a calm my other brothers and I have to fight to keep in check. And there is a part of Boris that enjoys what he does. If he believes it's justified, every slice of his knife or pound of his fist is tranquil liberation, as if it's sweet relief for him to continue to survive.

I have to bring out, then fight, the raging beast within me. I need him to do what I have to do. At the same time, I have to tame the animal inside me, and I struggle during every kill I've ever been a part of to do so.

When we killed Lorenzo and his thugs, I told myself this was it, and the killing was over. I knew deep down it wasn't. Zamir is still around. We were creating a mafia war. At some point, we will be stepping in to keep the powers in balance. At any moment, I will need to be able to drop everything and tap into the monster I wish didn't reside within me.

The more days that went by and the Rossi family didn't find the evidence, my nerves only grew. From time to time, my brothers and I would have short conversations about it. It always ended in us changing the topic since there was nothing we could do, except wait.

"The war has started. We must be prepared," Boris states, his eyes cold and emotionless.

No matter how much I waited for this day to come, chills still run down my spine. I didn't like it before I had my krasotka in my life, and now everything seems even more dangerous. It's why I would never have approached her in Vegas without the agreement I made with her friends. No matter how badly I wanted her, I warned her to run from me.

I should have tried harder to make her detest me.

Who am I kidding? I should have never touched her in Vegas. I was a goner the moment I laid eyes on her.

I'm a selfish bastard for allowing her to stay with me, but I can't let her go. Her protection will be my number one priority. Making sure Zamir goes down is more important than ever, and at some point, I'm going to have to tap into my beast, possibly more than once. After it's done, I'm not sure how I'll still be able to look at her.

I cross my arms tight to my chest, breathing through the stale air in my lungs. "I'll call Tolik. We need Obrecht back in Chicago to monitor the situation. Zamir will be recruiting harder to build his troops. Ensure our guys on our construction payroll know if they need overtime or advances, to talk to us. Nobody becomes so desperate they need to deal with Zamir or his men."

"On it," Sergey says.

"We need to solve this zoning issue ASAP. Our guys need to stay working," Dmitri states.

I pace. "We still don't have proof Zamir and Lorenzo were working together, but it's too big of a coincidence Lorenzo knew about our properties when he convinced the mayor to give him that lot. It reeks of Zamir."

"We're the largest employer for Russians, and even the Polish, in Chicago. He's been utilizing more and more of them," Boris points out.

The better people in our community do the less desperate they are. Zamir thrives on others' desperation. It makes sense he would try to create chaos within our company. He not only hurts us but those he wants to take advantage of. Now, more than ever, we have to keep our community of people working. "I'll talk to Aspen tonight to see if she has any other ideas on how to push this zoning issue through faster. The board doesn't meet for another three and a half weeks. There would have to be an emergency situation for them to meet sooner on this issue. I'm not sure how we could make that happen, but let me pick Aspen's brain."

Boris cracks his knuckles. "Might be time to have some discussions with the board members."

I step so close, I'm face-to-face with him. "We do not become thugs. Our businesses are legitimate. We have worked hard to not become men who we despise."

Boris's voice matches the darkness in his eyes. "We already are those men. When you go to sleep at night, you know who you are and what you are capable of. If it is for the greater good—"

"No! We do not cross the line in our business. We will not fall farther into the pit of hell."

"We're already in it, brother, and there is no getting out."

Boris is right. I can't kid myself about who I am when I shut my eyes. I do despise myself for all the men I've killed even though they were bad men. But I won't allow my brothers, or any other Ivanov, to become anything like Zamir, or the Rossis for that matter.

Sergey clears his throat, and I tear my gaze away from Boris. "I'll call the foremen today and put a schedule together to walk through all our sites this week. I'll talk to the employees one on one and feel them out. If Zamir's already started to recruit harder, we need to know."

"I'll help you. I'll take the North side crew, you take the South," Boris tells him.

Dmitri sighs. "We need to beef security up. I hoped we'd scrape by without having to deal with this until after the weekend. The last thing I want is Anna worrying on her wedding day."

"I'll handle it. We'll make sure everyone blends in," I assure him.

He gratefully nods. "Thanks."

I've got two days before the wedding to get Tolik's extra guys here.

The rehearsal dinner is tomorrow night.

It isn't as big as the wedding. Our local security can accommodate.

"Anything else? If not, I need to get on security," I say.

Boris nods. "One thing."

"What?"

"Killian has Liam watching Giovanni's visitors." Liam is Killian's third cousin, who's serving time with Giovanni. He only has a year left on his sentence. We grew up with him.

My gut drops. "And?"

"Bruno Zielinski showed up."

Dmitri's color drains from his face. "Visiting with Giovanni?"

"Yes."

My brothers and I stare at each other. Bruno is the head of the Polish mafia.

I finally say, "If the Zielinski family is making any alliances with the Rossis, we need to know."

"Killian is already on it," Boris replies.

My brothers leave, and I spend the next few hours dealing with security and reviewing my notes and task list I made during my meeting with Aspen.

When she walks through the door, I should go through zoning issues with her and find out if there is anything we missed that we could use to our advantage.

If intentions were all that was required, I'd be golden. But implementation is necessary, and the only thing I can think of when I see her is how much I missed and crave her. And I shouldn't kiss her. I have no control around her when I do. The moment our lips and tongues collide, the desire within me takes over, and I fall into the ecstasy of losing myself within her.

For several hours, I forget about all the stress of everything around me. The only thing that matters is her, and I do everything in my power to show her how much I want her to always be mine.

17

Aspen

MAKSIM TAKES ME TO A RESTAURANT I'VE NEVER BEEN TO. IT'S a five-star steakhouse with a Japanese flair and an extremely private environment. The entire restaurant is dimly lit with candles on the tables. The hostess leads Maksim and me to a small room with only enough space for the table. It's a semi-circle, and the luxurious booth forms around it. The chocolate-brown leather is tufted and thickly padded. Soft indie music seductively fills my ears.

Maksim helps me out of my coat and hangs it on the hook. He motions for me to slide in. He follows, and the hostess hands us menus. "Your server will be with you shortly, Mr. Ivanov."

"No rush," Maksim replies and puts his arm around me.

She smiles then blushes, continuing to stare at him instead of leaving. She finally says, "Would you like me to put your drink order in?"

Are you kidding me?

I drape my hand on Maksim's thigh. I didn't realize I was a jealous person, but the way she's looking at my man, like he's her eye candy, sets something off in me.

She's younger than me by at least ten years.

The ghost of my past and Peter's infidelity with Ms. Co-ed is a demon I don't even try to fight. "We're good, thanks," I snap before Maksim can reply.

Her hazel eyes widen, and she breaks her drooling gaze away from Maksim and focuses on me.

Yep, I'm in the room, and you can get your flirty ass away from my man.

She takes a nervous breath and addresses Maksim. "Would you like the door left open or shut?"

"Shut," I answer, forcing a smile and inching my fingers on Maksim's inner thigh toward his cock.

She scurries away, closing the door behind her.

He turns to me, raising his eyebrows.

"She can find another daddy somewhere else."

He breaks out in laughter.

"It's not funny."

His face falls. He traces my jaw. "My krasotka, I told you I would never be unfaithful to you. It's not the type of man I am."

I focus on the door, trying to calm my shaking insides.

Why do Peter's actions have to affect me?

Maksim's lips brush against my ear. "I have everything I want with you."

I take a deep breath and turn to him. "I'm sorry."

His eyes twinkle. He teases, "It's okay. Your jealous side is cute, too." He pecks me on the lips, and the waiter comes in.

"Krasotka, do you drink wine?"

"Yes."

"Red or white?"

"Either. Surprise me."

Maksim scans the wine list. "A bottle of the Chateau Lafite Rothschild Pauillac, please." The words roll effortlessly off his tongue.

When the waiter leaves, I ask, "Do you speak French, too?"

"Yes."

"Wow. I feel super uncultured with you." I say it jokingly, but a part of me does. We're in two different worlds. He's rich, multilingual, and powerful in too many ways to count. I'm the woman trying to keep her rent paid and the cockroaches under control.

"Do you want to learn Russian or French? I'll teach you."

"Is it hard?"

"Not if you break it down and take it one word or phrase at a time."

"Okay. Teach me Russian."

The waiter returns and uncorks the bottle. He pours a small amount into a glass to try. It's so dense it's almost black. Maksim pushes it to me. "You taste it, my krasotka."

I pretend to know what I'm doing. The juicy but tart aroma of currants flares in my nostrils. I inhale the intoxicating smell then take a sip. It's smooth and luxurious with the right amount of everything, but I really have no clue what I'm supposed to be tasting. Whenever I see people do it, I always wonder if anyone sends the bottle back.

"This is delicious," I say. It might be the best glass of wine I've ever had.

Maksim smiles and nods to the waiter. He fills two glasses, leaving me with the one I tasted the wine in. And that is another thing I never understood. Why doesn't he pour me more in my tasting glass, which is the same as the one he's filling?

"Did you want to order appetizers?" the waiter asks.

"Is there anything special you like, or do you want me to order?" Maksim asks.

"You can. I'm not picky."

He rattles off several things, and the waiter leaves.

I take a sip of my wine. "I didn't ask you how your meeting went with your brothers. Is everything okay?"

Something crosses in his eyes. As quickly as it comes, it goes, so I'm unsure how to take it. He replies, "I do have a problem. I wondered if you could help me."

"Sure. What is it?"

"I need to get the zoning issue solved. That project keeps our men working. They must have incomes to feed their families and not have any lapses in paychecks." Worry laces his voice.

"I understand your concern. It's nice you care about your employees so much."

The same thing that entered his expression is back, but this time, it doesn't leave.

"Maksim, what else aren't you telling me?"

He taps his long fingers on the bottom of his glass then swirls it on the table. "There is another issue I can't go into with you. But it has never been more important for us to keep our projects going. Not for our bank accounts but for our community."

My stomach twists. I want to ask him what he means, but I also promised him I wouldn't require his disclosure on every situation if he deemed it unsafe for me to know.

"It's something dangerous?"

His face is solemn. He pins me with his gaze. "Not just for my brothers and me. For our community of people but also others who are at risk."

"Such as?" I don't know why I'm pushing. I should respect the boundary he's trying to set. He already told me he couldn't tell me.

He takes a sip of wine. I almost tell him I'm sorry for asking, but he turns back to me. "From the moment we stepped foot in America until Boris gave me his gambling winnings to build our real estate business, we lived in poverty. No matter how hard my mother or father worked, they could never get ahead. The struggle was a daily occurrence. I used to hear my parents arguing about it. My father knew Zamir and his men were not good. He warned my mother over and over not to ever get involved with the Petrov family. When he died, there was a new sense of desperation."

I put my hand on Maksim's cheek. "I'm sorry about your parents."

His face hardens under my hand. He redirects his attention to his wine glass, swirling it some more. "It was a long time ago." He takes another mouthful.

I choose my words carefully. "Zamir is part of whatever is going on?"

He briefly closes his eyes. "Yes."

"So you need to keep your employees working so they don't become desperate and turn to him?"

He spins in his seat toward me. "Yes. But not just our people. The Polish as well. Zamir has been preying on their bad fortune lately. And a lack of money drives people to do things they never believed they could. We are the largest employer for both Russians and Polish men in Chicago. We are a natural target for Zamir to hit. If he hurts us, he increases his recruits quickly. Men, who would otherwise have no reason to join him, will."

"I will do whatever I can to help you. The hurdle is the board. Do you know if any of them could be in Zamir's pocket?" I may be naive to mob business, but I understand the dirty politicians that run Chicago. I've seen too many outcomes not make any sense for there not to be under-the-table deals.

Maksim snorts. "Possibly all of them. But I will look into it."

"We need to come up with a reason for them to have an emergency meeting. I will research more when I get to work tomorrow."

"Thank you."

"Of course."

The waiter comes in and sets down three dishes. He points at each. "Salmon tartare, tuna tataki, and sushi platter. Did you want to order now?"

"Aspen?" Maksim asks.

"You keep ordering," I tell him. I hate looking at menus, especially in a five-star restaurant. I've not been to many, but I'm immediately going to look at the prices of everything and pick the cheapest items since I've had to do that for the last twenty years. By letting Maksim decide, I avoid the stress. Plus, I like to try new things, so I'm interested to see what he chooses.

Maksim quickly selects, and the waiter leaves. Maksim picks up his chopsticks, secures salmon tartare on it, and holds it to my mouth.

"Mmm," I groan as the salmon melts in my mouth.

He smiles. "Good?"

"Mmhmm." I finish chewing, swallow, and wash it down with another sip of wine. "This is all delicious. Thank you."

He puts another mouthful of food to my mouth.

"Aren't you going to eat?"

"Yes. After you try everything first."

I don't argue and let him feed me the tuna. It, too, melts in my mouth.

"Are you free this weekend?" he asks.

I swallow. I tease, "Oh, I don't know. I might need to wash my hair."

He grins. "Dmitri's wedding is this weekend. The rehearsal dinner is tomorrow night, and the ceremony and reception are Saturday. Will you come with me?"

"That depends."

He raises his eyebrows. "On?"

"Are you wearing a tux?"

"Yep."

"I'm definitely in, then."

"Do you have a thing about tuxedos?"

"Nope. But I think I'm going to have a thing about you in a tux."

He softly laughs. "Guess you're in luck, then. Every month or so, I have an event to go to where I need to wear one."

"Is this a blanket invitation?"

He drags his finger from my forehead and down the side of my face. "No. If I have an event, I'll ask you to go. But you will be asked to all of them."

"Isn't that the same thing?"

"Not at all. I think it's easy to take advantage of someone you're in a relationship with. And I won't assume you'll go somewhere with me without asking."

My insides flutter. "You're old-school, aren't you?"

"Is that your way of saying I'm an old man?"

"No. But I like old men, remember?"

His lips twitch. "Ah. Yes. I forgot about your resistance to being a cougar."

"Makes you a lucky man."

Amusement fills his eyes. "That I am."

"So, what time is the dinner tomorrow night?"

"Seven. When do you get out of work?"

"Probably four. Most people leave around then on Fridays."

He pecks me on the lips. "Good. I think you should stay at my place all weekend, too."

"Okay. I'll need to go to my apartment and figure out what to wear."

"I'll order you something."

"You don't have to. You've already bought me enough things."

He leans into my ear and nibbles on it. His hand slides to my inner thigh.

I squirm in my seat.

He murmurs, "Do you have a problem with me buying you things?"

"Ummm..."

Do I?

His tongue flicks the back of my ear like a snake.

"I'm not sure."

His mouth moves across my jaw. He pauses when he gets to my lips. His eyes meet mine. In a no-room-to-argue voice, he says, "You should have the best, my krasotka. And I will give it to you."

I don't respond. I've never had anyone give me nice things before. Some women would fight him and claim they don't want it or need it. But I love everything he's given me. Maybe I'm a bad woman for it, but I also think Maksim will do what he wants. He seems to enjoy spoiling me.

I say, "I might be a horrible woman for admitting this, but it's nice to be taken care of and spoiled for once."

His eyes darken. "As you should have always been."

My chest tightens, and I wish it wouldn't. I don't want to feel any emotions from my past, especially not sadness, when I'm with Maksim. But baggage is hard to escape. Years of not having anyone to rely on and making everything work for both Peter and me rears its ugly head. I turn away from Maksim, embarrassed that I'm tearing up. I blink hard. I put my fingers over my eyes to stop the tears from falling, and my lip quivers.

Like everything Maksim does, he takes control of the situation and pulls me into his chest, covering my cheek with his palm, and kissing me on the forehead. "Everything you've not had, I will give you. And I will love every moment of taking care of you. You are not on your own anymore, my krasotka."

I want to believe him and that it can be that simple. That all he has to do is snap his fingers, and we'll live happily ever after. But I'm not the only one with baggage. And when two people's issues intertwine, good intentions and promises become almost impossible to keep.

18

Aspen

COFFEE WAFTS IN MY NOSE. I GO STRAIGHT TO THE CAFE. Maksim and I were up late. He finally insisted I go to sleep around two a.m. so I wouldn't be exhausted all day. But then we woke up around five and couldn't keep our hands off each other again.

"Double espresso," I tell the barista then turn to Adrian. "Do you want anything?"

"I'm good."

I'm still uneasy about bringing Adrian to work, but Maksim insisted. He told me to explain my ex was bothering me and that Adrian would stay in my inner office lobby once he checked the premises. I think it's a bit overkill, but I still don't know what is going on.

I probably never will.

I agreed to it.

Better to be safe than sorry.

I pull the new wrap Maksim had flown in from Vegas around me. After dinner, we stopped by the front desk so he could add me to his security. That way I could come and go as I please. The package was waiting for me.

"You didn't have to get me a new one," I said when we got into his penthouse and removed it from the package. I was in awe he replaced it and that it got to Chicago so quickly.

"You seemed genuinely upset it got ruined," he casually said, as if it weren't a big deal.

I tore my eyes off the cashmere wrap. "I was. I truly love it."

"Well, then, it's good they had one left."

I set the wrap aside, straddled him, and showed him how grateful I was for his thoughtful gift.

The barista calls out my name, tearing me out of my flash-back. I pick up my coffee and lead Adrian to the elevator.

My phone vibrates, and I hand Adrian my cup. "Hold this for a second, please."

He takes it. In his thick Russian accent, he teases, "At your service."

I pull my phone out of my purse. Skylar texted me.

Skylar: *Are you with Mr. Bend Me Over?*

My face heats up. I glance at Adrian. He's concentrating on his job and is scanning our surroundings.

Me: *Yes. You need to stop calling him that.*

Skylar: *Why?*

The elevator door opens, people get off, and Adrian escorts me in.

I step as far away from Adrian as possible and try to hide my phone screen so he can't see. Actually, he's being very respectful and hasn't attempted once to glance at my phone. I text back.

Me: *He's with me all day long.*

Skylar: *Lucky you.* She adds some hands-in-the-air emojis.

Me: *Not interested. I have a man, remember?*

A burst of giddiness surges through me, thinking about Maksim as mine.

Skylar: *I didn't forget you're getting hot sex all day and night, and I'm not. So, did you find out if Mr. Bend Me Over is single?*

The elevator opens, and Adrian steps out first, holds the door so it doesn't close, then glances around. He looks back at me and motions for me to follow him.

Me: *No. Don't make me ask him, either.*

Skylar: *Do it. I'm curious if he's taken.*

I catch Adrian's cocky expression and type back.

Me: *I'm sure he is.*

Skylar: *Ask.*

Me: *Then what?*

Skylar: *Hmm... You can slip him my address for work, and he can come service me at lunchtime on my break.*

I burst out laughing.

Adrian turns and arches an eyebrow.

"Sorry. My friend. She's texting me."

He nods then continues scouring the office.

Me: *I need to go. Talk to you later.*

Skylar: *Aspen, find out!*

Me: *Have a good day. Bye!*

Skylar: *Aspen!*

Me: *Jeez. Okay!*

I throw my phone back in my bag then say to Adrian, "My office is over there." I point to several feet in front of us.

Adrian escorts me down the hall. I ignore the curious looks from my coworkers. The only person I need to tell about Adrian is my boss. It's no one else's business.

We get to my office, which is the size of a shoebox, and Adrian deems it safe.

"I will go sit in the lobby now."

"Wait!"

He stops. "Yes?"

"Ummm..."

This is so uncomfortable. He's Maksim's security guy.

Adrian crosses his arms. "Are you okay?"

"Yeah. So...ummm...are you married?"

His lips twitch. "No."

"In a serious relationship?"

Amusement crosses his face. "Why the interest in my love life?"

My cheeks burn. "Just curious. We do have to spend a lot of time together. So...anyone special?"

Adrian's blue eyes grow cockier. "Does this have anything to do with your friends?"

"My friends?" My heart beats faster.

Why did I let Skylar talk me into this?

I have nothing to be embarrassed about.

More arrogance fills his expression. "Which one were you texting?"

"Huh?" I'm not sure why this is embarrassing me, or why I'm trying to cover for Skylar.

"Pink, dark, or blonde hair?"

Oh, jeez. What's the point? Skylar didn't say not to tell him she asked.

"Pink."

His lips turn up. "Tell her I'm single." He winks and walks out of my office.

I remove my phone from my bag and text Skylar.

Me: *You owe me. That was super embarrassing.*

Skylar: *Why?*

Me: *He asked which of my friends wanted to know. And when I said pink hair, he said to tell you he's single.*

She sends me a graphic of a girl cheering.

Skylar: *Did you tell him where I work?*

Me: *No. And I'm done playing matchmaker. You're on your own from here on out. He's my bodyguard, not bestie. Plus, he's super cocky.*

Skylar: *I know. It's freaking hot.*

I groan, and there's a knock on my door.

Me: *Gotta go.*

I turn to my boss, and my stomach flips. I don't like having to explain why Adrian is with me. "Morning, Fred. I was going to come chat with you."

"Everything okay?"

"Yes. Have a seat." I motion to the chair.

He sits and waits for me to speak.

"I had an issue with my ex."

Concern fills his face. "Are you okay?"

"Yes. But I also want to disclose something else to you." My pulse beats quicker. I'm not doing anything wrong, but it feels strange.

"What is it?"

"I'm seeing Maksim Ivanov."

His eyes widen. "Oh..."

"We met in Vegas before he came into the office. I didn't know he lived here. Anyway, he's a bit overprotective, and he is insisting his bodyguard stays with me right now."

I've never seen Fred speechless before now. He recovers and looks behind him. "Where is he?"

"He's in the lobby if that's okay? He won't bug anyone."

"Sure. Your security is important. Whatever will keep you safe."

I release a breath. "Thanks."

"So..."

"What?" I ask.

"You and Maksim are serious?"

Heat burns my cheeks. "Yes."

"Well, I hope you don't get sick of him."

"Why would I?"

"From now on, we're only working on his project. The mayor called. He wanted to know if we solved the zoning issue yet."

Something nags at me, but I'm not sure what it is. "It's not even been twenty-four business hours. No one was in the building yesterday due to the snow."

"Yep. You know the mayor and his unrealistic expectations."

"How does he expect us to get the zoning changed before the board meets? He knows how this works. Does he have any suggestions, or is he going to call the emergency meeting?"

"Of course not. He doesn't want to look partial."

The nagging feeling inside me grows, and I sit back in my chair. *What am I missing?*

Fred scratches his cheek.

I lean forward. "Fred, why does the mayor care so much about the Ivanov's getting their zoning changed?"

He scrunches his forehead. "I'm not sure. But I can't question him. I'll lose my job. Ask your boyfriend. I have to meet with Sally on a different matter. Let me know if you find anything out." Fred rises and leaves.

I call Maksim.

"Krasotka, is everything okay?" he answers in a worried voice.

"Yes, of course."

"You just missed me, then?" he teases.

I bite on my smile and turn toward the window. "I'd prefer to be with you right now."

His voice drops. "Why? What's wrong?"

"Nothing. Just...well, my boss told me the mayor called and is demanding we figure out your zoning issue, but of course, he isn't going to stick his neck out. It made me wonder something."

"What's that?"

"Why is the mayor pushing for this to happen?"

The line goes silent.

"Maksim, are you still there?"

He clears his voice. "Yes. I'm trying to figure out the answer to your question."

"You don't know?"

"The land needs to be cleaned up. When we bought it from the city, the mayor reminded us we must start the process in the next ninety days. We are contractually obligated, or the property goes back to the city, and we only receive ninety percent of what we paid for the lot."

"Is the mayor pushing so the land is no longer toxic?"

Maksim's voice is full of doubt. "Possibly. But I need to think about other reasons and speak with my brothers. I did not know he was putting pressure on your office."

"Maybe I'm looking into things too deeply? I don't want to cause an issue if there isn't one."

"No, my krasotka. You are correct to come to me with this question. Let's not discuss this over the phone any further. We can talk more about it this evening."

Does he think our phones are tapped?

Don't be silly. He's cautious, that's all.

Still...

"Aspen?"

"I'll see you tonight."

"Okay. Have a good day, my krasotka."

"You, too. Bye." I hang up and turn on my computer. I spend the entire day researching how to help Maksim. I decide to focus on the cleanup since it seems to be a reason for things to happen faster.

My alarm rings around four, and I turn my computer off. I have a few pieces of information I printed off. I'm not sure if they will lead anywhere, but I put everything in a folder and stick it in my bag.

When I get to the lobby, Adrian rises. I had forgotten about him. He leads me out of the building and into the car.

It doesn't take long to get to Maksim's. He lives closer to my office than I do. I go into the penthouse and pull out the folder. I study the information again but can't seem to find the answers I'm looking for. The nagging question about why the mayor is insisting on getting this done won't leave my head.

Around five, I put it on the table and go to get ready.

When Maksim comes home, I'm sitting at the vanity, finishing my makeup. He comes into the bathroom and leans over me.

I look up, and he pecks me on the lips.

He strokes my cheek. "How was your day, my krasotka?"

"I still don't have any answers for you."

He nods and smiles. "We will find the answers. I appreciate you helping me."

I put my blush brush down and rise. He slides his arms around my waist, and I put my palms on his chest. "Did you figure anything out?"

"I'm not sure yet. My brothers and I were supposed to buy the land before. Everything was agreed upon, and at the last minute, the mayor sold it for barely anything to Lorenzo Rossi. We negotiated with Lorenzo for months and then he flipped on us. He started offering to buy our other parcels and kept lowering the price, along with threats. We still don't know why the mayor sold it to him under our noses."

"Guess it's good for you that Lorenzo ended up dead," I blurt out in a teasing tone.

Hardness fills Maksim's face. His eyes turn cold.

My mouth goes dry. Blood pounds between my ears. I once again don't think before I speak. "Did you..." I can't finish my question. The words "kill him" won't come out of my mouth. I swallow hard as Maksim continues to intensely pin me with his gaze.

He doesn't finish my question, nor does he confirm or deny what I'm insinuating.

My belly quivers so much, I drop my hand off his chest to hold it. He's told me he tortures and kills men. I know this about him. Lorenzo Rossi wasn't a decent human being. He hurt too many people to count. I don't know a lot about him, but I do believe the earth is a better place without him on it. But did Maksim kill Lorenzo for a piece of land? Did I give him a pass to kill people but not even think about why he might murder them? Does he kill for selfish reasons, such as things like money?

Dizziness overpowers me. I grip Maksim's shirt, breaking our gaze and focusing on my clenched hand.

He tightens his arms around me, fists my hair, and gently tilts my head up. "I will not go into details with you about why or how things occurred. But I see fear in your eyes. Tell me what you are thinking right now."

Panic continues to spread through me. It becomes harder to breathe. I don't want him to be any less than the man I thought he was. If he killed Lorenzo for money, I can't condone it.

Time passes. It's so quiet, the ticking of his Rolex watch seems to get louder.

"Are you scared of me, my krasotka?"

Am I?

No. He won't ever hurt me.

But if he killed Lorenzo to make money, can I still believe that?

Hurt fills his face. "You believe I could harm you? That something in me would ever turn against you so much, I would give you anything but pleasure?"

My chest is tight, and my lungs can't take more air, but I also can't seem to release any of it.

Pain laces his voice. "I have been honest with you. I told you all my demons that reside within me. We agreed to be truthful with each other, but you won't tell me what is causing you to suddenly fear me?"

He's right. I should ask him my question. And I don't believe he would ever harm me. I wish the words would come out. Instead, I remain unable to speak.

The look on his face slices me. Pain and disappointment swirl in his expression.

He releases me and steps back. "I see I've been wrong about us." He turns and walks out of the bathroom.

I should follow him.

I don't.

I stay frozen, unable to do anything, and try to put my thoughts together. Questions I should have asked before surface. Things I assumed about Maksim makes my mind spin. I debate in my head about what is acceptable and not, regarding his sins.

When I'm able to breathe again, true fear hits me. I don't want it to be over with Maksim. Life only began when I met him. But every moral boundary I've ever held makes me a hypocrite. I've moved from the black and white and into the gray. How do I return to clarity on what is right and wrong? Is it even possible to have a right or wrong on murder?

The more time that passes, the more confused I am. There seems to be no answers. The only definite thought is I don't want to be anywhere he's not.

But when I finally leave the bathroom and approach him, I see the damage I've done. And I'm not sure if I'll ever be able to repair it.

19

Maksim

SCALDING WATER SCORCHES MY SKIN, ROLLING DOWN MY BACK. The pain it gives me does nothing to dull the sting of my heart.

She's betrayed me. I saw it on her face. She thinks I would hurt her.

I didn't try to cover up what I did to Lorenzo. Since I disclosed to her all that I am, there was nothing to hide. Yet something in her turned.

Was it the reality of what I'm capable of? Maybe it's the fact she can now put a face to one of my victims. Either way, she isn't able to see past my darkness. She is now fearful of me.

I turn the water off and wrap a towel around me. Since she was in the bathroom, and I can't be late to Dmitri and Anna's rehearsal dinner, I showered in the guest bathroom. I don't know if she's still here or not. Part of me wants her to be. The other part of me doesn't want to see her. It's a slap in the face that I can no longer have her.

I'm not sure how I ever believed someone as good as her would be able to love me. I can't deny the man I am. The darkness that resides in me isn't something I can excuse or forget. It's never going to suddenly disappear.

Every time a situation pops up that I need to call upon my demon, I'll always be able to. And I can't just ignore problems when they appear.

The war has started. Boris's baby ties the Ivanovs to the O'Malleys. The beginning of the end is here, and I'm not sure how all of this pans out. When it's over, it might be the Ivanovs and O'Malleys in body bags.

Or sliced to pieces and sunk in Lake Michigan.

This is the time to let her go. Everything is only going to get more dangerous and darker.

Don't try to convince her to stay or not be afraid of you.

I need to protect her always, including shielding her from me and my reality.

My stomach lurches over these thoughts. I convinced myself we were real. That no matter what, we were able to sustain the cruelty of my past and what's ahead. But I've lied to myself. I knew better the moment I heard her voice and laid eyes on her at the pool in Vegas.

The reflection staring at me in the mirror doesn't convince me it can be any other way. I'm the same man I was before Vegas. She hasn't changed my darkness to light, nor can she.

The devil is still in my eyes. I see him. I know him. I can't escape him. And bringing her into my world was selfish.

I leave and go into my room, no longer able to avoid her, if she's even still here. I scan the room but don't see her. The light is on in the bathroom, but I avoid it, going straight to my closet and selecting a fresh suit.

I wish I could crawl in a hole and never come out. Moving forward without her seems impossible. But I'm an Ivanov. It's not in my blood to wallow in sadness. And I won't be the cause of any unhappiness or worry when it's Dmitri's special moment.

Keep moving. The situation isn't going to change if you fall into self-pity.

Jade never reciprocated my deep affection for her. It hurt. Aspen giving me all of her then fearing me cuts at me in ways I didn't know existed. I would die protecting her. But somewhere within her, she believes I could hurt her.

I may be a ruthless man, but I have lines I will never cross. Hurting women and children is one of them. But my commitment to Aspen goes beyond any general rule I live by. I thought she would never be able to fear me, knowing my truth and still staying, but I was wrong.

I put my underwear on and step into my black slacks. I pull my zipper up and reach for my belt.

"Maksim."

I freeze, closing my eyes. Her voice alone dices up my soul.

She wraps her warm arms around me and presses her cheek against my back. "I'm sorry."

Blood pounds into my skull like a hammer. It's loud and throbbing. Her heart beats into my spine, stirring the craving I always feel for her.

It will never be. She will always fear me.

I hold her hands in mine, and with every ounce of courage I have, I remove them, step forward, and put my shirt on, keeping my back to her. "There is nothing to be sorry about. I shouldn't have expected you to understand my world or me. This is all my fault. I knew better in Vegas. I'm the one who should apologize." I focus on fastening my buttons.

"Don't say that. Please." Her voice is desperate and full of agony entwined with fear. And I can't ignore that she is still scared of me. It destroys any piece of my heart that remains.

Be a man, not a coward.

I spin. Her eyes glisten, and her lip shakes.

She's so scared of me.

"I will never, ever, hurt you. Not now, not when we are no longer together. I should not have allowed this to develop between us. It was irresponsible of me."

Her eyes widen. She steps toward me. She reaches up and holds my cheeks.

I stare over her head, not able to look at her, in fear I may not be strong enough to let her go.

"Maksim—"

"I cannot be late. I will not allow my issues to stain Dmitri and Anna's happiness." I can't hold back anymore and tilt my head down.

Tears stain her cheeks. Betrayal and regret are in her eyes. It tears me to pieces to hurt her, but how can we be if she fears me?

"Tomorrow, when you wake up and are no longer in this world, you will be relieved."

"You're throwing me away? Just like that?" she chokes out.

"No, my krasotka. I'm allowing you not to live in fear. No one should have to be afraid of the man they are with."

"Is that what you think? That I am afraid of you?"

"It's not what I think. It's what I see. Even at this moment, your eyes tell me everything."

"I don't know what you think you see"—she takes a deep breath and swallows hard—"but you don't know what is in my head or heart. And I am trying to process so many things—"

"About me."

She angrily spouts, "Yes, about you, Maksim. And me. And what everything means."

She can't understand any of this. She's not meant to be anywhere near this world. No amount of analysis will lead her to honestly believe what is in me is acceptable. She will always have the same confusion about us she does now.

"I'm not sure how to let you go, my krasotka, but—"

"Then don't!"

I stare at the ceiling, dying inside, wondering how to keep her and give her everything she deserves.

But nothing appears. My ability to shower her with gifts and protection and love will never compensate for the dangerous world I live in. None of it can erase the man I am. A man whom she will never fully trust.

I kiss the top of her head. "Let's not make this harder than it already is. I need to go." I step away from her, struggling to breathe, feeling the death that's always a part of me rise from my core and strangle me.

She's better off without me.

"Maksim," she calls after me, following me through the penthouse.

I walk faster, but she grabs my bicep. In a harsh voice full of agony, she yells. "Do not treat me like I'm disposable."

I stop. My heart beats too hard in my chest.

What am I doing?

The right thing for her.

I'm hurting her.

It's now or later. The future will hurt worse.

I spin. "My krasotka—"

She slaps me so hard, my head jerks to the side. It echoes in the air and stings my cheek.

I put my hand to my face and slowly look at her.

Her tears fall so fast, they roll off her chin and onto the wood floor. She glares at me. "I see I've put my faith in the wrong man. You are no different from the one I gave twenty years of my life to. You tell me you will be mine, and I will be yours. But the first moment we have any issue, you toss me to the curb like a cheap piece of furniture you no longer want. You give me no chance to ask you any questions or try to decipher pieces of information that I don't know what to do with. And you want me to accept you, yet you don't give me the same courtesy. All you can think is that you know what is inside my head, but you know nothing."

Her words are a bullet, and they hit my artery.

Have I been wrong?

"You can't tell me you aren't scared of me."

She shakes her head in disgust, and new tears fall. "I have never been afraid of you, Maksim. Trying to understand the depths of who you need to be at times is not something I can grasp in one moment. But you expect me to never have any questions. To be blind to things and trust you, yet the things I am privy to, you don't allow me to fully decipher. The self-hatred you have for yourself, you use it to determine what I'm capable of, regarding us. And you're wrong. You're so very wrong and unfair." She turns and walks to the elevator.

I don't move, letting the words sink into my thick skull, hating myself even more for continuing to hurt her.

What am I doing?

She's right. I've made assumptions about what she is thinking and never allowed her to tell me.

I've never been more wrong in my entire life.

I can't let her leave.

"Aspen," I call after her, rushing to the elevator.

But I'm too late. The door has shut, and it's already moving down. I call her phone, but it rings in her purse, which sits on the coffee table.

By the time I get outside, she's gone.

I pick up the phone to call Adrian. Boris calls on the other line, but I ignore it.

"Boss," Adrian says.

"Tell me you're with Aspen."

"She wouldn't come with me and is in a cab. I'm following her."

"Good. Her purse is here. She has no money. Pay for the cab when she stops and don't let her out of your sight. If that jackass or anyone else comes near her, protect her at all costs."

"Got it."

I hang up, cursing myself and texting my other driver to pull the car up.

I get in, am about to follow Aspen, when Boris texts.

Boris: *Where are you? Everyone is here.*

Shit.

I'll talk to her after dinner.

She's never going to forgive me.

Me: *Traffic jam. Be there soon.*

My brother has been through too much for me to do anything to ruin his and Anna's weekend. With my chest tight, heart pounding, and regret spinning in all my cells, I go to the dinner and through the motions, wishing Aspen was with me. I avoid the questioning looks my brothers give me about her not being here. I can't text her since her phone is at my place. There is nothing I can do until the event is over.

My remorse and fear that I'll never be able to win her back and make what I've done right only grows throughout the night.

Around midnight, I'm getting ready to leave, and I text Adrian.

Me: *Is she at her apartment?*

Adrian: *No. She went to her friend's, and they went out.*

Me: *Which friend?*

Adrian: *The blonde. But now all four of them are together.*

Me: *Where?*

Adrian: *Cat's Meow. They aren't in the best shape, either.*

You have to be kidding me.

My pulse increases. I try to call Adrian, but he doesn't answer.

Adrian: *Too loud to talk.*

Me: *What did you mean?*

Adrian: *They're pretty hammered. I think I'm going to need some back up to get the four of them out of this place. Aspen is pissed I'm here, and the more she drinks, the more I can't do anything right. I'm pretty sure if I have to drag her out of here, it's going to get super ugly.*

Anger flares through me.

Me: *Don't leave. I'm on my way.*

I caused this.

I go over to Sergey. "I need you to come with me."

"Where to?"

"Cat's Meow."

He raises his eyebrows. "Seriously?"

"Yep."

"This your way of trying to get over whatever is going on with you and Aspen?"

"Not funny," I growl.

He holds up his hands. "Easy there. All right. I'm not doing anything exciting. Guess it's a night at the Cat's Meow. But do you want to tell me why we are going there?"

"To get my woman."

20

Aspen

MY TEARS TURN INTO ANGER. MAKSIM TOSSED ME ASIDE LIKE A dirty dish towel. He gave me no time to explain anything. Instead of telling me his worries, he made assumptions and the decision to be done with me.

I deserve better than that.

At least I didn't waste another twenty years of my life.

But this feels worse than anything Peter did to me.

I'm halfway to my apartment when I realize I left my purse and phone in his penthouse.

I'm not going back there.

I tell the cabbie to go to Hailee's instead. I have no idea if she's home. When the cab pulls up, I start to tell the driver I have no money and to wait for me to get Hailee.

Adrian flings the door open. He asks the cabbie, "How much?"

"What are you doing here?"

Adrian cockily smirks and pulls out his wallet.

More anger builds that Maksim thinks he can dump me but still have Adrian watching my every move.

I don't wait and get out of the cab and run up to the door. I buzz Hailee's unit, and she answers. "Hello."

"Let me in!"

"Aspen! What are you doing here?" She releases the lock, and I step in. Unfortunately, so does Adrian.

"You don't need to be here."

He snorts and steps in the elevator with me.

"Did you not hear me?"

"Until Mr. Ivanov tells me I am to no longer protect you, I will continue my duty."

"I'll call the cops. You can't just stalk me," I threaten and push the button for Hailee's floor.

Adrian sighs but gives me another cocky expression.

"Give me your phone," I say and hold out my hand.

"Why?"

"So I can report you to the police for harassment."

He grunts, and the door opens.

I stalk past him.

Hailee is already waiting in the hall for me. "Aspen, what's wrong?"

I walk past her into her apartment. When she steps in, I shut the door so Adrian can't come in.

Hailee's eyes fill with concern. "Aspen? Your mascara is all over your face."

"Maksim broke up with me."

"What? Why?"

I never considered what I would tell her. I can't tell her the truth. Even though Maksim and I are through, I would never disclose his secrets.

"We got into an argument." It sounds weak.

"Maybe you'll be able to work it out?" she suggests.

"No. He's done with me."

"That seems harsh."

"Well, he is a ruthless man."

Hailee's eyes widen. "What do you mean?"

I need to shut up.

"Nothing. I...I..." My tears flow, and I can't stop them.

Hailee pulls me into her arms. "Oh, girl. I'm so sorry."

"He just tossed me aside like I was replaceable. As if nothing we had was worth even the energy of a discussion," I sob.

She hugs me tighter. "Shh. Come in and sit down."

I let her lead me to the couch.

"Why is Adrian here if you broke up?"

It only makes me cry harder. I know Adrian is here because Maksim cares about me. It's his self-loathing that made him act rashly. But he doesn't have any faith in me to love him. And I can't even explain to Hailee the truth, which makes me feel even more alone.

There isn't a lot for me to tell her. I don't want to lie, so the only truth I reveal is how much it hurts.

Her phone rings, pulling me out of my pity party. "Skylar, I don't think I'm coming. Aspen is here. Maksim broke up with her and—"

Skylar speaks so loudly, Hailee cringes and moves the phone away from her ear. It's muffled, so I don't know what she says, but Hailee puts it on speaker.

"...talk to her," Skylar demands.

"You're on speaker. But calm your voice down. I think you blew out my eardrum," Hailee reprimands.

"Sorry. Aspen, what happened?"

I sigh and try not to cry. "I don't want to talk about it. But my purse and phone are at his house. I can't even get into my apartment."

"Want me to go get it?"

I sniffle. "No. I'll get it tomorrow when he's at his brother's wedding." More tears flow at the thought that I won't be there with him. I cover my face. Everything was new with Maksim and me, but I wanted to be part of his life and his family's. It made me feel important to him that he wanted me by his side at Dmitri's wedding.

Hailee slides her arm around my shoulder and hugs me.

"Okay, well, we aren't letting him win," Skylar says.

I catch my breath. "What are you talking about? I don't think either of us is winning or losing. This isn't a game."

"No, but where is he right now?"

"His brother's rehearsal dinner."

"Yep. And where are you?"

I glance at Hailee.

She rolls her eyes. "What are you getting at, Skylar?"

"Get ready. We're all going out. I'm already texting Kora."

"Where are we going?" Hailee asks.

"I think this calls for the Cat's Meow."

"No," I state.

"Yep. Kora just said she's on her way. We aren't letting you sit around and cry all night. And if you do, you can do it over drinks and entertainment."

"At the Cat's Meow?" Hailee huffs.

"Don't be a snob or prude. See you there. Bye." Skylar hangs up before Hailee or I can object any further.

"I'm not going," I say to Hailee.

She tilts her head, scrunches her forehead, and stares at me.

"What?"

"Don't move." She gets up and walks toward her bathroom.

"Where am I going to go?" I mutter.

I can't believe that's it. One situation where I needed a few minutes to process things, and he dumped me.

How could he be so cruel?

I thought I meant something to him.

Why would he tell me his truth then give me no chance to ask him questions or explain my thoughts?

What do I think? Do I even know who I am anymore?

Maybe he's right, and I am better off not being with him.

How am I going to even get through the night without him?

I start to cry again, and when Hailee comes in, I'm in a full-blown sob.

She tries to comfort me, but it doesn't help.

"How could he do this to me?" I wail. "This is why I didn't want to touch any man. I thought he was different, but he made me disposable, just like Peter did."

"Shh. I'm so sorry. Are you sure there's no way to work it out?"

"No. He won't. I'm not good enough again." My body erupts in tremors as I drench Hailee in my tears.

When I finally calm down, she says, "Let me call Skylar back. We aren't going anywhere."

I almost agree but then say, "No, don't. I can't sit here all night, or I'll keep crying. Let's go."

Hailee hesitates. "We don't need to go."

"No, Skylar's right. But I need you to float my drinks until I get my purse back."

Her blue eyes glisten. "Are you sure? We can eat ice cream and watch sappy movies instead."

I straighten up. "No. I did that when Peter cheated on me. Let's get out of here."

A sympathetic smile forms. "Okay. Let me clean you up."

I release an emotion-filled laugh.

Hailee pulls out the makeup bag she got from her bathroom, cleans up my face, and replaces my makeup. "There. All fixed."

I draw in a deep breath. "Thanks."

"Are you sure you want to go?"

I rise. "Yes. Self-pity isn't going to help me."

We open the door. Adrian is against the wall with his arms folded.

Annoyed, I say, "You can leave."

"I'm sorry, but I can't."

I stomp past him. "You're really pushing it, Adrian."

"I'm doing my job."

"Why are you here if Maksim broke up with Aspen?" Hailee asks.

Adrian's cocky expression falls. He seems speechless for a moment then recovers. "I take orders from Mr. Ivanov. When he tells me to protect Aspen, that is my job until he tells me otherwise."

I push the elevator button. "So you're going to follow me all night, no matter how many times I tell you to get lost?"

"That is correct."

"You can't do that," Hailee says.

I'm about to give Adrian another mouthful when I realize something else. "Are you reporting my location to Maksim?"

Adrian's words slice me. I should be happy, but it makes our breakup even more real. "No. I don't report unless Mr. Ivanov calls or gives me instructions to send him updates, and he has done neither."

"But earlier today, you sent him updates?"

"Yes."

My chest tightens. The elevator opens, and I get outside as fast as possible. Cold air hits my lungs, and without thinking, I get into the car when Maksim's driver opens the backseat door.

Hailee slides in next to me. "Why are we in Maksim's car?"

"I don't know. But there's no point taking a cab. If Adrian is going to follow me, we might as well save on the fare."

Hailee pats my hand. "Good thinking." She rolls the divider window down. "Cat's Meow."

Adrian turns from the passenger seat and raises his eyebrows. "Cat's Meow?"

"Is your job to judge me or guard me?" I ask.

Adrian snorts, shakes his head, and I roll the divider back up.

"Is he always so cocky?" Hailee asks.

"Yep. Skylar is going to go nuts when she sees he's here."

Hailee groans. "This should be interesting."

It takes a while to get to the Cat's Meow, which is on the south side of Chicago. The neighborhood isn't great. Metal bars cover almost every window and door. It's about four steps below the safety level of where my apartment is located, so I don't venture on this side of town unless we're coming to the Cat's Meow, which isn't very often.

"I can't believe we're going in here," I mutter to Hailee when we pull up to the neon flashing sign.

"At least we have Mr. Russian Badass in case things get dicey," Hailee replies, right as Adrian opens the door.

He reaches in to help me out, but I ignore his gesture, pushing past him. Hailee follows me, and we stand at the back of the line.

Adrian makes a clucking noise and puts his hands on both our backs.

"What are you doing?"

"Not standing in the cold. Let's go inside."

"Do you not notice all the people?" The line is fifty feet long.

"Yep. But I'm a man who makes things happen. Let's go."

"We better not lose our place in line," I grumble but let him lead us toward the front.

We pass Skylar and Kora halfway to the bouncer. They both hug me as people yell at us not to cut in line.

"Ladies, you come, too," Adrian demands while eyeing Skylar over.

They don't argue and walk in front of Adrian.

"You might want to keep your eyes on our surroundings instead of my friend's ass," I hiss.

He smirks and focuses on Skylar's backside again.

When we get to the front, Adrian high-fives the bouncer, then speaks fast Russian. The bouncer motions for us to go in. There's a cover charge, but Adrian slaps cash down as my friends pull out their wallets.

"You need to go," I tell him again.

"Wasting your breath," he barks out above the music.

Shaking my head in annoyance, I step farther into the club. It's not our everyday hangout, but the girls and I come here every now and then. It started after Peter and I split. Kora said we needed to stir things up and have a wild night out. I'm not feeling like doing anything but running back to Maksim's and begging him to keep me, but I know he won't. He's made up his mind about me and us. He isn't a wishy-washy man.

Emotions grow in my chest, and I push them down.

Do not break down here.

Why did I think coming out was a good idea?

Kora puts her hand around my back and leads me farther into the club. A red glow illuminates the dark area. Poles, cages, and small stages surround the perimeter. A dance floor is in front of a bigger stage. Private booths, VIP areas, and bars are expertly laid out. Three floors get more exclusive as you go up.

Topless strippers, both male and female, dance in cages and swing on the poles. A new show starts every half hour on the main stage. Shot girls wearing lingerie so skimpy they might as well have nothing on roam through the club.

Everything from hip hop to country music plays at the Cat's Meow, depending on the show taking place on the main stage. The current one consists of two males and one female in a provocative striptease.

We find a table, and Skylar orders shots. She asks Adrian, "You want one?"

Adrian gives her a set of fuck-me eyes, and she blushes. He leans toward her ear. It's not on top of it, but it's enough to notice. And I'm not sure if he intentionally knows how to do it, but his Russian accent seems to get thicker, as if he knows it makes him sexier. "Not while on duty."

I'm not sure if it's Adrian himself, or because he's Maksim's bodyguard and still following me even though Maksim booted me to the curb, but I don't want Adrian anywhere near me.

Maksim let me go.

He doesn't want me anymore.

"Go away," I order Adrian.

Skylar only encourages him. "What time would you be getting off?"

He licks his lips at her.

Adrian is a reminder of everything I lost tonight.

Pissed, hurt, and trying to keep it together in public, I rise and jab his chest. "Leave. Now."

"Aspen, cool it," Skylar says.

I spin. "Are you here for him or me?"

She scrunches her forehead. "You, of course."

"Then he goes or I do."

Adrian holds his hands in the air. "I'll be against the wall if you need me."

"I won't," I assure him, and he walks away.

Hailee takes my hand and gently says, "Sit down."

I sit as the shot girl puts four glasses down. "Another round," I tell her, pick mine up, and swallow the liquor. The alcohol burns my throat as it slides down. I don't usually drink shots, but I take it as soon as the next one is set down.

"Slow down," Kora warns.

I point to the six shots sitting on the table. "Are you going to drink with me, or am I by myself?"

Skylar holds hers up. "I'm with you, girl." She downs it, and the others follow.

My buzz hits my head like a baseball bat. "Good. I'm either going to spend the night crying or enjoying the amenities. Which one do you want me to do?"

"Enjoy the amenities," Kora replies.

I glance around the room. I find the most muscular guy I can and make eye contact. It's not anything I would ever do. "Good. Let's start now." I motion for the stripper to come over and also for the waitress. I turn back to my friends. "Who has dollar bills on them?"

21

Maksim

I TEXT ADRIAN THAT I'M HERE. MY STOMACH IS IN KNOTS, AND I'm trying to calm down before I see Aspen. But I'm not happy she's wasted and at the Cat's Meow. It's in the roughest part of town, and I know what happens in that club. While a lot of it is innocent fun, it doesn't take much for patrons and the strippers to cross the line in the private rooms. And if Aspen and her friends are as intoxicated as Adrian claims they are, it's a recipe for trouble.

Adrian: *Pavel is at the door. We're upstairs, third floor. I couldn't stop all of them. They just went in Wes Petrov's suite, and I'm not allowed in. Aspen wouldn't listen to my warnings. Wes's thugs surrounded her and her friends.*

My heart races so fast, I think I might have a heart attack. Wes is Zamir's son. He's as heartless as his father and just as dangerous. "Fuck!"

"What's going on?" Sergey asks.

"They're in Wes Petrov's suite."

Sergey's eyes turn to cold slits. "How are we handling this?"

The beast in me awakens. I close my eyes and take several breaths, trying to tame him. My fingers trace my pocket knife through my suit pants. "We need to get them out of there with no incidents." I reach into a hidden compartment under the seat and hand Sergey my gun.

"Shit," Sergey mutters, and we step out. I motion for my driver, Bogdan, to follow.

We waste no time getting past Pavel and ignore the women who approach us for lap dances or shots. We go straight to the third floor. Adrian is pacing in front of the closed door of the VIP room.

"How could you let this happen?" I bark.

He holds his hands in the air. "There are four Petrov thugs, plus a bodyguard and four women. I'm not Superman. I do have some limits."

Sergey snorts. "You should have called for backup."

"It just happened. They've only been in there for two minutes."

I step closer to Adrian's face. "How did you let my woman get near a Petrov?"

"Your woman?" He raises his eyebrow in question. "She seems to think she's not."

Anger bubbles, and I clench my fists at the sides of my thighs. I'm not used to Adrian doing anything but obeying me, and his comment stings. He's one of my toughest men. He can sweet-talk anyone, but don't get on his bad side. He'll have you in a body bag in seconds.

Sergey steps between us. "This isn't the time for this conversation."

He's right.

"Take the bodyguard, Adrian. Bogdan, get your gun."

Adrian obeys, opening the door to the VIP room, stepping in, and head-locking the bodyguard in one swift move.

My pulse beats so hard in my neck, I'm sure everyone can see it. I retrace my knife as my inner beast tells me to tear every man in this room to pieces.

The first person I see is my krasotka. She's in the dress I bought her to wear to the rehearsal dinner.

She should have been there with me.

God, I was such an idiot.

How did she get anywhere near a Petrov?

Wes Petrov's tattooed arm and fingers wrap around Aspen's waist. She sits on his lap, and he licks his lips, his face close to hers.

My fists curl at my sides. Heat and anger churn in my gut, and the monster inside me is ready to unleash its fury on him.

My krasotka is in danger. I need to be smart.

She's mine. He's touching my woman. I swallow the bile rising in my throat and try to control rage I usually only feel before I'm about to slaughter my enemy.

It may not be tonight, but he will receive my consequences.

It would take me minutes to slice him to pieces and never have one ounce of guilt over ending his life. So it's never been more challenging for me to contain my demons. Any violence puts my krasotka in danger.

I need her back in my arms, not his.

"Whoa." Wes laughs and pulls Aspen closer to him when she sways backward.

She puts her hand on his shoulder to steady herself.

Watching her touch him is torture. My blood turns to flames, searing under my skin. I stop myself from stepping forward and pulling her off his lap.

If I do that, she could get severely hurt or even killed.

This is my fault. How could I ever put her in a situation to run into his, or any other man's, arms?

I'm going to kill Adrian for letting her get wasted like this.

Aspen's friends aren't in any better shape. All are on Wes's thug's laps.

Bogdan aims his gun at Wes and his thugs. He growls, "Hands up."

The women gasp with eyes wide. Wes's thugs slowly put one hand in the air but keep another one on each woman's waist. Wes keeps both his hands on my krasotka. His dark, cold eyes fill with surprise. He glances at his bodyguard who's turning red, then back at me. A sinister smile forms on his face. "Maksim. Sergey. Did you come to finally pay your dues?"

Aspen slowly turns her head and blinks, catching my eye. Even in her drunken state, I see pain, confusion, and fear. But this time, I know it's about the situation and not me.

What have I done?

I step closer, tearing my eyes away from her. "We have a deal with your father and it's very clear. Ivanovs are off-limits. I suggest you release our women, now."

He snorts. "Your women? Maybe you should keep better track of your women."

My beast claws in my gut, awakening further from hibernation and ready to slaughter its first meal.

Sergey steps next to me with my gun in his hand. He growls, "Release them."

"Or what?" Wes asks and trails the back of his fingers down my krasotka's arm.

She scrunches her face and wobbles on his lap, staring at me as tears begin to fall down her face. "Maksim," she barely whispers.

My heart cracks. *I've done this. This is all on me.*

I reach for her, and Wes tightens his hold on her. Aspen's friends try to get up, but they are held down as well.

"Let go of me," the pink-haired woman shrieks. The thug holding her laughs.

Adrian drags the bodyguard closer and stops more airflow to his lungs. He turns purple. "Ten seconds and I snap his neck."

Wes's dark eyes pin mine. "Release the whores."

Sergey steps forward, and I hold him back with my arm.

Adrian counts backward in a gruff voice. "Ten...nine..."

Kora, Hailee, and Skylar stumble over to the door behind Bogdan. Wes doesn't let go of Aspen.

I remove my knife, step as close to him as I can, and put my hand on Aspen's shoulder so my palm lays flat on her chest. Her back is flush to my thighs. I hold my right hand with the knife in the air. "Last warning."

"Seven..." Adrian growls.

"You will incite war between the Ivanovs and Petrovs. Are you sure you want to do that by killing me?" Wes cockily asks.

"You want to take your last breath tonight?" I seethe.

Aspen's heart pounds into my palm, and she shudders.

He starts to chuckle and releases his hand from Aspen. I pull her up and into me. She's shaking and can hardly stand, I'm sure from a combination of too much alcohol and fear. Sergey steps forward with his gun pointed at Wes's head.

I walk backward with my krasotka, keeping my knife out, and order Bogdan, "Give your gun to Adrian and take the women to the car."

Bogdan does as he is told. Adrian keeps the thug in a choke hold and holds the gun out at the others. I guide Aspen out of the club, following Bogdan and her friends.

None of the women say anything. They are all shaken up. Bogdan texts our other driver to pull up.

He puts the women in the car, and I steer Aspen to mine. "Get in," I order her.

She obeys and turns to me once she's seated. "Maksim," she cries with tears streaming down her cheeks.

"Shh. Stay here. I'll be back in a moment." I shut the door.

Bogden and I stand in front of the vehicles, staring at the building. I grip my knife in my pocket tighter.

Sergey, come on, little brother.

My insides are flipping. I've never left my brother behind before. And Adrian is my cousin. I'm not ignorant to the fact there are five Petrovs and only two Ivanovs.

Sergey and Adrian come out of the club, and I breathe in relief. I nod to them. They get in the other vehicle, and I get in mine.

Aspen's makeup is all over her face. She's shaking and can't stop crying.

I pull her onto my lap, and she curls into me.

"I'm sorry," she cries.

"Shh. This is my fault." I stroke her head, trying to stop my pulse beating at a rapid speed in my neck.

Any run-in with a Petrov is bad, but we just held them at gunpoint. I threatened to slice Zamir's son into pieces. There are going to be consequences at some point.

And he knows who my krasotka is.

We go directly to my penthouse. I lead Aspen to my bathroom and turn the shower on. When the water is warm, I undress us both and pull her into the shower.

She sobs in my arms, and I hold her as tight as I can. I stroke her hair. "Shh."

"How could you throw me away?" she cries out, and my heart breaks.

"I haven't. I never could. I messed up," I tell her. It sounds pathetic and only makes my disgust for myself grow.

Every tear reminds me of my mistake. I curse myself for my stupidity while holding her until the water gets cold. Somehow, I manage to clean the makeup off her face and dry her off.

I put her in my bed and tug her into my arms. Her sniffles become farther apart, and when she's finally asleep, only then do I reach for my phone and text my brothers.

"A second war has started. We must prepare."

22

Aspen

A HAMMER IS HITTING MY HEAD OVER AND OVER, AND NAUSEA sets in. I slowly open my eyes, but it's so dark I can't see anything, so I shut them again.

Where am I?

Maksim.

The comforting smell of bergamot and cardamom wafts in the air. His strong arms cradle me, and his heart thumps against my ear. I snuggle into his soft chest hair, and he strokes my back, then kisses my head.

Wait. He dumped me.

I sit up too fast, causing my stomach to lurch and head to feel like a Mack truck rammed into it. I hold my skull with one hand and put the other over my stomach.

Maksim sits up and tugs me to his chest. His deep voice is low, his accent thick. "Slow down, my krasotka."

I breathe for a moment then slowly turn to him. The faint outline of his chiseled cheeks and square jawbone is barely visible. Like I did so many times while blindfolded, I reach for him, needing to verify he's really in front of me. I whisper, "Maksim."

His hands slide through my hair, firmly holding me. It's possessive, giving me the false sense that I'm his, and he never let me go.

But he did. The cruel reality crawls across my heart, scraping the already-torn pieces to shreds. My mouth is dry from the alcohol I drank. A lump grows in my throat, and I struggle to swallow it.

Maksim puts his forehead on mine. "My krasotka." His voice pricks my heart. I'm unsure what it means.

The events of the night come rushing at me: too many shots to count, strippers, and dancing. A man with a Russian accent who felt just as dangerous as Maksim, if not more so, invited me into his VIP room, then pulled me onto his lap before Maksim took me away. The blur of guns and knives then Adrian counting loudly from ten down, stirs in my mind.

I don't know the name of the man whose lap I sat on. But I remember the way his hand gripped my waist when Maksim came in. The fear I felt wasn't like anything I had ever felt around Maksim. I realized, even in my hazy state, the man was dangerous but a polar opposite to Maksim. I don't doubt he is every bit of a killer Maksim is, but he has no boundaries regarding what he would do and why. He would hurt me if the opportunity came up and not even think twice about it.

I shudder thinking about how I wanted every morsel of attention that man would give me before Maksim came in. That man was the closest thing I could get to Maksim, with his Russian accent and dangerous flair. And if I hadn't been drinking, I want to believe I wouldn't have given him two seconds of my time. Surely, I would have seen the difference between him and Maksim? But I can't be sure because I couldn't escape the devastation growing in my heart from Maksim disposing of me like a useless piece of trash. "Everything ached so badly," I whisper in a barely audible, raspy voice.

Maksim's eyes shut. "My krasotka—"

Hurt, I cry out, "No. You created a hole in my heart, and it only got bigger as the night went on. You threw me aside. Why were you even there?"

"I came as soon as Dmitri's event was over. Adrian didn't tell me what was going on, or I would have left the restaurant immediately. I planned on coming to your apartment after, but if I had known you were at the Cat's Meow, or with Wes Petrov, I would have left the rehearsal dinner."

My chest tightens. "Petrov? The...oh God. Is that...?"

Maksim's voice is emotionless. He confirms, "It's Zamir's son."

My nausea takes hold, and I try not to get sick. Sweat breaks out on my skin. I close my eyes and hold on to Maksim's shoulder, but my head keeps spinning. Several days ago, I had never heard of the Petrovs or had anything dangerous in my life. Now, it seems to surround me. And when I had Maksim as mine, it was okay. I could accept it and compartmentalize it because he would always protect me. Now, I don't know where we stand or if there even is an us anymore.

"Breathe, my krasotka."

The knowledge of who I was with, and what could have happened in Wes's room, hits me, along with the betrayal I feel about Maksim breaking up with me. It spirals like a tornado, mixing with confusion. I'm scared to ask it, but the courage appears somewhere within me. "Why am I here?"

"Because I love you. This is where you belong...with me."

My lungs constrict until it hurts. Blood pumps between my ears, intensifying my headache. Any hydration left in my mouth is gone. "How can you love me when you let me go only a few hours ago?"

His warm palms cup my cheeks. I close my eyes, wishing I didn't want every touch he gives me. But I do, and I hate that he has the power to release me, pull me back, and still affect me so much.

His Russian accent intensifies. "I wish I could redo the evening."

"But we can't."

"I'm a fool. I acted rashly. I can't tell you how sorry I am."

I wish my head would stop pounding so I could think. I want to return his admission and tell him I love him, too. That the only thing I want is to be his and with him forever. But something stops me. All I keep remembering is earlier in the night when he put on his shirt and threw me out of his life in a matter of moments.

It hurt a thousand times worse than losing Peter. So I pull away from him. I don't want to make a mistake and lose him, but the trust I gave him cracked. He threw the stone to start the fissure. Somehow, he needs to find the glue to repair it. I can't fall back into a relationship where he can destroy me in seconds then drag me back to being his. But now isn't the time to figure it out. I'm too sick. "I need water and something for my head. I can't talk about this right now."

He reaches toward the nightstand and hands me two pills and water. "You weren't in good enough shape to take this earlier."

I say nothing, accept the water, and refrain from guzzling it, taking small sips so I don't get sick everywhere. I get the pills down and hand the glass back to him.

He sets it down and weaves his fingers through my hair once again, holding my head, as if I'm his.

My emotions can't handle it anymore. Tears escape, rolling so fast, they slide off my chin and drip on my thighs.

"Forgive me, my krasotka. Please." His voice is gravelly, full of remorse, and a hint of desperation lies within it.

"I hate the fact I want you so much," I barely choke out.

He pulls me into his arms, wrapping me in the immediate safety I always feel with him.

I mumble in his chest, "You don't get to do this to me."

He stiffens then tightens his arms around me, pressing his lips to my head. His chest rises and falls faster. He finally says in a tone laced with fear, "Do what?"

"Dangle the promise of a life with you. Then cast me away, only to drag me back and tell me you love me."

"I do love you. I've been beating myself up all night since you walked out of here. It's not a question if I am at fault. I know I am. Don't let my mistake destroy us."

My headache only intensifies. I want to be with Maksim. The pain I felt without him when I left Vegas, and last night, isn't something I ever want to feel again. But how do I know he isn't going to quickly dispose of me the next time we have an issue? "Every fiber of my being wants you...no, wants us. But I can't think right now."

He releases a long sigh then tilts my head up. He brushes his lips against mine. "You need rest, and I'm being selfish. We will talk tomorrow when you feel better. But I promise you, no matter what happens, if you forgive me, I'll never let you go again." He slides down under the covers, taking me with him and cocooning his body around me.

"I already forgave you. But forgiveness and trust are two different things," I murmur.

He slowly inhales. So much time passes, I am almost back asleep when his voice, full of agony, cuts through my heart. "Whatever I have to do to gain it back and keep you forever, I will, my krasotka."

I want to believe him. Nothing in me wants to hold a grudge or not move forward with him. So I kiss his chest and fall asleep on his promise, secure in his arms, telling myself everything will be okay when I wake up and can think again.

The problem with trust is, once it's broken, it's hard to repair. Anything that threatens it again can take the fracture and break it in two, even if the truth isn't what you perceive.

23

Maksim

MY ALARM RINGS. I GRAB IT AND TURN IT OFF. I'VE BEEN awake all night and curse myself for not thinking about it when Aspen's eyes flutter open. She needs her rest. I'm hoping she can sleep off her hangover, find a way to move past my stupidity, and come to Dmitri and Anna's wedding with me.

I stroke her cheek. "Go back to sleep. I don't want to leave you, but after everything that happened with Wes last night, I need to meet my brothers for our workout."

I don't take the damage I've created in our relationship lightly. However, I can't ignore the threat that now looms over our family and her.

She sits up, and her eyes widen. "There will be ramifications for my actions?"

My stomach twists. "Nothing that happened last night with the Petrovs is your fault, my krasotka."

Something passes in her eyes. "Did you only come to get me because you couldn't stand the thought of me being with him?"

Her question alarms me. The jealousy and rage I felt seeing her in Wes's arms reignites. My voice comes out harsher than I should allow it and grows the more I speak. "I did not know you were with him until I arrived. You are here because I love you. Did I enjoy finding you sitting on his lap, with his face inches from yours? No. Would I have thought you would replace me so quickly? No. But I will take the blame for it."

She quickly looks away and squeezes her eyes shut.

This isn't the way to win her trust back.

I move her chin toward me so she can't avoid me. Her brown eyes glisten, and I soften my voice. "I apologize. It did not come out right."

"It's the truth."

There is no denying it. "You cannot expect me not to be jealous."

"You want my full loyalty, but you don't give me yours. You hold all the cards to my heart, and yet, at any moment, you can fling them on the ground. That's what you showed me last night. I didn't think you ever would, but you did."

"And you fled to another man's arms," I angrily blurt out, unable to get the vision of her with Wes's arm secure around her out of my head.

She closes her eyes, and when she opens them, all I see is more pain. Hurt emanates in her voice. "It doesn't excuse me getting drunk or allowing another man to touch me to try to forget about you. All I wanted was you, and anything resembling you seemed like a good idea in my intoxicated state. But you made it clear we were through. I begged you not to end us, and you did it so easily."

Rage digs into my bones. "You think that thug resembles me?"

"Maybe not in daylight, but all I heard was the Russian accent. I felt his danger how I feel yours, which I never felt with any man before I met you. And he had tattoos, like you."

I should remember I caused this. I should step back, cool off, and approach this conversation again when my emotions aren't running on all cylinders. Except should and reality are two different things. My jaw twitches, and I growl, "You compare me to a Petrov?"

She gets on her knees and straddles me. Her heavenly hands hold my face, and as angry as I am, I immediately put my hands on her ass, tugging her as close to me as possible. "There is nothing I want from a Petrov or any other man. I'm trying to explain to you how I got to be in his room. Are you not hearing everything I'm saying? Can you only focus on my mistake and not why I did what I did, which is that I was trying to find anything similar to you?"

"From a Petrov," I bark but don't push her away. The need to hold on to her intensifies even through my disgust.

She winces, then tilts her head, bites her trembling lip, and slides her hands to my shoulders. "If you can't understand what I'm saying, we will never move forward." Her voice cracks. "Maybe we are past the point already, and this is just harming both of us further."

"No. We aren't doing this again," I firmly say.

She misinterprets my words. Her entire body trembles. "Oh...ummm... I..." She tries to climb off me, and I slide my arm up so she can't move.

"I mean, we aren't going to not figure this out and let each other go. So tell me you still want me, my krasotka. Tell me, even though you know I'm an ass at times, you're still going to trust me again. And I will promise you I will do better. There will be no more talk ever again about ending us. We will never utter those words, or anything close to them, ever again."

A tear drips down her cheek, and her chest heaves when she inhales.

"Tell me," I demand, my lips brushing hers, my palm fisting her hair.

"I'll never stop wanting you, I already know this."

Her words are more than I needed to hear. I kiss her, and she returns my affection. "Can you trust me again, my krasotka?"

She slowly nods her head. "I don't have a choice. I want us." She opens her mouth but then shuts it.

"What do you need to ask me?"

She hesitates.

"Go on," I instruct her.

Her face darkens. "Yesterday, when I asked you about Lorenzo..."

My stomach flips. "What about him?"

"I'm not sure how to ask you this."

"Just ask. I won't get mad."

She furrows her eyebrows. "Did you kill him to get his lot?"

Things become clear. What I saw on her face wasn't fear about me. It was fear about the motives behind my actions.

"No matter what you tell me, I will deal with it. I won't leave you," she claims.

Would she really not despise me if I was a man who killed for greed?

She believes you may be.

I haven't told her the facts for her to piece it together. I would come to the same conclusion she has if I only had the limited information she does.

God, I was such a fool.

I swallow the lump in my throat. "I do not kill for money. He didn't only threaten my brothers and me. He crossed the line and harmed Boris's girlfriend, Nora, then began sending threats to Anna. There are many other reasons I do not regret his death, but those two things led to his demise."

She releases a breath. "Okay. Thank you for telling me."

"This information would have avoided our issues yesterday?"

"Yes."

I close my eyes.

She weaves her fingers through my hair. "Maksim."

I open my eyes.

"Did you mean it when you said you love me?"

"I am not a man who would ever lie about such a thing."

Her lips form a tiny smile. "I love you, too."

My heart soars. I didn't expect her to reciprocate my love. For years, I told Jade I loved her and never once heard it back. And I fight the emotions forming in my chest.

She kisses me, and I deepen it, growing hard under her. My alarm rings again, reminding me that I still have issues to deal with. I groan and turn it off. "I don't want to go—"

She puts her finger over my lips. "Go."

"You'll be here when I get back?" I'm not sure why I ask, we've moved into a better space, but something inside me says not to leave her.

Her eyes twinkle. "I prefer your bed to mine."

"Good. Get some sleep. I'll be back as soon as I can."

She slides under the covers. "Done."

I tuck a lock of her hair behind her ear. "Does this mean you'll still go to the wedding with me today?"

She smiles. "Are you going to dance with me?"

"All night."

"Guess I'll slum it and be your date, then," she teases.

I lean down and kiss her. "I'll be back soon."

Relieved we've worked through some of our issues, I get changed and go to the gym my brothers and I own. When I walk in, my brothers are already talking.

I pat Dmitri on the back. "You nervous?"

"About marrying Anna? No. About this other shit with Wes? Can't say it doesn't worry me."

My pulse increases. "Wes isn't going to allow this to disappear."

"Why was Aspen in his VIP room?" Boris seethes, his arms crossed tightly to his chest.

The self-loathing I have reappears. "It's my fault."

"How is that?"

I explain what happened. "She didn't know it was him."

"Since when is it okay for your woman to be in another man's VIP room and on his lap?"

"Watch it," I threaten Boris.

His eyes turn to slits, and he steps forward. "She's put all of us, and by extension, our women, in more danger. Nora is pregnant with my child."

I move closer to him. "You think Aspen did this on purpose? It was an accident."

"Knock it off, you two," Dmitri warns.

Sergey steps between us. "This isn't helping."

I step back. "We're already at a maximum level for the wedding security. We'll need to continue it after tonight."

"So now we have two wars going on. Goddamnit," Boris growls.

Nothing about this situation makes me happy. Boris's reaction isn't helping matters. I point at him, angry. "Sometimes, you're such a hypocrite."

"What does that mean?"

"Maksim," Dmitri growls.

I shake my head at Dmitri. "No. He's not innocent in any of this."

"What are you talking about? My woman didn't sit on a Petrov's lap last night," Boris seethes.

I lunge toward him, and my body hits Sergey's. "Do you forget what family your woman belongs to? Hmm?"

Boris's eyes darken. He sniffs hard. "You got something you want to get off your chest?"

"Maksim," Dmitri warns again.

"Don't ever disrespect my woman. And don't you dare sit on your high horse when the O'Malley's issues are now part of ours."

Boris's face hardens further. "I didn't ask you to take on anyone's issues. You're free to remove yourself at any time."

"Boris!" Sergey yells.

"What? He's not obligated."

"You speak in anger, so I'm going to give you a pass," I threaten him.

Boris grunts. "I don't need anything from you."

Dmitri steps behind Sergey and pushes Boris back to the wall. He puts his hand on his cheek and firmly states, "We are brothers. Our blood is thick. It does not separate, no matter what the circumstances. Do not ever lose sight of this. If one of us has a problem, we all do. And you know we do not keep score. We sacrifice for each other without thinking twice. You have demonstrated this your entire life. This is not the time to change or break our bond."

Dmitri refers to the debt that Boris pays off to Zamir each year for our freedom. And guilt crashes through me before Boris speaks.

"Tell that to our fearless leader."

I step around Sergey. "Dmitri is right. I should not have spoken about the O'Malleys. You know I am happy for you and Nora."

Boris stares at me but says nothing.

Dmitri pats his cheek and steps away. He spins. "Do not get upset, but what is going on with you and Aspen? It is fair for us to ask you this after the events of last night."

Sergey surprises me and comes to my defense. "They disagreed. She went out with her friends, and all the ladies drank too much. No one knew who Wes or his thugs were. It was an innocent mistake. They were only in the VIP room for a few minutes. Adrian should have had more backup. In the future, we need to be better prepared."

I nod gratefully at Sergey. "I agree. Adrian shouldn't have been in that situation on his own. We're lucky things ended how they did last night."

Dmitri says, "Call Tolik. Tell him we need a tail on Wes. Obrecht is focused on the Rossi/Petrov war. We can't take his attention off that."

"Agreed," Sergey says.

"At this point, all we can do is add the tail and keep security beefed up. If he makes any moves or threats, we'll know," Dmitri states.

I wish there were something else we could put in place, but he's right.

Boris pats him on the back. "Let's work out. We have a wedding today."

Dmitri grins. "And nothing is stopping me from saying, 'I do.'"

24

Aspen

MAKSIM LEAVES, AND I CAN'T FALL BACK TO SLEEP. I SHOWER and put on a black silk robe he bought me at some point in the last few days. I'm drying my hair when he arrives home. I turn off the dryer.

He leans down and pecks me on the lips. "How do you feel?"

"Better. My headache is gone. Whatever you gave me seemed to work. Plus, I've gotten an entire glass of water down."

"Do you think you can eat?"

"Maybe toast?"

"All right. I'll make some." He kisses the top of my head and leaves.

I finish my hair and go out to the kitchen. I sit on the barstool.

"Just in time." Maksim sets a plate of toast in front of me then puts his plate of eggs and toast next to mine. He comes around the island.

I take a bite of the bread. My stomach is still a bit queasy, but I'm hoping food might help settle it.

Maksim puts his arm around me, and I lean into his chest. "I hated not being with you last night."

I glance up and confess, "It really hurt you didn't take me."

Remorse covers his face. "Can I admit something to you?"

I sit up straighter. "Yes."

He hesitates then says, "You know that woman I told you about in Vegas? The one I said wouldn't love me?"

My stomach twists. "Yes."

"For eleven years, we were on and off. She isn't a bad person, but her past isn't as innocent as yours. In some ways, being with her was easier. I didn't ever question whether she would be able to handle my truth if she knew it."

His admission is a hard pill to swallow. It makes me wonder if a part of him thinks she is a better match for him, even if it's deep down. A nervous stirring occurs in my chest. There's so much about Maksim and his truth I'm still trying to process. I want to talk to him about it, but I don't want him to think I'm going to run from him.

He strokes my cheek and softly says, "I've offended you."

"No. Offend isn't the right word."

"Then what is?"

I clear my throat then take a sip of water. I avoid Maksim, trying to figure out how to have a conversation without him feeling like I'm judging him or wondering if his ex is a better woman for him than me.

He puts his hand on mine. "Aspen, can we go back to you and me? Before I screwed up, we weren't worried about what we said to each other."

I turn in my chair. "Okay. I am nervous. I don't have anyone to talk to about all the things you've told me. I want to discuss it with you and sort out my thoughts, but I'm afraid you'll take what I say the wrong way. Or worse, you might think I'm not able to handle things, and you made a mistake telling me your truth."

"I see." He stares at me for a moment. "Finish eating then let's talk. I promise not to get upset."

I obey, and we eat in silence. My stomach flips but not from nausea. *What if he does think she's a better fit for him than me?*

Maksim told me he loved me, and I don't doubt it. Yet, it doesn't remove my insecurity from his admission.

When we finish, he takes my hand, leads me to the couch, and pulls me onto his lap. He waits for me to speak.

"I thought I knew where I stood on certain issues, and life was black and white, but I feel like I've moved into a gray area."

"Yes. You cannot be with me and not be. You're too good to move from one end of the spectrum to the other. And the things I have done..." He trails off for a moment, and his jaw clenches. "The things I cannot guarantee you I won't do

264

again, represent everything you were clear on before meeting me."

He will kill again. I need to be prepared and okay with it.

"How do you know this is what is going through my head?"

His thumb strokes my spine. "When my mother was kidnapped and held hostage, everything changed for me. The morals my father had instilled in us no longer existed. I was a torturer and murderer. It is not anything my father or mother raised me to be." There's disappointment in his eyes. I wish I could remove it and replace it with pride so he didn't have to feel this way about himself.

I quickly insist, "It wasn't your fault."

His voice is stern. "The circumstances do not erase the sin, my krasotka. And the choices I have made in the last twenty-plus years were my decisions. While there are reasons I can justify for every man I have killed, who Zamir did not direct me to, I still broke my old moral code."

I didn't have any expected answer from Maksim, but his response makes his truth even more real. I suspected he had killed men, besides Lorenzo, not under Zamir's orders, but hearing him confirm my suspicion increases my pulse.

"What would make you kill someone?"

He doesn't hesitate. "Survival. Sometimes revenge."

My blood goes cold. I shiver and get goose bumps.

Maksim's eyes darken. "Anyone who comes after my family or our women suffers the consequences. We don't kill for reasons some men do. Money or other material possessions are never a motive. And our businesses are all legitimate. Every penny we have, we earned through our hard work and sweat."

"Is this your new moral code?"

He sighs. "If you want to call it that."

If anyone would have told me a month ago that I'd be in love with a man who's killed not one but multiple men, I wouldn't believe it. I would tell them they were crazy, and I would never condone any such thing. I'm not sure when I mentally crossed the line. Was it when I first met Maksim and could feel he was dangerous? Did his constant reminder to me about how ruthless he is move me across it over our brief encounter? Or did it occur when he told me his story?

Either way, it doesn't matter. I no longer believe what I used to. I can't, because I'm still here, with him, not wanting to be anywhere else. I have never had an urge to run from him, and I never will. I slowly say, "I'm not the person I thought I was. The fact you don't kill for possessions but only to protect those you love makes me fall deeper for you. It tells me what kind of man you are. But I can't lie to myself. If you told me you did kill for other reasons, I still would not be able to stop loving you. And I'm not sure what that makes me."

There. I said the truth I've been afraid to admit.

Maksim spins me and yanks my knees on the sides of his hips. His hands slide into my hair, and he holds my face close to his. "Do not take my sin and let it taint any part of you. I cannot live with myself if my actions cause you to despise yourself."

My heart pounds from the quick way he pulled me to him. Bergamot and cardamom grow stronger in my nostrils. "I don't want my internal confusion to cause you to regret choosing me over her." It's another admission I was scared to say out loud.

His face falls. "There has never been a choice, my krasotka. Not one moment since I met you has there been one thought I want her over you. It's always been you. And while it might have been easier for her to stomach the truth of who I am versus you, that doesn't make me wish I told her over you."

"But you said—"

"I know what I told you. I had eleven years to trust her completely. But I never did. And you..." His eyes sear into mine. He swallows hard.

"I what?" I whisper, my lips brushing against his.

His thumbs stroke my cheekbones. "I've known you for a second. Yet, I've bared every part of my ugliness to you. Instead of running, you stay. You declare your love for me and take every twisted piece of my soul and accept it. Then you tell me if I was an even more horrible man, you'd still not leave me."

"I wouldn't."

He closes his eyes. "When I think of what could have happened to you last night...with him..."

"I don't want him. I've only ever wanted you. I'm sorry, I—"

He drops his hand, sliding it under my robe and firmly palming my ass. His other hand fists my hair, and his eyes light with dark fire. He growls, "You're mine, krasotka. No other man will touch you. I will be the only one, going forward, do you understand me?"

I reply with a kiss, parting his lips with my tongue, grinding my lower body against his hardening erection.

He pulls back, breathing hard. "Answer me. I will not allow there to be any confusion on this."

"Yes, I understand."

He takes a few breaths, scanning my eyes, then lips, then back to my eyes, before sliding me off him, so I'm facing the back of the black leather couch. He spins quickly so his body is behind mine. The sound of him releasing his belt and zipper rings in my ears. The metal of his belt clangs on the wood floor.

He slides his palms between my thighs, widening me and pulling my hips toward the end of the seat so my ass is in the air. Then he bunches my silk robe and rips it off. His large hand splays on my back, pushing me into the tufts.

His erection slides into my folds, deliciously hitting my clit.

"Oh God," I moan.

He thrusts but not in me, holding me down while teasing and taunting my clit until it's so swollen, I'm sweating and begging him to release me.

"Who do you belong to?" he growls.

"You!"

"And who's the only man who touches you?" he barks, gliding his stiff shaft over my pulsing nub.

"Only you!"

"Whose cock do you want buried deep inside you?"

"Yours! Oh God...please, Maksim," I cry out.

"I'm a jealous man, my krasotka. If anyone lays a finger on you, I'll kill them. I mean it."

I whimper, on the edge of climaxing, inhaling the leather and smell of my arousal.

He grabs my hips and shimmies me over his cock, faster and faster until I'm screaming his name, and my body is trembling in ecstasy.

When I begin to slow, he slides into me in one thrust. His warm skin hits my back. He growls in my ear, "You will always be mine. Do you understand?"

"Yes," I whimper, my insides spasming against him, unable to stop as he pounds into me.

"I'm never letting you go. I won't be a fool twice."

"Oh fuck!" I scream when he hits my G-spot. I unravel like never before. Fire boils my blood, permeating my veins, and flicking across my skin.

"Krasotka!" Maksim yells and pumps his hot seed deep inside me, creating a high so euphoric, my head spins.

I collapse against the sofa, barely able to get oxygen, my one cheek resting against the leather with Maksim's breath tingling on the other.

His eyes meet mine. With labored breaths, he says, "There will be no more secrets. No lies, no outside forces to come between us. You are mine. I am yours. Do you understand, my krasotka?"

I nod.

He kisses me. Possessive. Hungry. So deep, new tingles form in my toes. When he ends our kiss, he flips me over. "Do not have any confusion around this, my krasotka. Any man who tries to harm you, or touch you, I will kill. There will be no warning. You need to understand what I'm disclosing to you."

Goose bumps pop out on my skin. "I wouldn't have ever allowed any man to touch me if you hadn't broken up with me."

His jaw twitches. "There will be no more breakups. I am not telling you this to make you feel guilty. I am warning you about what I will do so it will never be a reason for you to leave me."

My stomach twists.

"I won't back down on this. Yet, I see this as something to possibly destroy us. So I want your word if something happens, you are not going to hate me or stop loving me."

Since we aren't breaking up, I don't have any reason to engage in any man's attention aside from his, sober or intoxicated. *There's nothing to worry about.* "You have my word."

He studies my face for another moment. "Good. Let's get ready for the wedding."

25

Maksim

ASPEN STEPS OUT OF THE BEDROOM. SHE'S A STUNNING specimen of beauty and grace. Her black satin dress hugs every curve. Spaghetti straps wrap around her creamy shoulders. The front of the dress V's down, displaying enough cleavage, it's going to drive me crazy all night. When I chose the dress, I imagined her in it. She exceeds every expectation I had.

I step forward and circle my arm around her waist. "You only get more gorgeous, my krasotka."

She beams. "I was right."

"About what?"

"I have a new thing about you in a tux."

I drop my palm to her ass and survey every inch of her body. Meeting her eyes again, I trace her strap. "I think I'm going to have fun removing this dress tonight."

She moves her hand up my chest and inside my tuxedo jacket. Her fingers inch between the buttons of my shirt and through my chest hair. "Is there a dark corner at this wedding?"

I grunt. "If there is, I'll find it." I kiss her quickly. "We need to go." I help her into her coat and lead her to the elevator.

We leave the penthouse, and my bodyguard Kazmir, whom Aspen hasn't seen before, joins us in the lobby and escorts us outside. He's not there to protect me. He's there because if anything should happen to me, I need to make sure my krasotka is protected. We can't take enough precautions right now.

As soon as the door shuts, she nervously asks, "Is Adrian in trouble for my actions last night?"

Recalling the heated phone conversation between Adrian and me only creates a wave of bubbling anger in my veins. It took place after my workout. While I should be a rational man and give him a pass since he was outnumbered, it burns me Aspen ever got into a situation with any Petrov, much less Wes. In fairness, there wasn't anything he could have done without backup. But the mixed visuals of Aspen on Wes's lap and the real danger she was in then and now only made me lash out at him.

It's rare for Adrian and me to butt heads. He's the head of my security and usually my most reliable man. It's why I assigned him to protect Aspen.

Adrian may be on my payroll, but he's also not one to lie down and get attacked. If I look back at our call, it was pointless. All Adrian and I did was get into an argument. Everything he said was accurate. I should have been discussing how we are going to add the extra layers of security to Aspen. But the conversation couldn't even get there since I was so red with anger.

"No. Adrian's our cousin. He will be at the wedding." I scowl.

Aspen shifts in her seat. "I didn't know you were related."

I snort. "Some days I claim it more than others." It comes out bitter. I need to let what happened last night go. Adrian was outnumbered. He would have gotten himself, and possibly any of the women, killed if he had done anything. Yet, all I still see is my krasotka in Wes's arms.

Aspen sighs. "Things got out of hand last night. There's no way he could have stopped any of us from anything. And I wasn't very nice to him."

"It doesn't matter. His job was to protect you." As I say the words, I know it's unfair. But I can't seem to give him a pass. I need to know at all times Aspen is protected when she's not with me. While I don't want anything to happen to Aspen's friends, he wasn't being paid to protect them. He had strict orders and should have stopped Aspen and let the other women do whatever they wanted, no matter the consequences.

Aspen would be hurt if anything happened to her friends.

They all were in danger.

He's an Ivanov. It's not in Adrian's blood to let any woman be in danger.

273

According to Adrian, he was putting out fires all night with Aspen and her friends. But his admission only made me angrier over the phone since he wasn't told to protect them.

I would have done the same thing he did.

Aspen puts her hand on my thigh. "Maksim, don't be mad at Adrian. Especially if he's family."

I grunt. She's right. I need to get past it.

"This is a happy occasion. Let's celebrate and not feel anything but joy today," she says.

I lace my fingers through hers, my palm on the backside of her hand. "You're right. Dmitri and Anna deserve everyone to be in a good mood today."

"That's the spirit," she teases.

"See? I'm a rational man."

Her eyes twinkle. "I'll remember that in the future." She stares at me a moment then asks, "What's Anna like? I don't know much about your brothers, but at least I've met them. Do you get along with her?"

I chuckle. "Yes. Very well. Although at first, I wasn't too excited Dmitri hired her."

"Why?"

I pause, wondering how Aspen is going to react. "She's not Russian."

As expected, Aspen's eyes widen a bit. "I didn't realize you only hire Russians. Well, you did say Polish, too, I guess."

"We hire non-Russians and non-Poles. But we like to keep as much money in the Russian community as possible so they don't have to turn to the Petrovs."

Understanding crosses her expression. "Ahh. I see. So you didn't hit it off with Anna right away?"

"There wasn't anything major. And I learned within a few days how exceptional her talent is."

"What does she do?"

"She's an interior designer."

"Wow. That's awesome."

I can't help but smile. "Once I saw her skills and how bad Dmitri had it for her, I got over it. She's like the sister I never had now. You'll love her. The two of you will get along great."

Aspen strokes my cheek. "I can't wait to meet her. And I'm glad you're close."

I nod. "We are."

The car pulls up to the building. Snow falls, so we don't get out until we're directly in front of the doors. There are six men with shovels keeping the path and steps clear. I step out, reach in for my krasotka, and we hurry inside.

Sergey is the first person I see. His date is a woman named Eloise, whom he tends to see whenever she's in Chicago. I internally groan. It's not a surprise she's his date. He told me last night she was flying in this morning. I can't help wishing her flight was delayed and she wasn't here.

On the outside, Eloise is beyond beautiful. I understand my brother's attraction to her. But inside, all I see is ugliness.

She's one of the most in-demand black runway models in Chicago and also travels to New York and L.A. often for work. She has a thick, French accent and only moved to the U.S. a decade ago. Sergey's been obsessed with her since he met her a few years ago.

But I don't care for how she treats my brother. She acts annoyed with him every time we're together. Her actions tell me she thinks she's better than Sergey, which disturbs me. They aren't together, but every time she leaves town, he seems to have a harder time dating anyone else. And I wonder if he's falling into the same trap I created with Jade.

Regardless, I bite my tongue. Just like I wouldn't tolerate anyone speaking ill of a woman I date, he wouldn't, either. The last thing I'll do is let a woman come between my brothers and me. So, I put on my smile, and we all exchange greetings. I introduce the ladies. Sergey kisses Aspen on her cheek, and I do the same with Eloise.

"Dmitri here yet?" I ask.

"Boris just texted to meet them in the back room," Sergey confirms.

"Is Nora with them?" I would rather give Aspen the option to talk with Nora than subject her to Eloise.

Sergey's face lights up. He's grown just as close to Anna as I have. "She's with Anna. Should we peek in on her? Then we can rub it in Dmitri's face we've seen her in her dress."

I tug my krasotka closer to me. "Yes. Let's stop by, and I can introduce Aspen to Anna."

There are two main areas and several private rooms—one for Anna and one for Dmitri. The room the ceremony will take place in is also where dinner and dancing will be. The second area is for appetizers and cocktails. Each location is a nighttime winter wonderland. Fake trees covered in ice glow blue. Their limbs stretch over where the guests will sit and the aisle. Long icicles hang from the ceiling over candlelit tables. Luxurious, padded chairs face a small stage.

"Wow. This is incredible!" Aspen gushes and stops to take it all in.

I can't help feeling proud. "Anna designed it all."

Aspen gapes. "You're right. She is very talented."

"Dmitri said it was going to be amazing," Sergey follows, glancing around with a huge grin on his face.

"Hmm." Eloise's haughty sound is loud enough for all of us to hear then she purses her lips together.

Sergey arches an eyebrow. For the first time ever, I hear disgust in his voice where she is concerned. "You don't like it?"

She gazes around again then shrugs. Her French accent seems to thicken. "Fake trees? Eh."

Aspen blurts, "They don't look fake. I can't get over how real they seem."

I take a deep breath. "I think it turned out incredible."

"Agreed," Sergey growls, and I don't miss the tiny scowl on his face as he focuses on Eloise.

I clear my throat. "Should we go see Anna?"

"You go ahead. Eloise and I will catch up in a moment," Sergey orders.

I study my little brother's face. He's upset and pissed. The expression he holds is neutral, but I understand his look more than anyone. It's the disguise he puts on when he's raging inside. After so many nights with Zamir, he learned to cover his emotions. He may have only been twelve, but he saw the value in not reacting like a crazed lunatic.

Maybe it's because he and Boris were younger when everything first happened, but they have a naturally calmer demeanor than Dmitri and me. We have to work harder to cover up our emotions. But not Boris and Sergey. They can torture a man and not raise their voice once.

Right now, I see the same anger in his eyes as when he kills a man. I don't know if something is going on between Eloise and him, or if maybe he's finally had enough of her years of negativity, but I don't miss the smoldering disgust surrounded by his deadpan expression.

I pat him on the back. "I'll see you soon." I lead my krasotka away.

When we're out of earshot, she says, "Is she always like that?"

"Yep."

"I've never seen anything so amazing as this room. I don't understand how she can criticize it."

"That's Eloise. Normally, it's just directed at Sergey."

Aspen tilts her head. "She's disrespectful toward him?"

"In my opinion."

"Why does he put up with her? He's a grade-A stud. Girls must throw themselves at him."

I chuckle. "Takes after me, right?"

Her lips twitch. "There is no doubt you and your brothers are all Ivanovs." Her face falls. "So why is he letting her treat him badly?"

I sigh. "I can't say he's in love with her. I'm not sure if he is or not. They only date and have never been exclusive, but I think Sergey's always been holding out for more from her. But I'm not one to talk after my past. I just hope he isn't following my relationship footsteps."

She gasps dramatically. "But you have me."

I dip down and kiss her. "And I'm so glad I do. Present relationship excluded from my statement. Come on. I want you to meet Anna." I knock on the door, and Anna's friend, Harper, answers.

"Hey!" she chirps.

I bend down and kiss her on the cheek and introduce Aspen. Harper steps aside, and we move through at least a dozen women, ranging from Anna's friends to her mom, and some other ones I believe flew in from New York, where Anna is originally from.

Anna's mom is holding a veil and talking to her. Anna's back is to us. Her hair is blonde again. She had it dark for a while but recently switched it back. It's in an updo, showcasing her form-fitting, open-back dress. The expensive lace hugs her ass. I can't help but think about how much Dmitri will like it. He worships her ass as if it's a piece of art Michelangelo sculpted.

I clear my throat, and Anna spins. Her face lights up.

"Wow. You're stunning," I tell her, step forward, and kiss her on the cheek.

She takes a deep breath. "Thanks."

I turn. "This is Aspen. Aspen, Anna."

Anna smiles bigger. "It's so nice to meet you."

"You, too. You look gorgeous. And I can't believe you designed all that out there. It's amazing."

Anna blushes. "Thank you." She turns to me. "Have you seen Dmitri?"

"Not yet. We're making our way back there."

She takes Aspen's hand. "Okay. Well, you go hang with your brothers. Aspen can stay with us."

"Oh. I don't want to impose," Aspen says.

Anna snorts. "You aren't."

Nora steps next to Anna. "Maksim."

I kiss her on the cheek. Her red hair hangs in long curls. Her green eyes are bright, and her baby bump is barely showing. After I introduce her to Aspen, I say, "You look beautiful, Nora. How are you feeling?"

"Great."

Anna waves. "Bye, Maksim. Don't worry. We won't bite Aspen. Will we?"

"Nope," Nora replies. "Plus, we can hear all the juicy secrets Aspen knows about you."

Aspen laughs. "Well, guess I have to stay now."

I glance at her. She looks happy to be staying with the women. I peck her on the lips. "I'm in the other room down the hall if you need me."

"She'll be fine," Anna sings and shoos me away but not before Sergey and Eloise enter the room. She seems to look a bit nicer than when we left. Anna and Nora are just as friendly to her and tell her to stay as well.

I almost tell Sergey not to leave her so she doesn't say something nasty to Anna on her big day, but I bite my tongue. Sergey follows me out of the room.

"Everything okay between you two?" I ask.

He shrugs. "I'm not sure what I'm doing with her anymore."

I stop. My heart beats faster. "How long have you been feeling like this?"

He looks at the ceiling. "I'm not sure. But I don't get excited when she comes to town anymore. And she won't commit to me. She won't give me that. I'm good when she's here and wants to fuck, and that's about it."

"Ouch. You really believe that?" I would like to think there's something more. Even though Jade wouldn't fully commit to me, we were more than what Sergey is describing.

His face turns to steel. He meets my eye. "At some point, you have to stop pretending. And you know what? I used to care. I wanted more. She didn't. I told myself she eventually would. But she is never going to. I won't lie to myself anymore. And the thing is, I don't think I want her, either."

My stomach flips. I hate seeing my brother hurt. He deserves to be loved. Out of all my brothers, him maybe the most. I wish I could wave a magic wand and figure out how to help him be happy and find the woman who will adore him as much as he loves her. I put my arm around him and quietly say, "Sometimes you have to let someone go to open up space for the one who has the capacity to love you. And when you find her, you'll know. I won't tell you what to do. I spent eleven years waiting for Jade to love me. But you, my brother, don't need to make my mistake."

He closes his eyes briefly then says, "I think I just need a break. No Eloise. No women. No drama."

"Take one. You're allowed. If you're meant to be together, you'll figure it out."

He releases a big breath. "Let's go see Dmitri."

I pat him on the back, and we go into the room Dmitri and Boris are in.

Like Anna's room, his is full, too. The guys who were in Vegas are all here. Killian and his two brothers, Adrian, Tolik, Obrecht, and a few of our other cousins.

My blood boils at the sight of Adrian, but Aspen's words about this being a happy occasion ring in my head. From the look on Adrian's face, he's not excited I'm here, either.

He's your blood.

You would have done what he did.

It's my krasotka.

I ignore Adrian for a moment and hug Dmitri. "You ready?"

"Can't walk down the aisle soon enough."

Sergey hugs him and says, "Your bride looks amazing."

Dmitri's eyes light up. "You saw her?"

"Yep. She seems just as ready as you are."

Adrian's phone rings. I glance at him, and his face hardens. His eyebrows furrow, and he excuses himself and leaves the room.

Anna's brother, Chase, and his friend, Noah, start passing out shots of vodka.

Killian pulls out a flask. "Think I'll stick with whiskey." His brothers, Declan and Nolan, pull theirs out as well.

"To your last moments as a free man," Noah shouts.

Everyone takes their drink. I engage in small talk until Adrian comes back into the room.

"Maksim." He nods for me to step out into the hall.

I glance at my brothers, who all give me questioning looks. I follow Adrian and shut the door.

He checks to make sure we're alone. "Aspen's apartment has been broken into."

"What? Who did it?" I growl.

He raises his eyebrows.

I should know better than to ask. Wes Petrov, or any Petrov for that matter, isn't someone you cross. "I'll kill him."

"Shh," Adrian warns.

I fill my lungs with oxygen, letting it sit until I can't hold it anymore. "This is a direct attack on my krasotka and us."

Adrian crosses his arms. "It wasn't the Petrovs."

"No? Who then?"

"Her ex. The neighbor interfered, and he left with a full backpack."

"What did he take?"

Adrian shifts. "I don't know. But our guys assumed he would hang out, realize she wasn't there, then leave. When he ran out of the building, they went in to check things out and spoke with the neighbor. The surveillance pictures clearly show he had something in the bag. It wasn't full when he went in."

"Where is he now?"

"At a friend's apartment where he's staying. He hasn't come out since he left."

My inner beast riles. "Pick him up. Take him to the garage. Let me know when he's there."

"You want the guys to handle it or me?"

"No. I'll be the one dealing with him. No one touches him, except me."

Adrian nods. "All right."

"Get the backpack and whatever was in it back. Strip him down and tie him up so he's on his tip-toes."

"Done."

The clawing at my stomach starts. I go into the restroom and splash cold water on my face.

You can't kill him. Aspen will never forgive you.

I already warned her and made her promise me.

She didn't think you were talking about Peter.

He was warned.

He violated her space and stole from her.

What did he take?

What if she had been there?

I stare at my reflection, telling the monster within me to go back to hibernation. But he's been woken too many times in the last twenty-four hours. And once you wake a bear, it's hard to get him to go back to sleep.

Aspen

ANNA AND NORA ARE BOTH REALLY NICE. SO ARE THE REST OF the women. Eloise seems to be on her best behavior, keeping her side comments to herself.

The wedding ceremony is beautiful. Anna and Dmitri's happiness radiates off them. Maksim and Dmitri's brothers stand next to him, looking just as happy as he does.

I can't help but think about them as young men and the trauma they survived. I see Sergey at twelve, and I glance at Eloise, who sits next to me. She's got her lips pursed and looks as if she's annoyed to be here.

He deserves better than her.

I shouldn't judge Eloise or pretend to understand their relationship. I barely met her and don't know anything about their situation. Yet, everything in my gut says Sergey deserves to be loved, and she isn't treating him as she should be.

I don't look at her too long, in fear she might catch me and bite my head off in the middle of the ceremony, causing a scene.

Okay, now I'm being dramatic.

I wouldn't put it past her though.

I focus back on Maksim and his brothers. You wouldn't choose to mess with them, but you would never think they would have gone through what they have, either.

And they're all so handsome in their tuxes. Each of them has features of the other, creating no doubt they are brothers. But their bond is recognizable even in a room full of people. If Maksim hadn't told me anything about them, I would see it.

I haven't been to a wedding in a few years. The look on Anna and Dmitri's faces makes me wonder if I looked as happy as they did when I said my vows to Peter.

Peter's goofy grin as he slurred his words flashes before me. The embarrassment I felt, and the smell of beer and whiskey, floods my senses.

Nope. I definitely wasn't as happy as Anna and Dmitri.

I should have known then.

I was only eighteen.

I concentrate on the ceremony. When it's over, Maksim stops to escort me down the aisle. All of Anna's bridesmaids are married, and each of them collects their husband as they follow the bride.

As soon as Maksim puts his hand on the curve of my waist, his lips brush against my forehead. I tilt my head up, and he winks.

My insides turn to Jell-O. I lean into him, wondering how it's possible I've felt so comfortable with him since the moment he first touched me. Even when I was blindfolded and didn't know what he looked like or his name, our bodies melted together.

All night, Maksim and I have fun talking with the other guests and dancing. No matter what conversation we get into, his focus is always on me, making me feel important to him. And I notice the same with his brothers. There's an intensity about all of them, but each gives all their attention to their woman.

Especially Boris. I don't know why I can't seem to turn away from him and Nora, but the way he looks at her gives me the impression he wants to fuck her right on the table.

I often catch him dragging his finger down her bare shoulders, or wrapping his arm around her and stroking the curve of her waist. Every touch he gives her seems to light her up. She quietly gasps and closes her eyes at times, as if his touch alone is about to give her an orgasm.

After Anna and Dmitri cut the cake, I tell Maksim I'm going to the restroom.

"I'll take you," he says.

I give him a kiss. "No, continue your conversation. I'll be right back."

"You sure?"

I laugh. "Yes. It's only over there." I point toward the hallway.

He smiles, and my insides throb. Maksim's straight out of a GQ magazine in his tuxedo. "Okay."

I go down the hall and am almost to the bathroom when I hear muffled noises. I pause, not sure if I really heard something or not. The music isn't as loud as in the reception area.

"Jesus, Mary, and Joseph!"

That's Nora!

Should I get Maksim?

No. Someone is hurting her. There isn't time.

I open the door all the way and step in and freeze, just as Nora yells, "Don't make me wait. Oh…Jes…oh…"

She's up against a wall, her dress is bunched to her waist, and her legs are over Boris's shoulders. She's gripping his hair. One of his hands is over her neck, pushing her chin toward the ceiling. Two of his long fingers slide into her mouth and she sucks on them and moans. His other hand is over her breast, his thumb roughly circling her nipple through the fabric of her dress. His face is buried in her sex, and he's eating her out and grunting while she grinds into him like the Energizer Bunny.

Her cheeks match her red hair, and her whimpers get louder.

Boris growls something in Russian, and she cries out, "Please!"

Holy…oh my…holy shit! Why am I still here?

I tear my eyes away and back out into the hall, run into the bathroom, and lock myself in the stall.

That was hot.

Oh God. It's Boris and Nora.

They could make a porn movie.

Shit. I need to stop these thoughts.

Oh, jeez.

I finish my business, wash my hands, and pat my face with a cold towel.

Go directly back to the table, and do not open any more doors!

As soon as I step outside, Adrian and I bump into each other.

"Hi," I say, embarrassed from the previous night's events.

His face stays neutral. "Aspen." He starts to pass me.

I grab his arm. "Adrian."

He blows out a breath of air and spins. He raises his eyebrows.

My cheeks grow hot. "I'm sorry about last night."

He nods. His voice is low. "I'm sure you are."

"Adrian—"

"We're fine, Aspen. Let's not rehash it. I shouldn't have said that."

"Are we?"

"Yeah. But next time you go out with your friends, I'm bringing more of my guys with me."

My lips twitch. "Is that a joke?"

His expression stays serious. "No. It's a promise."

"We aren't always like that."

"Like what?" Maksim's voice booms.

I turn and smile. "I was telling Adrian my friends and I normally behave when we go out."

Maksim raises his eyebrows.

"Why are you giving me that look?"

"Your girlfriends are a wild bunch."

"Yes, they are," Adrian agrees.

"Are we?"

"Yes," Maksim and Adrian say in unison.

I wince at Adrian. "Sorry again."

He glances at Maksim then me. "Like I already said, we're fine. Excuse me." He passes Maksim and me.

"Are you and Adrian at odds still?"

Maksim sighs. "Don't worry about Adrian and me."

"But—"

"I don't want to talk about him." He kisses me, stepping back until I'm against the wall, deepening it until he's hard.

I breathlessly say, "This reminds me of our first kiss."

"But you can see me."

I cup his cheek and look into his beautiful blue eyes. "I prefer to see you. All of you."

He kisses me some more. "Let's get out of this hallway." He guides me a few steps when a disheveled Boris and Nora step out into the hall.

Her face still looks like a cherry tomato and Boris's mouth and beard are wet.

Boris cockily nods to Maksim. Nora avoids looking at us and rushes into the bathroom. Boris goes into the men's room.

Maksim's lips twitch, and he guides me out to the dance floor. I don't say anything and try to get the thought of Boris and Nora out of my head.

It's late when the wedding is over. We stay until the end and are part of the last group of guests to leave. Anna and Dmitri have just left. Maksim and his brothers' drivers are all waiting at the curb. We all get into the vehicles and part ways.

Maksim pulls me onto his lap.

"I had a great time. Thanks for taking me."

He traces my jaw. "I wouldn't have wanted to be there without you."

We make out the entire way home, lips locked, hands all over the other, hot and hungry. We're so wrapped up in each other, we don't notice the car stops until Maksim's driver opens the door.

Maksim escorts me inside. As soon as we get in the elevator, he pushes me against the wall. His hands slide my coat off. Our lips reunite, greedy and full of need. The elevator stops and dings. Maksim turns me, and I walk backward while he guides me inside the penthouse, our mouths never leaving the other.

He tosses my coat on the floor, and his hand reaches around me and unzips my dress. It shimmies down my body. His fingers dip inside my panties, gliding through my wet heat.

He groans, saying something in Russian, and continues kissing me while moving me through the apartment and circling his finger inside my sex.

We're in the living room when he freezes. His head turns, his finger slides out of me.

I glance across the room. An Asian woman with a sleek, chin-length bob is stretched out seductively on the couch in a black leather lingerie set. She has a garter belt, fishnet stockings, thigh-high boots with a six-inch heel, and her panties are crotchless.

It's the same couch Maksim fucked me on earlier in the day.

"Jade, what in God's name are you doing here?" Maksim barks then shimmies out of his jacket and wraps it around my shoulders.

I glance down and realize I'm in my bra, panties, and stilettos. I suddenly feel very exposed and self-conscious.

Of course. She's Jade. The *Jade. The woman who had his attention for eleven years.*

Why is she in the penthouse?

She does nothing to cover herself, trails her fingers on her thigh in a circle, and gives me a stare-down like I'm no one. "You said you missed me. When I saw you after your Vegas trip, I told you I'd give us a few weeks to think about things. It's been a few weeks. My answer is yes."

Yes? What is she telling him yes to?

A few weeks ago? After Vegas? He told me he hadn't seen her for months before meeting me.

Maksim's color drains from his face. His eyes turn into slits. "Put your clothes on, Jade."

Her cold eyes widen in surprise. "Did you hear what I said?"

Maksim steps forward and picks up her clothes, which are folded neatly on the coffee table. He tosses them at her. "You're too late. I made it clear we weren't doing this again."

"No, you said you weren't going to continue seeing me if things didn't change between us. I'm telling you, I'm ready. And I won't hold"—she cranes her neck and drills her eyes into mine while pointing in my direction—"whatever this is, against you."

The quivering of my insides gets worse. I close Maksim's jacket around me tighter.

Maksim growls, "Put your clothes on. Don't make me tell you again. Then get out of my house. We're over, Jade."

She confidently rises, slinks toward Maksim, and puts her hands on his chest. "You're acting rashly."

He grips her wrists and pushes them away from him. "Don't."

Her eyes turn soft. She looks up at him through her long lashes, and I want to rip them out. She softens her voice. "Eleven years, Maksim."

He takes a deep breath and stares at her.

I can't see his face. I don't know what he's thinking, but I'm suddenly scared he's reconsidering whether he should be with her over me.

His comment earlier about how it was easier to be with her flies into my mind, and I cringe. She's offering him everything he's ever wanted from her. And while I don't think ill of my looks or body, she's an edgy, sexy woman. There's nothing besides her cold eyes to find fault in.

"You're too late, Jade," Maksim's repeats, his deep voice firm, but I also notice this time there is sympathy in it.

A new pang of jealousy hits me. There's heart in his sympathy. I shouldn't want him to be cruel to her, but I don't like her getting any piece of his heart.

She breaks her gaze and stares at his chest. A moment passes. Maksim steps to the side and picks up her clothes.

Jade's eyes meet mine in a glare so cold, I shiver.

He puts his hand on her back and leads her out of the room and to the elevator.

I don't move. I don't follow him or turn to see them. Instead, I stare out into the lights of the surrounding buildings.

He lied to me.

Did they sleep together when he got back from Vegas?

Why didn't he tell me the truth?

A tornado of hurt and betrayal spins in my gut. Blood pounds hard against my ears. Maksim's voice cuts through it.

"Don't come here again, Jade. There is nothing left between us."

"Maksim, you don't believe that."

"I do."

"Because of her?" Her voice is sharp as a knife and slices through the air, giving me goose bumps.

"Yes. I love her."

She firmly says, "No. You love me. Only a few weeks ago, you loved me."

"No. I didn't. It's been months. And we both know it's when this ended between us."

I take a deep breath. Happy he claimed me as his and isn't wavering about choosing her over me. But I'm still not sure how I'll get past his lie. I hate he slept with her after we were together.

I don't know if he did.

How could he not have? She's sexy, and he was in love with her.

"Goodbye, Jade," Maksim states, and the elevator doors shut.

I still don't look behind me. I smell bergamot and cardamom first. His hands slide over my shoulders and to my stomach. His body moves flush against mine.

"I'm sorry you had to see that, my krasotka."

My heart thumps harder. "Did you sleep with her?"

"We were together for eleven years."

I shut my eyes, but a tear escapes. "Why did you lie to me?"

He spins me. "When have I ever not told you the truth?"

I stare at his chest, wanting to touch it, but I don't dare. "I asked you when you were last with her. You said months before you met me."

He tilts my chin up. "Yes. That is the last time I slept with her."

"I'm confused."

He sternly says, "I have touched no woman since I met you in Vegas. Nor have I wanted to. That is the truth."

"But you saw her?"

"Yes. She was waiting in the lobby when I got back from Vegas. I told her to go home."

"And you haven't seen her since?"

"I have. We had dinner a few days later. She asked, and I thought it might give us both closure."

"What did she mean when she said her answer was yes?"

His jaw clenches. "When we went to dinner, she told me I was creating issues when we didn't have any. She said things were good how they were between us, and there wasn't any reason to change them. I told her it wasn't a point I was willing to compromise on anymore."

"But you asked her to reconsider?"

"No. She asked if we could talk again in a few weeks. I didn't see the point, but I also didn't want to hurt her. I must have given her the impression I still wanted her, and I'm sorry about that."

I want to believe him. But did he really not want her anymore? Is there any part of him that is rethinking letting her walk out of here?

"Come sit down." He guides me to the couch.

"No. I don't want to sit where she was. Not tonight."

"Okay." He leads me into the bedroom, sits against the headboard, and pulls me on top of him. He flips the switch next to the bed, and the gas fireplace, that's the length of the room, lights up.

His strong arms are warm. I sink into his body, which feels like heaven next to mine.

Nothing has changed.

Or has it?

"Why was she here? How did she get in?" I ask.

He closes his eyes then opens them. "It's my fault. I meant to remove her access from the security list, but I forgot."

I stare at the fire dancing along the wall.

Or did he not do it because he didn't really want it to be over and was secretly hoping it wasn't?

Maksim pulls his phone out of his pocket and tightens his arm around me.

I don't look at him. I shouldn't be mad. But everything about Jade makes me self-conscious. And she's so opposite of me. I don't understand how he could be so infatuated with her then be with me.

Am I second best? Did he settle for me? Is he going to wake up tomorrow and change his mind about her?

"Marcel. It's Maksim. I need you to remove Jade's access to everything," he demands while his thumb strokes my waist.

I close my eyes, wishing I didn't feel jealous, hating the vision I now have of her in thigh-high boots wrapped around Maksim's waist.

"Thank you." Maksim tosses his phone on the nightstand. "She no longer has any access."

I stay silent, my worries and unwanted visuals spinning in my head. I finally speak, my voice cracking, "We're so different."

Maksim flips me over onto my back. He pins me with his body and gaze. His heart beats into my breast. His hand cups my cheek. "Yes. You are. And I'm nothing like your ex-husband. I think we've both decided what we had in the past isn't what we want for the future. Or am I wrong?"

He's right.

Instead of agreeing with him, I admit my insecurities. "There isn't any part of you that wants to take her up on her offer? Now that she's willing to give you what you asked for all those years?"

"No. I have you. And even if I didn't have you, I'm over her." There's no room in his voice to question anything.

I release a shaky breath. "That's good."

His lips twitch. "Only good?"

I smile.

He kisses my neck under my ear then murmurs, "Should I show you how crazy I am about you?"

I reach for his face and hold it in front of mine, taking in every part of his gorgeous features—the iciness of his eyes, his chiseled cheekbones and jaw, and his lips, slightly swollen from all our kisses earlier.

His expression turns to worry. "My krasotka—"

"I don't want to wake up tomorrow and you regret choosing me over her," I blurt out, my face growing hot.

"Listen to me. There will be no regrets. I love you. And you love me, hmm?"

"Yes. So much."

"Then I think it's time we both trusted in us together, don't you?" He arches an eyebrow and strokes my cheek.

I nod. "Yes. You're right."

His lips twitch next to mine. "Then kiss me and use your sexy little body to show me how much you love me."

Maksim

MONDAY MORNING COMES QUICKLY. MY KRASOTKA AND I went to brunch at Dmitri and Anna's. My brothers and Anna's family were there. After the party was over, Aspen and I came back to my place.

We avoided further talk of Jade, Wes, and her ex. Peter's still in my "garage." It's where my brothers and I take men who we need to deal with when we can't deliver our wrath in another location. It's an old building past the Chicago limits, almost in Indiana.

I didn't take Adrian's call on Sunday morning. He texted me immediately. Adrian: *Want to know the contents?*

Me: *No. I'll handle it on Monday. Deliver the essentials.*

Adrian: *Got it.*

The essentials were minimal food and water, along with intimidation. And once my brothers learned we had a guest in our garage, they didn't hesitate to visit at separate times. Well, Dmitri didn't because he left for his honeymoon.

Boris and Sergey didn't leave any scars or inflict any pain on Peter, but their mere presence made him piss his pants during both their visits.

When I woke up this morning, the growling in my head got louder. My beast is ready. It's time to take care of my issue, and I can no longer avoid it.

Sergey, Boris, and I work out first thing in the morning. I already told Aspen I wouldn't be back before she left for work. When my brothers and I finish showering, Sergey crosses his arms. "You going to take care of him now?"

"Yep." My beast is already awake. The intense cardio and heavy weights I lifted did nothing to sweat any ounce of rage out of me.

Boris slings his bag over his shoulder. "Is Adrian going to be there?"

"No. He's guarding Aspen." I'm still fuming over the events at the Cat's Meow, but Adrian is my best guy. A few days of being away from the situation made me realize there is no one else I trust as much as Adrian to watch over my krasotka. She also agreed not to give him a hard time today.

"You want us to come?" Boris's dark eyes shift, itching to be part of it.

I shake my head. "You two talk to our workers as planned. We can't let this coward sidetrack us from keeping our men safe."

"Are you going to kill him or give him a warning?" Sergey asks.

Boris grunts. "He threatened and stole from his woman. I know what I would do."

"What does Aspen think?" Sergey raises his eyebrows.

"She doesn't know anything about it." Guilt stews inside me for selfishly enjoying our time together over the weekend, living a normal life, and not dealing with problems.

"You aren't going to tell her he broke into her place? Don't you think the neighbor will talk when she goes back there?" Surprise fills Sergey's face.

It's a question I've been asking myself all weekend. As much as I tried to avoid thinking about anything except Aspen, it nagged at me. I should have told her, but so much had already happened in a short time frame. She was so happy on Sunday. I didn't want anything to interfere with it. "I will. We agreed not to have lies or secrets between us. But I want to know the entire situation first before I tell her."

"Back to the original question. Are you killing him? Do I need to prepare to come by later and help clean up?" Boris asks.

I inhale slowly then release it. The monster within me is ready to tear Peter to shreds, inch by inch, then hold his heart in my hand while it takes its last beat. I want to believe my krasotka won't hold it against me since I already warned her I would kill any man who touches her. But my heart is telling me she will never be able to forgive me. She already made it clear she didn't want me to hurt him. Killing him seems to be the one thing that could break us.

I take too long to answer, and Sergey advises, "You better be clear before you leave here what you are doing. In fact, we're going with you."

"No. We must stay the course. The war is not stopping for my personal issue."

"You hesitate about whether to kill him or not. It is better to teach him a lesson in this case. Without full surety, you will regret your actions. We will go with you."

"Our men—"

"A few hours will not make any difference. Our men are working right now. They have paychecks to feed their families. You do not have the restraint Sergey and I have. He is right. You are not doing this on your own," Boris states.

They know me better than I sometimes know myself. I'm grateful they see my weakness and are stepping in. I nod. "Then let's go."

We leave and pile into the back of my vehicle.

"Aspen has warned you not to harm him?" Sergey asks.

"I told her I wouldn't lay a hand on him if he left her alone, and it was his choice to heed the warning or not."

"She still didn't like your response?"

I sigh. "Little brother, you are not helping me be confident in the actions I will take."

He snorts. "I like Aspen. You two looked happy together. In fact, I've never seen you look so happy with any woman before. I wouldn't want you to destroy something good."

"I'd still kill the guy. But I guess it's why I'm with Nora and not someone like Anna or Aspen. Nora knows exactly who I am and how I respond to threats. Still wish Dmitri would have finished Anna's ex off," Boris states.

"Aspen knows everything," I blurt out. "And Anna may not have ever forgiven Dmitri. It's better he lived. And Dmitri and Anna are happy."

"You told Aspen everything?" Sergey asks, surprised.

"Yes."

The car goes quiet. I glance out the window at the blur of buildings passing us by, wondering what the best route to deal with Peter is.

Sergey lowers his voice. "How did you date Jade for eleven years and never tell her but meet Aspen and disclose all our secrets within under a month?"

I can't help but notice the worry in his voice. I don't blame him, either. If Aspen weren't mine, and he told a woman he just met about our secrets, I would be concerned, too. "It wasn't fair for me not to tell her. And she's not Jade. We can all trust her. She would never betray us."

"You always felt Jade would?"

Sergey's question takes me by surprise. Is it the real reason I never told Jade? Do I believe Jade would ever cross me? I glance at my knees, thinking about when I put Jade in the elevator the other night. Her glare, usually reserved for everyone except me, was exceptionally cold. I assumed it was from how hurt she was from me rejecting her.

"What aren't you telling us?" Boris asks.

I shake my head. "Jade was lying on my couch in lingerie when Aspen and I got home from the wedding."

"Ouch," Sergey blurts.

Boris whistles.

"Yep. Jade wasn't happy when I sent her on her way and reinforced we were over."

"Well, it's good she doesn't know our truth, then," Boris states.

Several minutes of silence pass.

Sergey asks, "So what are we doing to this dickhead?"

"*We* aren't doing anything. I'll be dealing out his punishment," I claim.

Boris groans. "You take all the fun out of it."

"Okay, so what are you going to do? What is the point Boris and I need to step in and stop you?"

My monster stirs. I fight him, not giving in to what he wants me to do. I begrudgingly admit, "I can't kill him."

"There are a lot of things before death," Boris points out, his eyes gleaming with ideas I probably wouldn't even think about.

"Simmer down. Maksim said he's the only one touching him," Sergey reminds him.

Boris grunts and taps his fingers on the armrest. "What's the hard limit? Organs? Limbs? His tongue?"

I want to say it's all available for me to do with as I see fit at the time, but I know myself. If I don't give Boris and Sergey a line I can't cross, I'll end up killing Peter.

"Fingers and toes."

"Right. All of them?" Boris asks with hope in his eyes.

I don't answer, not sure where I want to draw it.

Sergey shakes his head. "You just told a woman you've only known a short time all of our secrets. I think it's best if you think about what she would want in this situation."

I groan. "Sometimes, I wonder if you're the only smart one out of all of us."

"Speak for yourself. Smart would be finding a woman who understands how you operate," Boris replies.

"Enough. Figure out your limit, Maksim. We're almost there," Sergey demands, annoyed.

My phone rings. I glance at it and answer. "Everything okay, my krasotka?"

"Maksim, Peter broke into my apartment Saturday. My neighbor left me a message. Since I didn't turn my phone on yesterday, I just listened to it."

My stomach flips, and I stay silent.

"Maksim? Are you there?"

I clear my throat. "Yes."

Her voice dips several octaves. "My neighbor also said a guy with a Russian accent questioned her. Do you know anything about this?"

She asks in a question, but we both know the answer. "We will talk about this tonight."

She inhales sharply. "Maksim..."

"He was warned. He stole from you."

"What did he take?"

"I don't know. I will find out shortly."

"Where are you?"

"We will discuss this tonight," I repeat.

In a stern voice, she says, "Maksim, please. Don't...don't..."

I can picture her squeezing her eyes and trying to get the words out with distress smeared across her expression. It tugs at my heart and weakens my resolve to inflict massive amounts of pain on him.

I hate she still cares about his well-being, but I don't want to hurt her.

"He will still be breathing when I am done with him," I state.

"What does that mean?" she whispers.

"This is the man I am. I will not let others harm you in any way."

Sergey raises his eyebrows, as if to tell me he told me so. Boris crosses his arms and taps his elbows.

"This is not the same as the situation I got us in on Friday night."

The visual of her on Wes's lap riles my inner beast. I struggle further to tame him, trying not to make a decision I'll regret.

Silence fills the line. My pulse continues to increase. She's right. Peter isn't anywhere close to the caliber of Wes or any Petrov. But he's still a threat to my krasotka. And he hasn't respected her wishes to stay away or taken Adrian's warning seriously. I cut through the quiet. "I cannot let his actions go unpunished."

My brother's eyes are so different. Boris is annoyed. Sergey is worried. Neither gives me any comfort. I turn toward the window.

"Maksim, I'm begging you..."

I can't ignore the desperation in Aspen's voice. It tears at my heart. And I don't want to lose her. The thought is all it takes to set my limit. "There won't be any permanent damage. You have my word."

"What does that mean?" she quickly asks, her voice a mix of relief, confusion, and fear.

"We will not discuss this any further over the phone. Do not worry. I give you my promise."

"There is nothing I can say to make you turn around and forget about this, is there?"

I shut my eyes for a moment, avoiding my brother's stares. I will not allow any man to get away with what he has done to her. "I cannot give you more than I just did. We will talk tonight. I love you." I hang up, not waiting for her to respond, knowing there is nothing else to say. I have a job to do. It's to protect her. I've already allowed her wishes to reduce the severity of the message I will send.

The driver parks the car outside the building. I take a deep breath and turn to my brothers.

"What's the limit, Maksim," Sergey asks again.

Boris cracks his knuckles and raises his eyebrows.

"No long-term health issues. Scars are okay. Limbs are off-limits, including fingers and toes."

"Bones?" Boris asks.

"Acceptable," I state and open the car door. "Let's get this over with."

We go inside and lock the door behind us. The building has two parts. Both parts are nothing special with cement floors and walls. The front room has a desk. Peter's backpack sits on it.

I open it up and empty the contents. Aspen's laptop and charger, wedding rings, and a box of checks for her bank account are inside.

Nothing about the items helps to squash the growing rage I feel. My guess is he took the only things of value Aspen has and then planned to keep stealing from her.

"So, it's all about money, then?" Sergey asks.

"Lazy bastard," Boris seethes.

All the years she supported him, and he still wants to take from her.

"Limits still the same?" Boris asks.

"Don't tempt him," Sergey replies.

I take a deep breath. "Nothing has changed. I won't lose my krasotka over him."

Sergey pats me on the back. "Good choice."

I step forward and open the door. This room is the same as the front one, minus the desk, and has plastic covering the walls, floor, and ceiling. A rope hangs in the middle of the room, attached to Peter's wrists. He's naked and stands on his toes. Any amount of movement can cause him to twirl or sway, pulling at his arm sockets and risking to dislocate his shoulders.

His bloodshot eyes widen when he sees the three of us walk in. Exhaustion is all over his face and slowly morphs into fear. His light hair is greasy, and he smells like urine. Sweat pops out on his skin. He manages to ask, "Who are you?"

I step forward and hold my knife blade against his cheek. "I'm your worst nightmare."

He swallows hard then tears begin to fall. "What do you want from me?"

"What do I want?" I growl, pressing the knife lightly into his skin so a drop of blood pops out on his cheek.

His body shakes and begins to move in half circles.

"She's not yours anymore. You spent twenty years taking from her. Now you steal from her. There are consequences to your actions."

"You can have it all back," he cries out.

Boris begins to tsk, and Peter glances over at him with his eyes, not moving his cheek due to my blade. He cries harder. "Please let me go."

The man in front of me is a coward and thief. He's a pathetic waste of space. But he isn't a Wes Petrov. He doesn't have the balls to be a genuine threat.

My krasotka's face won't leave my mind. I want to inflict pain on him for the years of sorrow he gave her. But it's suddenly clear, no matter what I do to him, I risk losing her. She knows he's weak and nothing like the men I usually dole out punishments to. And the satisfaction of hurting him isn't worth risking her.

I thought I needed my brothers to stop me from crossing the line. I now can't seem to make a move. My krasotka is everything to me. The line isn't clear enough, and I won't let him destroy us.

I lower my knife and step so close to him, I can taste his stale breath. "You will never look at or speak to her again. You will leave Chicago. If you even think about reaching out to her, or taking another penny of her money, I will find you. Your death will be long and painful."

His lip quivers.

"Do you understand me?"

"Y-yes."

I shake my head in disgust and step back. I turn to my brothers and motion for them to follow me. When we get in the other room, I say, "Sergey, brand him to give him a reminder for life. Get him dressed and put him on a bus as far away from here as possible. I need to take the car. I'll send another one."

Boris growls. "You're getting soft, my brother."

"No. He is not the type of man we are used to dealing with. I will not destroy my relationship over a coward."

Sergey takes his knife out of his pocket and opens it up. "Where do you want it?"

"On his chest, so every time he looks in the mirror, he sees it." The nice thing about being an Ivanov is the letter I looks the same when you look in the mirror. You can't escape it.

Sergey nods and goes into the other room.

"Wh-what are... Please let me go," Peter wails.

"I'm going to watch," Boris says and leaves the room.

"This will be better for you if you don't move," Sergey seethes.

"Who are you?" Peter cries out.

I sling the backpack over my shoulder. The last thing I hear before I step out the door is Sergey reply, "The enforcer."

Aspen

I can't stop pacing Maksim's penthouse. The churning of my stomach won't stop. I should be at work, but I called in sick.

Maksim said Peter wouldn't have any permanent damage.

What does that mean?

Why did Peter break into my apartment?

What did he take?

I don't know who Peter is anymore. The man I married at eighteen doesn't seem to exist. Or maybe he was always like this, and I didn't see it. I've never known him to steal anything.

Maksim told me he would kill anyone who harmed me. I assumed it would be Wes, not Peter.

He said he wouldn't kill him.

Oh God!

I crouch down, trying to breathe. No matter what Peter did, he isn't a Wes Petrov. I don't love Peter anymore. I don't want anything to do with him. I want him to stay as far away from me as possible. But I don't want him dead.

Why do I not believe Maksim when he promised me he wouldn't kill him?

He won't. He loves me, and we agreed not to lie to each other.

Why didn't he tell me about this over the weekend?

"Krasotka!" Maksim's voice cuts into my panic, and I glance up at him.

He rushes over, pulls me up and over to the couch, then onto his lap.

"Maksim...did you...oh, please, tell me you didn't..." I whisper.

Maksim's eyes darken. "I promised you I wouldn't kill him. And all I saw was your face. So I stopped myself from hurting him."

"You did?"

"Yes. You did not believe me when I gave you my word?"

"I...no. I can't tell you I haven't doubted your word. I'm sorry. I've been so scared about what you would do to him."

Hurt passes in his expression.

"I'm sorry. I don't want to lie to you."

He takes a deep breath and nods. Then he pulls me into his chest. "Okay, my krasotka. You're right. We shouldn't lie to each other. But if I give you my word, it's an oath. I won't ever break it."

I sink into his chest, letting him wrap me in his arms. We stay quiet for several moments. I finally lift my head.

"So, nothing happened to Peter?"

His face hardens.

My pulse increases again. "What did you do?"

"I didn't do what I wanted to him. But he won't be coming near you again. He's leaving town."

"What do you mean?"

"He won't be taking another penny from you, and you won't ever hear from him again."

"I pay him alimony. Of course he'll hear from me. It's not that easy," I blurt out.

Maksim's eyes turn to slits. "What are you talking about?"

"My divorce. I have to pay him alimony."

Maksim shakes his head and growls, "Not anymore."

"It's part of my divorce decree."

He picks up his phone, swipes it a few times, and holds it to his ear.

"Who are you calling?"

Maksim holds his finger up. "Boris. You left yet?"

The air in my lungs gets thicker.

His brother is with Peter?

"Good. Don't until I give you further directions." He hangs up.

"Maksim, is Boris with Peter?"

"Yes. And Sergey."

"Why?"

"To enforce our agreement."

A new fear grows. "What would that be?"

"I told you. Peter is leaving town. He is not allowed to come anywhere near Chicago ever again. My brothers will see to it he's put on a bus en route to somewhere far away."

I gasp. Maksim said he was leaving town, yet it didn't really hit me. I hesitantly ask, "Isn't that a bit cruel?"

"I am a ruthless man. There are other options I could have chosen for his consequences. Would you rather I pick one of those? Hmm?" Maksim raises his eyebrows.

"Ummm..."

He holds my cheeks. "I stopped from physically harming him how I should have. For you. No one will steal from or threaten you. I will not bend on his punishment. He will never come near you again, and he is not getting another penny of your money. Who was your attorney for your divorce?"

I swallow hard. *Why do I care about where Peter lives? He isn't exactly an angel. Did he ever love me, even when we first got married?* I sit straighter. "Kora. Why?"

"And she allowed you to owe him alimony?" he barks.

"She did the best she could. It's only ten percent of what I should have had to pay. I hate paying Peter, but Kora did an amazing job for me. I'm not sure what I would have done without her."

He holds out his phone. "Get her on the phone. Tell her you need papers immediately for Peter to sign to stop the alimony payments."

"What? He's not going to sign."

"Want to make a bet?"

"You can't force him. That's illegal." I don't know the law, but I'm pretty sure forcing someone to sign is criminal.

"Call her," he sternly replies.

"Maksim, I can't just—"

"Krasotka, I left before I hurt him. I did it for you. It was not an easy thing for me to walk away from. If I had known you owe him alimony, I would have sunk him to the bottom of Lake Michigan right now. Please call Kora."

"I don't know her number. Let me get my cell." I get up and hit the button for Kora.

She answers right away. "Hey. It's about time you called me. How many messages do I need to leave?"

"Sorry. I didn't have my phone on over the weekend, and this morning has been crazy."

"You can't just have your badass boyfriend, his stud brother cub—who kisses like a porn star...or what I think one would kiss like—and their muscle men bodyguards wave their guns and knives around in a club, then not talk to us all weekend."

She kissed Sergey?

"Kora, I can't talk about this right now. There's another reason I'm calling."

She drops her voice, and it fills with concern. "Are you okay?"

"Ummm...yes. I need something from you ASAP."

"Sure. What is it?"

I turn toward Maksim. He watches me intently and nods. I continue, "Can you write up papers for Peter to sign off on alimony?"

The line goes quiet.

"Hello?" I ask.

Kora clears her throat. "What's going on, Aspen?"

"I can't get into it right now. But how quickly could I get a document for him to sign?"

"I can create it in fifteen minutes. But you'll need two witnesses and a notary. When are you meeting him?"

"Today at some point. I need it as soon as possible."

"Aspen, where are you?"

I walk to the window and stare out over Chicago. Lake Michigan is a snowy mix of ice and cold waves. "I'm at Maksim's."

"Send me his address. I'll bring the forms."

"It's okay. Just email it."

"No."

"Kora—"

"I'm your attorney. I'm not sure what's going on, but text me the address, or I'm not writing up the document."

I close my eyes. "Can you just do it?"

"Send me the address."

"Kora—"

"Aspen, let me talk to Kora," Maksim says, wrapping his arms around me and holding his hand out.

I sigh, hand him the phone, then lean into his frame.

He puts it on speaker. "Kora, it's Maksim."

Kora turns her pit bull attorney voice on. "What's going on, Maksim? Why the secrecy?"

I wish I could be as confident as Kora. Most women would bend over to Maksim, but she doesn't even think twice to try and protect me.

"Peter has agreed not to take another penny from Aspen. Are you able to quickly draw up the paperwork?"

"I can. But as Aspen's attorney, I won't give her the form unless I witness him signing."

"Why? Is there a legal reason you need to be there?" Maksim holds me tighter to him and kisses the top of my head.

"It's not required, but I don't put anything past the weasel. I prefer to witness it all."

"He won't be giving Aspen any trouble again. We'll be fine with the paperwork on our own."

"Sorry, no can do."

"Kora, just send it," I say.

"Aspen, I'm your attorney and friend. I'm not budging on this."

Maksim surprises me and quietly laughs. "I can see we're going to waste a lot of time fighting, which I prefer to avoid. Draw the papers up. Are we able to meet at your office in an hour?"

Kora's voice changes back to her chipper tone. "And Peter will be able to make it, too?"

"Yes."

"Great. An hour works. I'll see you then." She hangs up.

Maksim says in my ear, "I'm going to need you to trust me a bit more."

I tilt my head toward him.

His blue eyes pierce mine. He gives me a quick kiss on the lips.

"I don't understand what is happening right now. My insides are shaking. I'm trying to be okay with everything going on, but..."

He spins me and slides his hands in my hair, holding my head firmly. "You will not pay another penny to him. He will not see you ever again once you leave Kora's office. I spared him his life so you wouldn't hate me. But he will not continue to bother you or steal from you."

"What did he even take? I don't have anything of value, and he knows this."

Maksim's face grows dark. "Your laptop, wedding rings, and a box of checks."

"What?" I put my hand over my mouth.

"Why is your face pale?"

"Do you have the rings here?" My eyes water, and I blink hard.

Something crosses Maksim's face. I don't understand what it is, but he walks to the table and opens a backpack. He removes the contents and hands me the rings.

I stare at the rings and can't stop the tears from falling. Emotions swirl so fast, I begin to sob.

Maksim pulls me into his chest. "I've never married. I won't pretend what it's like for you to look at your rings."

"They aren't mine. They..." I can't finish. I stain Maksim's shirt with my anguish.

"Shh." He tries to comfort me, but I'm a mess.

I clutch the rings. When I calm, I look at him.

Maksim wipes my face. "Krasotka, if they aren't your rings, who do they belong to?"

"My mother."

His expression fills with surprise. He leads me to the couch and pulls me onto his lap. "I have been selfish. I know nothing about your family. I have not asked. I am sorry. Please, tell me about them."

I look away as fresh tears fall.

He patiently waits for me to speak.

"My father is still alive. He has dementia and lives in a nursing home run by the state. I can't afford anything better for him. A year before my mom passed, his spot became available. It was hard for my mom and dad. She loved him, and they were super close. Then my mom..." I get too choked up to continue.

Maksim comforts me, and I mumble into his neck, "She had a heart attack and died. I didn't even get to say goodbye to her. She just...was gone one day."

It's been four years since my mom passed, but the grief never seems to go away. And when it hits me, I'm always amazed at how much it still hurts.

I open my hand and stare at her wedding band and engagement ring. "I can't believe he stole these. He knows they're the only thing I have of my mom's. I bet he wouldn't even get much for them."

"I'm sorry, my krasotka. I thought they were yours."

I shake my head. "No. I pawned those so I could pay the rent I was behind on after Peter cleaned out our account before he moved out."

Maksim's face turns red with anger. "This is the man you wanted me to show mercy to?"

I focus on my mom's rings.

How could Peter be so selfish and cruel?

He releases a long breath and strokes my hair. "Where is your father's facility?"

"Several hours away. It's the only opening they had. I don't get to see him as often as I should. I have to save to rent a car for the trip."

Maksim picks up his phone. "We will move your father."

"What? No. There aren't any state facilities with openings around here."

Maksim holds up his finger. "Manya, I need you to research the top five dementia facilities in Chicago and make an appointment for me to meet with the directors immediately."

I gape at him.

"Yes, clear whatever you need to. Let me know when it is set up." He hangs up.

"What are you doing?"

"Your father will not be hours away from you. We will move him to Chicago so you can visit as much as you wish. And he will have the best care possible."

I rearrange myself on his lap. "I don't think you understand how much these facilities cost. They're over six-figures a year."

"Yes. I am aware. Do not worry about the price. I will pay for it."

"You... It's too much."

Maksim cups my cheeks. "You will have the best. Your father will have the best. There is no more discussion on this. When Manya has the appointments scheduled, you and I will interview the directors and tour the facilities so you can choose which one you are comfortable with."

I stay quiet, stunned, and not sure what to say. "Maks—"

He puts his finger over my lips. "There is nothing to argue about over this. Now, I need to call my brothers regarding our other issue."

Peter. My chest tightens. He's stooped lower than I ever thought possible.

"Boris, we have some legal papers Peter needs to sign at Aspen's attorney's office. We need to meet at noon."

Muffled noises come through the phone.

"Tell Sergey to make sure he's presentable. Throw him in the shower. I'll text Sergey the address." Maksim hangs up.

"Why does Peter need a shower?" I ask.

Maksim hesitates then replies, "He's not had one since Saturday."

I suddenly don't seem to have any sympathy for him. I straddle Maksim. "You've had him since then?"

His icy eyes match the hardness in his expression. "My guys picked him up after he broke into your apartment. It was during the wedding. I didn't want to tell you there, and so much happened after...with Jade. You were happy on Sunday. *We* were happy. I didn't want to ruin our day."

I don't think long about what he disclosed. And I don't hold the fact he didn't tell me right away against him. "But you would have told me?"

"Yes. I wanted to retrieve what he took from you, and I would have told you tonight." He strokes my cheek. "Do you believe me?"

I don't hesitate. "Yes, I do."

"Good." He leans in and kisses me.

I pull back. "After the papers are signed, I never have to see Peter again?"

"No."

It suddenly seems like a great idea that Peter can't stay in Chicago. "Thank you." I put every ounce of affection I have for him into a kiss, trying to show him how much I love and appreciate him.

"You are not angry with me, then?" Maksim asks.

I shake my head. "No. I love you. And I don't have any respect left for Peter, but thank you for not physically hurting him. It might not make sense to you, but I don't want you to touch him and it to be my fault."

"Whatever he has done is his fault," Maksim states.

"You know what I mean."

"Then it is good I did not do anything. However, if he does not stay out of Chicago once my brothers put him on the bus, I will no longer hold back. And I cannot promise this with other men, my krasotka. If it had been Wes—"

"You can kill him. I will never hold it against you," I blurt out quickly.

Maksim looks at me in surprise.

Did I just tell him I was okay with him killing someone?

Wes is a Petrov. They are the scum of the earth.

I don't doubt Wes is just like his father. And everything Zamir put Maksim and his brothers through makes me have no sympathy for anyone in their family.

I admit, "I'm not sure at what point I changed, but I will not tell you to protect anyone who is a threat to you or your family. That includes the Petrovs or anyone associated with them." I scoot close so my knees hit the back of the couch, and my breasts press into his chest. I caress the side of his head. "I surprised you?"

"Yes."

"Maybe I'm not as good of a person as you thought?"

He fists my hair and holds my face next to his. "You are light mixing in my darkness. Don't ever forget it."

His phone rings, and he answers, "Sergey?"

I sit back on his knees.

"Yes, I will send it now. See you soon." He hangs up and hands me the phone. "Can you pull Kora's office up and text it to Sergey? We should go."

I do it, and we leave. Neither of us says much on the way. When we get to Kora's office, her assistant whisks us into the conference room.

She's standing at the window, overlooking downtown Chicago. Her designer pink tweed pencil skirt suit is made up of soft colors with a bit of blue and purple. Expensive gold buttons adorn the back of her skirt, leading up to the bottom of her ass. Her arms are folded, and she looks deep in thought.

"Kora, Mr. Ivanov and Ms. Albright are here," her assistant announces when we step in the room then she leaves.

Kora spins and comes over and hugs me. Maksim leans down and kisses her cheek.

She motions for us to sit, and we do. "Where is Peter?"

"Sergey will be here with him soon."

"Sergey?" she asks and flushes. It's faint. I don't even know if Maksim sees it. But I don't miss it.

I need to ask her how she knows how he kisses.

"Yes."

She recovers quickly. "Why is he with Peter?"

Maksim puts his arm around my shoulder and smiles. In a friendly but no-nonsense tone, he replies, "Kora, we won't be discussing any of the details. He will come in, sign, and then he will leave with Sergey. You are a smart woman and saw what I am capable of in the club. There are things you should not ask and questions I will never answer. This is one of them."

Kora sits back, crosses her legs, and gives Maksim a challenging stare. "Aspen is not only my friend but my client. If you are having Peter sign something and he is coerced, it could come back and hurt Aspen."

Maksim nods. "Yes. I'm sure you understand I will go to extreme lengths to protect my krasotka. She will not be in any danger now or in the future due to that man. If she ever is, I will take care of it."

She doesn't break her gaze with Maksim for several minutes.

I clear my throat then wave between them. "I'm here. In the room."

Her voice doesn't falter. "I think we should talk alone."

"No. Whatever you want to discuss, you can say it in front of Maksim. I will not hide information from him."

"I'm your attorney. This—"

"Mr. Albright and Mr. Ivanov are here," her assistant interrupts.

My stomach twists, and I close my eyes for a moment. Maksim kisses me on the head and releases me. I spin in my chair to face Peter, and my heart races.

"Kora. Good to see you again." Sergey stands behind Peter. He towers over him and cockily licks his lips while checking her out.

"Sergey. Peter," she coolly replies. "Have a seat."

Peter's blue eyes are bloodshot. He avoids looking in my direction. His hair is wet, and his cheek has a dried spot of blood, which could be from shaving. Deep down, I know it's not.

Did Maksim or Sergey cause the drop of blood?

It doesn't matter. The piece of shit stole my mother's rings.

Maksim puts his warm hand over mine, which rests on my thigh. I swallow the emotions popping up.

Sergey and Peter sit across from us. Peter still doesn't look at me.

Anger surpasses my grief. I'm not sure if I've just hit my limit with him, or if I've gotten a bit of Ivanov courage, but the longer it goes without him facing me, the more pissed I get. I slam my hand on the table. "Look at me."

He takes a nervous breath and slowly meets my eyes.

"How could you steal from me? And you took the only thing I have left of my mother's."

He says nothing. His lips quiver.

"Answer me," I seethe.

"He took your mom's rings?" Kora asks in disgust.

I glance at her and nod. "And my laptop and a box of new checks. The ones with only my name on them."

Kora's eyes turn to slits. She rips up the paper.

"What are you doing?"

"I'll be back in a moment." She rises.

"Kora—"

"I will be right back." She leaves the room.

Maksim squeezes my hand and kisses it.

Peter glares at us.

Maksim asks, "Did you enjoy your time with my brothers? Or did you piss yourself again?"

Peter squeezes his eyes shut.

Sergey leans into his ear. "We had fun, didn't we?"

Peter shudders.

"How could you do it, Peter? You know what those rings mean to me."

"You left me with nothing," he chokes out.

All I've ever been to him is someone to take from.

I ask him the questions I've wondered too many times to count. "Did you ever love me?"

He doesn't answer me. As I look across the table, I see a sad, pathetic man. But I don't know him. I'm not sure if I ever did.

I lean forward. "I used to cry myself to sleep over you. Every night, I blamed myself for our divorce. I thought I must not have been good enough for you. Now, I see how wrong I was. You weren't good enough for me. And every day, when you wake up or close your eyes at night, I want you to know I no longer care about you. I don't think about you. I don't love you. And I certainly don't want to ever see you again."

His eyes widen.

Kora comes back in with her phone and another piece of paper. Three of her coworkers are with her and take seats at the opposite end of the table. She sits, spins in her chair toward Sergey and Peter, and crosses her legs.

She puts a piece of paper and a pen in front of Peter. She sets the phone so it faces Peter and hits a button. "You are being recorded. Please state you agree to be on video."

Peter furrows his eyebrows.

Sergey gets another cocky expression on his face and states, "I agree. Don't you, Peter?"

Peter reluctantly states, "Yes."

"Please state your name," Kora says.

"Peter Albright."

"And do you admit you broke into your ex-wife's home on..." She looks at me.

I reply, "Saturday."

"This past Saturday and stole Aspen Albright's property? The contents were her deceased mother's wedding rings, laptop, and a box of checks for her personal bank account. An account you are not on? Is this correct?"

Peter's face reddens, and his jaw clenches.

"Please answer the question, Peter."

"Yes," he admits.

She nods. "And you agree to sign this form, giving up all rights to any alimony payments from your ex-wife in exchange for Aspen not pressing charges?"

His hand trembles. He stares at the form and clenches his fist.

"Answer the question. Yes, you agree? Or no, you do not agree?" Kora continues.

He clears his throat. "I agree."

"Please sign the form."

He closes his eyes, squeezing them, but then picks up the pen and quickly signs.

Kora points. "Please date it as well."

He obeys and puts the pen down.

Kora slides the paper over to me. "Please sign you agree to these conditions."

I don't even read it. I sign, date, and shove it back to Kora.

She rises, takes it to her coworkers, and says, "Please sign as witnesses." She addresses a woman on the opposite side, "Please notarize."

They sign and notarize then leave the room. When the door is shut, she turns off the video and glares at Peter. "You've always been a mooching piece of shit. I never thought you'd do something so hurtful to the only woman who's ever supported you no matter how awful you treated her. I hope you rot in hell."

Peter scowls at her, his eyes in flames. "Shut the f—"

Sergey's hand flies to his throat. He squeezes it until Peter is red and choking. Sergey leans into Peter's ear. In a low, controlled voice, he says, "You need to learn your manners in front of ladies. When I remove my hand, you're going to apologize. And if it isn't sincere, my hand isn't going to be any nicer the second time around." He releases him.

Peter holds his throat. His eyes are wet.

"Now," Maksim growls.

Peter looks at Kora. "I'm sorry."

She shakes her head.

"Are we done here?" I ask her.

She smiles at me. "Yes."

I return her gesture. "Thank you."

She winks.

I rise and put my hands on the table. I forget Kora's in the room and doesn't know anything about what happened and shouldn't. All I see is the pathetic human being I gave twenty years to. The man who watched me weep for my mother for months after she died. And the visual of me at the hospital, with my friends by my side when they declared her dead, while he was God knows where, only deepens my rage. "You were only shown mercy today because of me. I will never require it again. If you attempt to contact me or steal from me or break the terms you agreed to with the Ivanovs, I will lift any protection I have given you. Don't forget it."

"Aspen—"

"No. Don't you speak to me. We're done." I hug Kora. "Thank you." I spin to Maksim. "Ready?"

His lips twitch. He dips down and kisses me. It's deep and hungry and full of love. It's everything Peter never gave me.

Maksim pulls back but keeps his lips near mine. "You sure you don't want my brother to give him what he deserves? Hmmm?"

I can see the hope in Maksim's eyes.

I glance at Peter then back at Maksim. "No. Your brother has better things to do with his time today instead of stew with trash. Let's go."

Maksim grunts, spins me, and puts his hand on my ass while we walk out the door.

I don't give Peter any more attention. I've given him twenty years. And I've officially crossed the line from the woman who will bend over backward and not be treated right to one who no longer will accept anything but love.

When we get into the elevator, Maksim leans down into my ear. "You're pretty hot when you're all fired up, my krasotka."

I reach for the stop button and push him against the wall. "What do you want to do about it?"

Maksim

"WE'VE TALKED TO EVERY ONE OF OUR GUYS. THEY ALL SEEMED content. No one appeared to be desperate. Since work has been steady for so long, the foremen haven't heard of anyone struggling," Sergey informs us, conversing in Russian as we usually do when it's just the four of us.

It's been over a week since the situation with Peter occurred. Dmitri is back from his honeymoon, and the four of us are getting our morning workout in.

"Where are we at with the rezoning issue?" Dmitri asks.

"I've got a meeting today with Aspen and the mayor. She thinks she found a loophole, but he's going to need to sign off. He's told her boss he won't push this council meeting forward. He doesn't want to look biased."

Boris grunts. "It's time to show him who he's messing with."

"We don't cross the line in our business," I remind him.

"He screwed us over by selling the land to Lorenzo. He's already dirty. I'm with Boris," Sergey says.

Dmitri puts his weight on the rack. "I don't want to cross the line, but if we don't get this issue solved, our guys are going to suffer. I hate to say it, Maksim, but the ends justify the means in this situation. We can't lay our men off. They need to feed their families. That project represents two years of paychecks for them. And our other buildings are almost complete."

The dread I've felt has only been growing and becoming more intense every day. Dmitri is right. We only have a few months of work left and then we'll be forced to lay our crews off.

"If this lot stays industrial, no one is going to want to buy their home next to it. All the surrounding land we own becomes worthless. I say we agree right now to put our people first. Whatever we need to do to make this happen, we have to do," Boris insists.

I glance at Sergey.

"I'm with Dmitri and Boris on this one. We already have dirt on the mayor. If he can't help us willingly, then it's time to use it."

I sigh. Several months ago, I had Obrecht tail the mayor. It only took him two days to send me photos of the mayor and his favorite hooker. He also had an intense meeting with Lorenzo from the look on their faces. Unfortunately, without any further evidence of what they were discussing, it's not as powerful as the pictures of his prostitute and him naked in several different positions. "Once we cross this line, it's too easy not to do it in the future."

Dmitri nods. "If our community is in jeopardy, we have to do everything in our power to help them. You are the one who instilled in us to always put our people first."

"No, our father did."

My brothers and I stay silent for a few moments. The sadness about my father's early death never goes away. It washes over us and is visible on all of our faces.

Boris's voice is deadpan. "It is settled, then. We have no choice. Show the mayor no mercy. Make it clear to him that screwing with the Ivanovs is a bad idea. Otherwise, I'll show him my wrath."

"You will do no such thing," I bark.

Boris steps forward. His eyes darken into small slits. "I will not let our people fall prey to the Petrovs. Get it done, Maksim. Or I will."

"You are too eager these days."

Boris raises his eyebrows. "Oh? Do you prefer me to wallow in guilt and pretend I'm not the man I am?"

"No. I expect you to be the good man you are and remember we don't go looking for opportunities to release the monsters within us."

"Maksim," Dmitri warns.

I turn to him. "What? Should we all turn into raging lunatics?"

Boris grunts. "The lunatic I see when we need to get things done isn't me."

Dmitri spits out, "Enough, Boris."

Boris points at all of us. "None of us are good men. You all need to stop pretending you are. The mayor is standing in our way. He does what we need him to do, or you make him. Do it with the photos, or I will do it with my hands. Choose." He turns to the machine and starts racking the weights.

Sergey shakes his head and clenches his jaw. He glances at Boris then back at Dmitri and me. "Boris is right. We are out of options. Get it done, Maksim. I'm exhausted from this. We're already behind schedule for this project. Use the photos, or Boris won't be the only one of us you need to worry about."

Dmitri nods. He repeats, "The end justifies the means."

I heavily sigh. "Fine. You all win. But I want your word this doesn't become the new norm in our business."

"We only cross the line if our people are in trouble. This is an exception," Dmitri agrees.

I point to Sergey and Boris. "And you two? I have your word?"

"You have mine," Sergey agrees.

Boris snorts. "Fine. Grab that plate." He adds several to one side of the squat machine.

"You trying to hurt yourself before the fight tonight? Thought you were supposed to go easy before you get in the ring?" I remind him.

He ignores me and keeps adding to the bar.

I glance at my other brothers, and we all study Boris. His jaw twitches. I ask, "What else is going on?"

Boris points to the plate. "You going to rack that, or should I?"

"You've got a fight tonight. This is a bad idea, and you know it. So what's going on?" Dmitri follows.

Boris sighs and wipes his sweaty face on his shirt. "Liam is getting out."

Sergey steps forward. "Liam O'Malley?"

"Yes."

"Fuck," Sergey mutters.

"Nora's worried Killian's going to get pulled into more of his shit. I told her she's overreacting. I don't like her stressed out. It's not healthy for the baby."

"Did you talk to Killian?" Dmitri asks.

"I told him he's not a kid anymore. He swears Liam is going to stay out of trouble. But we all know Liam."

My chest tightens. "Boris, whatever you do, remember what you just said. Killian isn't a kid anymore. You can't save him if he isn't smart enough not to let Liam take him down."

Boris focuses on the ceiling.

Sergey warns, "Boris, you can't—"

"It's Killian. We aren't talking about a random person. It's Nora's brother. Hell, he's always been like a brother to me. I won't let him get pulled into Liam's world."

"Any of us would do anything for Killian. But he needs to be smart. You know this," Dmitri states.

"*You* need to be smart," I reiterate, worried Boris will get sucked into the O'Malley mafia issues. They've kept me awake too many nights lately. We're already too close to them with the war we created. We don't need to go any further in.

He scowls. "You have so much faith in me, dear brother."

"And welcome back to Ivanov land, Dmitri," Sergey says sarcastically.

Dmitri snorts. "Guess I didn't miss much while I was away?"

"Actually, you did. Maksim let me carve the I in Aspen's ex-husband's chest instead of Boris. I think Boris is still pissed off, and that's what this conversation is really about," Sergey teases.

"You did give Sergey all the fun," Boris states. "That cowardly prick cried for his mommy within seconds of Sergey's knife slicing his skin."

"I'll make sure you get the next one. Now get away from the squat machine. You have a fight tonight."

"Yes, boss," he grumbles.

"You'll thank me when Gus doesn't kick your ass."

"He's not taking me down."

"Jump rope, now." I point over to the area designated for this activity.

We finish our workouts, shower, and I get in my car. I call Aspen.

"Maksim, everything okay?"

"Yes. Are you on your way to the office?"

"Yes."

"Okay. If I ask you to leave the room during our meeting, I need you to get up and not ask questions."

The line is quiet for a few seconds. She lowers her voice. "What's wrong?"

"Nothing, my krasotka. Can you do this for me?"

"Follow your orders?" she teases.

I chuckle. "Yes."

Her voice turns serious again. "Of course."

"It's best if we keep things professional in front of the mayor. Let's not give him any indication we're together."

"Ummm... I disclosed to my boss we were together. I'm not sure if he knows or not."

Of course she did.

"No worries. If he knows, fine, but let's still keep it strictly professional."

"Okay. I'll see you at ten?"

"I'll be there. Bye." I hang up and tap on my thigh until I arrive at my penthouse. I go straight to my safe and remove the envelope of photos Obrecht gave me. There's no reason to look at them, but I double-check everything is still in it. Then I shove the pictures back in the yellow envelope and put it in my padfolio.

My brothers are right. We cannot let our people suffer or fall victim to the Petrovs. It doesn't make me feel any better about crossing this line. But everything in my gut tells me I'm going to have to.

I stew about it until it's time to go, tapping into my beast, who will allow me to be the person I don't want to be in business. By the time I get to the meeting, he's out in full force. I'm focused solely on doing whatever it takes.

When I get there, I refrain from kissing Aspen or showing any affection toward her. I intentionally sit across from her so she will be on one side of the mayor, and I will be on the other. Touching her alone will weaken my resolve. We both keep it professional while we wait for the mayor in a conference room.

He comes in. We go through the standard greetings, shaking hands. Mayor Dixon sits back in his chair and presses his fingertips together. He's in his late fifties, and his hair has turned almost all silver. He puts on his fake smile. "Have you found a way to rezone the land?"

Aspen opens her folder and puts a piece of paper in front of the mayor and me. "Yes. This statute from 1968 gives you the right to rezone property without the board's consent if it's in the best welfare of the community. Since the Ivanov's surrounding property has citizens living on it, the toxins in the land present a risk. Without the new development, the currently zoned industrial lot won't be cleaned. This will prevent the cleanup of the other land, which continues to put your voters at risk."

I can't resist chuckling inside. My krasotka knows exactly how to make it clear to the mayor what's important to him, which is getting reelected.

"The proper steps are to put this in front of the council. Making a move like this also sends voters a message I disregard the others they vote into office."

"Putting this up for a vote allows something to go wrong and my request to be denied," I state. "When we bought the land, you said it was a high priority to clean it. Is this no longer the case?"

The mayor keeps his face neutral. "It is. But it must be done with public approval. The board members know it is toxic. They have a duty to do what is best for their community as well."

"It's a risk we don't need to take," I firmly state.

"It's a risk *I* don't need to take," he replies.

I break my gaze from him and focus on Aspen. "Will you please give the mayor and me a moment alone?"

She nods and rises. "Sure."

When she leaves, I sit back and stare at him. He doesn't flinch and keeps his politician expression on his face. After several moments, I say, "I was hoping you would do what is right."

"I've done nothing wrong."

"You know what I'm still interested to know?"

"What's that?"

"Why did you sell the land out from under us to Lorenzo in the first place?"

There's a tic in his jaw. "My discussions with other citizens aren't your business."

I grunt. "Seems to me it is."

He says nothing.

"Tell you what, why don't you take a look at these and let me know if you're willing to stick your neck out." I drop the yellow folder in front of him.

"What's this?"

"Open it."

He hesitantly does. His face reddens, and his eyes widen. After he sorts through all the photos, he puts them back inside. "You're going to blackmail me?"

"No. I don't blackmail. I implement."

He clenches his jaw.

"Today. You sign the paperwork Aspen drew up by noon."

He leans forward. "You're messing with the wrong person."

I snort. "You underestimate me. It's about time you learn not to screw over an Ivanov. You've done it once, and it will be the only time. If you don't follow through by noon, these pictures will not be the only thing I release. This will be the beginning of your demise."

"What does that mean?"

"I don't show all my cards. You can be with the Ivanovs or against us. Take your pick."

He takes a deep breath and closes his eyes. When he opens them, he reluctantly says, "Fine. I'll sign it. I want the digital copies of these."

"Sure. But I'll still have a copy."

He scowls. "Then I'm not signing."

I tilt my head and wait several moments until he flinches. "There is no choice for you. I hold the cards. I own you. You obey, no one sees anything. You go against me, and all of Chicago will want to watch you burn, tied to a stake."

"There's nothing else you have on me."

I raise my eyebrows. "Isn't there?"

More uncomfortable silence passes. I don't move, watching him squirm.

He rises. "I'll sign by noon. You better keep my reputation clean."

"Not so fast. There's something else you're going to do."

He furrows his brows. In an annoyed voice, he says, "Oh?"

I point toward the door. "That woman out there knows more than anyone in her office. She runs circles around all of them. You will promote Ms. Albright to Senior Planner and pay her accordingly."

"I don't get involved in those types of activities."

"Too bad. Figure it out. You have until the end of the business day on Friday to make it happen." I rise and pick up my padfolio but leave the yellow envelope on the table. "Notify me when you've completed these tasks. And one last thing."

He sighs and seethes, "What else?"

I step forward so I'm right in his face. "Don't ever fuck with an Ivanov again. My wrath will make the consequences of those photos seem like Disneyland."

Aspen

"TIME TO SPILL IT. HOW DO YOU KNOW SERGEY KISSES LIKE A porn star?" I take a sip of my martini. The girls and I are having drinks then Maksim is picking us up. Boris is boxing tonight. When he asked me if I wanted to go, I already had plans with the girls. It morphed into them joining us.

Maksim seemed amused they wanted to come.

"Do women not go?"

His lips twitched. "Anna loves it. She brings her friend, Harper, a lot. Nora comes unless Boris is fighting Killian. Then she won't watch."

"So, why are you surprised my friends want to attend?"

He shrugged. "I'm not sure. Nothing should surprise me with those women though."

That was a few days ago.

"Oh no, you don't! You have a lot to tell us about Mr. Stranger Danger," Hailee says.

"What do you want to know?" I casually ask. It's been over a week since our night out at the Cat's Meow, and we haven't been together since. Besides my visit to Kora's office, I haven't seen any of them. I've been rehearsing what I'll tell my friends about Maksim all day, but it doesn't sound convincing in my head. And my friends aren't stupid.

Hailee lowers her voice even though we're inside Skylar's condo. Her tone is full of worry. "I researched the Petrovs. Apparently, Wes's dad is the Russian mafia king?"

"Yes," I admit.

"How does Maksim know him?"

I take another sip then shrug my shoulders. No matter how much I rehearsed it, my delivery sounds weak. "They're both Russian."

Kora snorts. "Aspen, you're going to have to give us more than that."

"What you just said is totally ridiculous. It's like saying anyone who is French knows all French people," Hailee adds.

I shake my head. "I'm not going to disclose Maksim's business."

"Is he part of the mafia?" Skylar asks.

"No." *At least that sounded confident.*

"Then why did he tell Wes they had a deal, and the Ivanovs were off-limits?"

I avoid their gazes. "I'm not going to discuss anything else. The Ivanovs are not mafia. End of story. Now, what happened in the car between you and Mr. Loverboy?"

"In the car? Nothing," Kora states.

I spin. "Then how did you kiss Sergey?"

Her lips twitch. "Let's clarify your statement. He kissed me."

I roll my eyes. "Okay. When did *he* kiss *you*? And you do know he's only thirty-three?"

"Jeez, Aspen. Get off the age thing. One, he doesn't look thirty-three. Two, he's almost thirty-four. Three, I'm thirty-eight—"

"Almost thirty-nine."

She slaps my arm. "Four, he could be twenty-one, and I'd give him a pass to do whatever he wanted with me for the night after experiencing those lips."

"Twenty-one," I screech in horror.

"If I could lock him in a cage and keep him as my cub to use and abuse me, I would."

Hailee spits out her drink.

"You need to stop spitting out your drink every time we get together," Skylar points out.

Hailee cringes. "Sorry. I didn't in Vegas."

Skylar pats her hand. "Yes, Hailee. You did a great job keeping your drink in your mouth while we were out of town."

She raises her hand in the air. "Score!"

"Can we take the focus off *Hailee's* spit and concentrate on how *Kora* ended up swapping spit with an Ivanov?"

"I wasn't the only one sampling the Russian goodies."

I turn to Hailee and Skylar. "One of you kissed Sergey, too?"

"Eew. No. We aren't into sloppy seconds," Skylar says, as if I insulted her.

"That's the truth," Hailee mutters and takes a drink.

I groan. "Then who..."

Skylar smirks.

"Oh, no. Please tell me you didn't get it on with Adrian."

Skylar licks her lips. "No, we didn't have sex. But why do you have a problem with him?"

"He's my bodyguard. I can't go pee without him standing outside the door."

"Now you're exaggerating."

"No, I'm not. I can't even come here."

Skylar glances behind her. "He's here?"

"Yes. Outside the door."

"Right now?"

"Did you not hear me confirm?"

She rises and paces the room. "Why didn't you tell me he's here?"

"What part of my bodyguard memo did you miss?"

"So anytime we're with you, he's going to be by your side?"

"Unless Maksim is with me, then he might or might not be. Why does it matter?"

She starts to walk to the door then comes back. "It doesn't."

"You're such a bullshitter," Kora says.

"Why are you freaking out right now?" Hailee asks.

"I'm not."

We all stare at her.

"I'll be right back." She disappears into her bedroom.

"What did she do with him?" I ask.

Hailee winces. "She kind of threw herself on him when we got into the car."

"What?"

"We were pretty intoxicated..." Kora adds.

"No kidding. Really?" I ask sarcastically.

Kora and Hailee exchange a look.

"What?"

Kora bites back a laugh. "She sort of straddled him and grabbed his face..."

I groan. "She didn't."

"She tried to remove his shirt," Hailee informs me.

"If I weren't into my cub, I'd have to give Adrian a shot. Skylar almost had his entire shirt unbuttoned. You could wash your clothes on his pecs and abs."

"They are pretty amazing," Hailee admits. "He had to practically carry her up here."

I put my hand over my mouth.

"Did she tell you what he said when he dropped her off?" Kora asks.

"No. What did she say?" Hailee replies.

Kora takes a really deep breath. "He said he would never be second to a Petrov, and she made her choice loud and clear."

"Ouch!" I say.

"Yikes," Hailee replies.

"Then he shut the door and left."

"Poor Skylar!" I rise and walk into her bedroom. The others follow.

Skylar stands at her window with her hand over her face.

I put my hand on her shoulder. "Hey, you okay? I heard what happened."

"This is so embarrassing."

"Did you think you wouldn't see him again?" Kora asks.

Skylar spins. "No. But I didn't expect to see him tonight. And I didn't want to go into the VIP room. You three convinced me and pulled me away from my conversation with him." She points to us.

"The night's still really fuzzy for me. I'm sorry," I offer.

She shakes her head. "It doesn't matter. I'm going to have to deal with it." She walks to her mirror, smooths down her hair, then turns. "Do I look okay?"

"Yes. You look smoking hot, like you always do."

"Agreed," Kora says.

"Eat your heart out, Adrian!" Hailee chirps.

My phone rings. "It's Maksim." I hit the button. "Hi!"

"I'm early. Are you ladies ready?"

"Yes."

"What is Skylar's unit number?"

"We'll meet you downstairs. Don't come up."

His voice drops. "Is everything okay?"

"Yes. We'll be right down. Adrian is here, so stay in the car."

"I'm already in the lobby."

"Stay put. We'll be down in a minute."

"Okay."

I hang up. "Maksim is in the lobby."

Skylar puts on a brave face. "I might as well face the music."

I hug her. "We were all drinking. I'm sure it wasn't as bad as you think."

"Mmmm...no, it was," Hailee says.

Skylar groans and leaves her bedroom. We follow her, and she opens the door. "Hi, Adrian."

There's a slight pause, and his eyes drift down her body and back to her eyes. His expression hardens. "Skylar."

We all step outside. Adrian glances at the rest of us. "Ladies. Are you going to behave tonight?"

"Yes, Dad," Kora jokes.

"Sorry about the other night," Hailee starts.

Adrian puts up his hand. "Let's not. Are you ready?"

"Jeez, Adrian. Way to forgive and forget," I mutter.

He scowls. "You don't forget incidents with Petrovs. You should know that if you're going to be involved with someone in my family."

I straighten. "Point taken. Let's go." I wish that night never happened. If I could go back and redo it, I would. Adrian has been cool to me ever since the incident. I don't blame him.

He escorts us down the hall, staying by my side but slightly behind me. We get in the elevator, and he gets in last and stands in front of the door.

Kora drags her finger in the air from the top of his shoulders down to his ass. "Solid," she mouths.

Skylar blushes.

I slap her upper arm.

"Ouch."

MAGGIE COLE

Adrian turns and raises his eyebrows.

"Sorry, neck cramp," Kora says.

He faces the door again as it opens.

We get out, and Maksim is waiting. He pulls me into his arms, gives me a quick kiss, then leads me out to the car.

Adrian sits in the front. The rest of us get in the back. When we get to Maksim's gym, the driver parks in front of the door. Adrian and Bogden both get out.

"Go straight inside, ladies. This isn't a good neighborhood," Maksim orders.

I glance outside. Bars cover the windows. Some are boarded up. There are no street lights, except for one several store-fronts ahead of us. Men in hoodies hang out on the corner.

Adrian, Bogden, and Maksim form a wall around us. When we get to the door, a man with the beefiest neck I've ever seen opens the door.

"Boss." His deep voice ricochets in the air. His Russian accent is thicker than Maksim's or any Ivanovs.

I wouldn't want to meet him in an alley.

"Leo." Maksim pats his back and motions for us to go inside.

The door opens to a stairwell. We move up the steps. The smell of sweat and the sound of grunts and punching bags fill the air. We get to the top. An open space full of different kinds of punching and kicking bags and a ring with a black-and-white rope in the middle creates the gym. The dark mat in the ring has something written in Russian on it. Two small offices are in the back. Men glisten with sweat, working out with trainers. Foreign words echo throughout the gym. I assume it's Russian and Polish since Boris's opponent tonight is from Poland.

"What does that say?" Skylar points to the ring.

"No past, no future," Adrian replies.

She looks at him and quietly asks, "What does it mean?"

His eyes roam over her body, as they always do. He meets her gaze.

"Without our past, we cannot have our future. It shapes us and determines what we will and will not tolerate going forward. We can never forget the past lessons, or they will be repeated in our future," Dmitri's voice booms.

I spin.

He and Anna are standing behind us.

"Hi! How was your honeymoon?"

They both beam.

"It was perfect," Anna replies.

I introduce my friends to them then ask, "You come to all the fights?"

She nods. "I love them. Boris is an animal. But you probably figured that?" She arches an eyebrow.

Is she referring to him or his boxing skills?

I keep my eyes locked on hers. "Yes. He gives off that vibe."

Nora arrives with her three brothers, Killian, Declan, and Nolan. I met them at the wedding. They give Anna and me a hug and kiss on the cheek then Killian says, "Maksim, did you tape Boris's ankle yet?"

"No. I just got here."

Killian helps Nora out of her coat. "I'm going to hang this up then give Boris my unsolicited advice."

Dmitri grunts. "Good luck with that."

"Time to inform him how the Irish would take him down," Declan asserts.

"I'll go with you," Adrian offers, and he leaves with Nora's brothers.

Maksim says, "Let me take your coats. I'll put them in the office. We're on this side of the ring. Grab a front-row seat."

He helps me out of mine, and the others hand theirs to him. He leaves with Dmitri.

Anna says, "Have you been to a fight before?"

"No, this is all of our first time."

"Sometimes the sweat and blood fly over the ring. If you're squeamish, you might want to go several rows back," Nora suggests.

"We usually end up standing next to the chairs the entire time, to be honest," Anna says.

"I have to use the restroom. Can you point me where I go?" Kora asks.

"I'll show you," Sergey's voice replies.

She spins and purses her lips. "Lead the way."

Skylar, Hailee, and I exchange a look.

"Do they know each other?" Anna asks.

"Not well. We...ummm... We all went out, and Maksim showed up with Sergey to pick us up."

Anna raises her eyebrows. "Was this the night of my rehearsal dinner? At the Cat's Meow?"

She knows about it?

Of course she does. Maksim told me Anna and Dmitri have no secrets. My actions put their entire family in danger.

My face heats up. "Yes."

"We didn't know who they were." Hailee comes to my defense.

"I didn't want to go into the room. They made me." Skylar sounds like she's joking, but I know it's still upsetting her about what happened between her and Adrian.

Anna and Nora exchange a glance. I can't tell if they feel sorry for me or are upset.

Nora studies my face. "Why were you in a VIP room with a Petrov or any man if you're with Maksim?"

"Nora—"

"It's a fair question, Anna."

Anna sighs then gives me a sympathetic look.

Skylar puts her hand on her hip. "Before you judge Aspen, you should get your facts straight. Maksim dumped her."

"Skylar!" I reprimand. The burning in my face grows hotter.

MAGGIE COLE

"No. They don't have a right to judge you. He broke up with you and went to the rehearsal dinner without you. We took Aspen out. And yes, we went to the Cat's Meow. Aspen didn't ask to go, but we weren't going to let her sit home and sulk. And we drank a lot. Way too much, okay? We all did stupid shit we regret. But we didn't know they were Petrovs or even what that meant. And none of us did anything with those men besides get manhandled on their laps, which wasn't fun, by the way."

"Shh. Keep your voice down," Nora orders and gazes over her shoulder.

"Why? Is the Petrov name a secret around here?" Skylar comes back at her.

"She said to keep your voice down," Adrian growls.

Skylar freezes then her expression changes.

Oh, shit. Now she's pissed.

Her eyes turn to slits, and she spins. She points in Adrian's face. "You don't get to tell me what to do."

"Don't make a scene."

"Leave me alone, Adrian. You've made it clear what you think of me, so keep your opinion to yourself." Skylar turns back to us, her eyes full of fire.

Adrian grabs her arm, spins her back to him, and in a low voice, says, "I need to talk to you."

"Let her go, Adrian," I say.

He snorts. "I'm off the clock. Stay out of it, Aspen." He maneuvers Skylar several feet away into one of the offices and shuts the door. He pulls the shade down.

"He acts like I boss him around or something," I mumble.

Hailee steps closer and puts her arm around me. "It wasn't Aspen's fault. And she didn't cheat on Maksim. She wouldn't do that. We aren't familiar with crime families and who they are. It was an innocent mistake. So, unless you're perfect, stop accusing her of things."

"I'm not accusing her," Nora says.

"No? Sounds like it."

Nora sighs. She closes her eyes. When she opens them, they are glassy. "I'm sorry. I get worked up over the Petrovs. I'm also pregnant, so raging hormones don't help."

"I think this is a big misunderstanding," Anna says. "If I insinuated anything, I apologize."

"Me, too," Nora replies.

I release a big breath. "It's okay. I understand why you would be upset. And I'm sorry for all the issues it's caused."

Anna stands straighter. "It'll be okay."

"How do you know?" I ask it before I think, forgetting Hailee doesn't know what I do.

Anna smiles. Her eyes are full of confidence, but I also see an immense amount of pride and love. "Our men are Ivanovs. They won't allow it not to be."

Nora nods. "Anna's right."

"Guess I need an Ivanov, then," Hailee mutters.

I turn to her and laugh.

"The O'Malleys can hold their own and aren't too bad looking, either. I've got several options for you if you prefer some Irish blood. My brother, Killian, is single. Plus, he checked you out." Nora winks.

Guess I wasn't paying attention.

Hailee's face turns crimson.

"Are you single? I'm sure he'll ask me."

"She is," I practically sing.

"Good to know. Come on, ladies. I need a chair before this starts. My feet hurt, and once it starts, I know my butt isn't going to be in the seat."

We sit down and talk until the guys come back out. Maksim puts his arm around me. I tilt my head, and he kisses me. He teases, "Did you miss me?"

I respond by giving him another kiss.

Boris and his opponent come out, and the fight starts. As I watch Boris in the ring, surrounded by Ivanovs and O'Malleys, I realize Anna is right. Boris is a beast in the ring, but there's no doubt every man surrounding me is just as fierce. And maybe it's arrogant, but I also believe, no matter what happens, none of them will allow anything to happen to any of us.

Maksim

"START MONDAY. WE NEED THIS DONE IMMEDIATELY."

"Give me two weeks. We're in the middle of another project," Sam Clauster, the head of the company we hired to clean up the land, replies.

"I don't give a damn what you're currently working on. My brothers and I paid you a hefty fee to keep you on retainer with the agreement you would drop whatever you were doing and get our project done. We're on a timeline, and we don't have a second to waste."

"I have four other projects. They will all take a backseat to yours. But it is customary to allow us to finish our current commitment."

My blood boils. I struggle to keep my voice stern and low. "You committed to the Ivanovs when you took our nonrefundable ten percent payment. We already discussed how this would work and put it in writing. You will fulfill your requirement."

"Don't be stubborn, Maksim. You understand how stopping in the middle of a project causes issues," he whines.

I run my hand through my hair and step in front of the glass. The waves from Lake Michigan are higher than normal. Whitecaps cover the water as far as my eye can see. "You will honor our contract. If you are not on our job Monday morning, there will be legal ramifications."

"Maksim—"

"Sam, how many deals have you done not only with Ivanovs but the Russian community?"

He sighs heavily. "I don't know."

"Too many to count. I highly suggest you remember who you're dealing with. We need our land cleaned so our men can keep working. If you do not fulfill your obligation as agreed upon, it won't only be the court you'll have to deal with. I'll make sure you never touch another Russian job in all of Illinois. Are we clear?"

"You don't need to be a bastard, Maksim."

"I'll see you bright and early on Monday." I hang up the phone.

Boris steps next to me. "I told you he would try to skate around the deal we made."

"He'll be there."

"How long did he say?" Sergey asks.

"Two weeks."

Boris snorts. "Two weeks out of work for our men, and Zamir will sink his fingers into them quicker than ever. Even if we keep them on payroll, the fear of not having work will drive them to listen."

I turn to my brothers. "You and Sergey go back to all the job sites this week. Inform everyone the project is moving forward, and the cleanup has started. There will be no layoffs, and remind them this next project will keep all of them busy for at least two years."

"What about the weather?" Dmitri asks.

"What about it?"

"If it snows, we're screwed. The ground can't be frozen."

"Sam gave us a three-week turnaround time when we did our due diligence. He's always been reliable on estimates. This next week's weather is supposed to be over forty, including nighttime. Let's hope we get an early spring and it stays that way."

"And if it doesn't?" Boris's eyes grow darker.

"We'll figure it out."

He shakes his head. "This is cutting it too close."

"What other options do we have besides moving forward?"

"At this point, nothing."

Sergey crosses his arms. "What if we do?"

"What are you talking about?"

"Hear me out."

"We're all ears," Dmitri states.

"We've relocated all the residents on the northern lot. Let's have Sam start there. Then we can begin construction while he's cleaning up the rest. Our guys stay working with no issues."

"Except we have the ninety-day stipulation with the city."

Sergey cockily smiles. "We only have to start the process. It doesn't say we have to finish it."

"Maksim, get out the contract," Dmitri says.

I go to my desk and pull out the file. I reread the section about the contingency.

"Well?" Dmitri asks.

"Sergey is correct. It clearly states we need to commence the cleanup. It says nothing about when we have to finish it."

"The cleanup on the northern lot was estimated only to take five days, correct?"

"Yes."

"So start the cleanup on the old city lot on Monday. Let's demolish the buildings on the northern land and then we'll pause the cleanup and have Sam move to the other lot if it's going to take longer than anticipated."

I rise and pat Sergey on the back. "Little brother, I think you might have just saved our asses."

Sergey holds his hand out to Boris.

Boris grunts, pulls his wallet out, and slaps a thousand dollars in Sergey's hand.

"What's that all about?" Dmitri asks.

"I bet him I could solve our problems today."

"I should've known. How long have you been sitting on this idea?" Boris asks.

Sergey taps his head. "Shower ideas."

"Well, you should shower more often, then. Good job."

"Maksim?" Aspen yells.

"In the office," I reply.

Aspen steps through the door and pauses. "Oh. Sorry. I don't mean to interrupt."

"You aren't. I'm glad you're back. Sergey just had a great idea to save our butts." I walk over to her and give her a quick kiss.

"Guess we both have good news, then."

"Oh?" I ask.

She bites her lip, trying to hide her smile, but she's unsuccessful. It grows until it can't get any bigger.

"What's going on, my krasotka?"

"Ummm...go ahead and tell me your news."

"No. You first."

She blushes. "I had something strange, but good, happen today at work."

"What's that?"

"I got called into my boss's office. The way he was talking, I thought I was getting laid off or something. But then he said the mayor was impressed with my performance and problem-solving skills and well... I got a huge promotion."

"You did?"

"Yes! You're looking at the newest Senior Planner!" She beams, and my heart soars.

I pick her up and lift her off the ground. "Congratulations. Much deserved."

My brothers all cheer in congratulations.

When I set her down, she turns a deeper shade of red, opens her mouth, then closes it.

"What is it, my krasotka?"

"My salary..."

"What about it?" I growl.

She better not be getting a penny less than their top paid planner.

Her eyes turn brighter. "My salary tripled."

I hold her cheeks and kiss her while my brothers shout some more. "I'm so happy for you. And very proud."

My brothers all come over and hug her then leave.

"Come with me. I need you for a minute." I guide her to my desk and set her on top of it. I put both hands on the desk next to her hips.

"Is everything okay?" She raises her eyebrows.

I lean into her ear and suck on her lobe. "I'm a starving man, my krasotka." I slide my hand under her dress, remove her panties, then glide my hands up the inside of her thighs.

She takes a deep breath and shudders.

I take my arm and shove the coaster, papers, and leather pad off my desk. They crash onto the floor.

My krasotka's eyes light with fire. I kiss her, moving her until she's on her back. I put my hands under her knees and pull them up until her feet are resting on the desk.

She reaches for my belt, releases it and my zipper, then palms my growing erection.

"I'm taking you out tonight to celebrate, Ms. Senior Planner." My impatience for her comes racing at me. I grip the top of her dress with both hands, rip it, then remove my knife from my pocket. "Stay still." I slide it through the cleavage of her bra, and she gasps.

I toss the knife on the floor then take her breast in my mouth and move my hand to her wet sex, rolling my tongue on her puckered nipple and finger on her clit.

Her eyes flutter, her moans get louder, and her hand strokes my cock faster.

I suck her breast harder and make her climax on my finger. She arches off the desk, crying out my name.

She begs, "Fuck me. Oh God, please!"

I fuck her hard but not with my cock. I drop to my knees and aggressively manipulate every part of her throbbing pussy until her juices and sweat are dripping on my desk, and her body is writhing so intensely she's screaming.

It only encourages me to make her orgasm over and over until her voice is hoarse. I'm not full. I'm never going to be satiated.

When my erection is on fire, pulsing to be in her, I rise, grab her hips, and pull her ass to the edge of the desk. I thrust into her, going as deep as I can in one movement.

Her gorgeous mouth forms an O. She laces one hand in my hair and the other over my ass, desperately pushing it and panting. Her tongue glides into my mouth, flicking fast, stoking the fire burning in my veins.

I groan.

"Maks...oh..." she moans, her eyes fluttering, face flushed, and body covered in sweat.

"God, you're sexy," I murmur to her in Russian then repeat it in English.

She clings to me tighter, shaking, and crying out in ecstasy.

I greedily steal her breath, sticking my tongue back into her mouth while detonating inside her, taking her climax higher.

Endorphins explode within me. I collapse against her, breathing hard, then I tuck a lock of hair behind her ear. I roll over on the desk then straddle her over me.

She kisses me, leaving no question how much she loves or wants me. She's the only woman who ever made me feel so alive.

And I need every breath of life she gives me. I mumble against her lips, "Move in with me."

She freezes and locks eyes with me.

My stomach twists.

Is she going to say no?

"Don't even go back to your place. I'll send movers and tomorrow have all your things here. Redesign whatever you want, I don't care, just stay here. With me."

She stays silent, staring at me.

My blood beats between my ears, pounding harder and harder until I feel dizzy. "My kras—"

"Yes."

"Yes?"

She nods. "Yes. I'll move in. But I'll meet with the movers. There aren't a lot of things I want if I'm living here."

I kiss her, and she pulls back. "What's wrong?"

She hesitates.

"Tell me what you want, my krasotka."

She takes a deep breath and nods. "Okay. There are two things I want."

"What?"

"A new couch. It can be the same one. I like the style. But I want one she wasn't on."

She meaning Jade.

"The couch will be replaced. What else do you want?"

"A new mattress and bedding. It can all be the same brand. I don't care about that. But I hated sleeping in the bed Peter and I had together. And ever since the night she came over, I think about her rolling around under your sheets with you."

"I'm sorry—"

She puts her finger over my lips. "It's not your fault. But you asked what I wanted."

"I have an idea."

"What?"

"Why don't you meet with Anna and redesign everything?"

"I don't need that. It's only those two things."

I stroke her cheek. "Let's start our life fresh. You. Me. Nothing else with memories of anyone else. Put your flair on the place."

She bites her lip and tilts her head.

"You don't like my idea?"

She smiles. "No, I do. But it's going to cost a fortune. Your place is huge."

I shrug. "It's not a big deal. Do you want to talk to Anna or go solo on it? I'll admit whatever you say you want, I'll agree to, so you can't depend on my design help."

She softly laughs. "Fair enough. I'd love to work with Anna."

"Good. It's settled, then. I'll call the movers and Anna."

"Just like that, huh?" she teases.

"I'm a man who makes things happen," I boast.

"Yes, you are."

I kiss her and squeeze her ass. "Let's shower and get ready. I'm taking you out to celebrate your promotion tonight."

We leave the office and get to the main room when the buzzer blasts through the air. I hit the button. "Yes?"

"Delivery. Should I bring it up?"

"Yes."

I meet one of the staff guys at the elevator. "Here you go, Mr. Ivanov." He hands me an expensive-looking black box.

"Thanks, Pete."

I take the box and set it on the counter. *Ms. Aspen Albright* is written on the card's envelope. I hand it to her.

Aspen scrunches her forehead. "Who would send me something here?"

"What about your friends? Did you tell them about your promotion?"

"I did send them a group text." She pulls out the paper, and the color drains from her face.

"What is it?"

She hands it to me.

My beast awakens as I read the card:

ASPEN,

Thinking of you.

Wes

I CRUMPLE THE NOTE IN MY HAND, TRYING TO CONTAIN MY rage.

I'll kill him.

Before I can tell Aspen not to open it, she lifts the lid. Everything happens fast.

A huge rattlesnake lurches out of the box. It bites her bicep and she screams in pain.

I grab it around the neck, reach for a butcher knife, and slice its neck. I drop the remains in the box.

Aspen holds her arm, crouching on the floor, crying.

"My krasotka!"

"It hurts...it..." She grabs her throat, and saliva starts seeping out of her mouth. Her skin breaks out in a sweat. She gasps for breath, and her eyes roll.

"Krasotka!" My heart races. I pick her up and run to the office to find my cell. When I get to it, she's convulsing. I call the front desk and tell them to send the medical team up and to send 9-1-1 for backup.

As I wait, I've never been more scared. She lays lifeless in my arms. Her arm is swelling. I'm worried about the poison going into her heart.

It feels like time moves slowly. The medical team comes in with Adrian. They demand I release her. Adrian pulls me off her. She passes out.

On the way to the hospital, I stare at her on the stretcher, with tubes hooked up to her. I barely comprehend what the EMT is saying. The sirens for the ambulance are loud, but drowning it out is my inner beast repeating, *"I'm going to tear Wes Petrov apart."*

And then there's the part of me trying to hold it together that keeps saying, "Please don't die, my krasotka."

Aspen

"I WANT TO KNOW WHERE THAT BASTARD IS NOW," MAKSIM'S voice growls.

A beeping noise gets louder. I try to open my eyes, but everything feels groggy.

"Aspen," a familiar woman's voice says, but I can't pinpoint who it is.

"I don't care how dangerous it is. Tell me his location," Maksim barks.

Another woman says, "Maksim, you need to calm down."

"Anna's right. You're going to get kicked out of here," Dmitri states.

I try to move, but pain shoots through my arm. "Ow," I moan.

Someone strokes my forehead. "Don't move too fast."

"My krasotka!" Bergamot and cardamom flare in my nostrils. Maksim's lips touch mine. He sternly murmurs, "Wake up, please."

I struggle and fight the bright lights but finally get my eyes to stay open.

Maksim leans over me and strokes my cheek. His eyes glisten. "Krasotka. I'm so sorry."

"Wh..." I clear my throat. "What happened?"

His face darkens. "Wes sent a snake. It bit you. You don't remember?"

I shut my eyes, and it comes flying back to me. I try to move my arm again, but it's too painful. I wince.

"Take it easy."

I glance past him. His brothers, Adrian, Anna, and Nora, stand near the bed. "Sorry to ruin your night," I joke.

Anna's face is serious. "Don't be silly. He could have killed you."

Maksim growls. It's low, but I hear it.

I reach for his cheek. Pain shoots through me again. I blurt out, "Why does this hurt so bad?"

"Snakebites and poison tend to do that," Nora teases.

"Not funny," Maksim snaps.

"Chill," Boris barks and tightens his arm around Nora.

Maksim takes a deep breath and closes his eyes. "Sorry."

MAGGIE COLE

"You're forgiven," Nora replies.

"Why does he get forgiven easily, and you hold grudges against me forever?" Boris asks.

She tilts her head up and smirks.

His expression turns cocky. He slowly looks at every part of her, lingering on her breasts and lower body, then drags his finger over her collarbone.

I don't miss the way her chest fills with air or the slight flush in her face.

The vision of them getting it on at the wedding fills my mind, and I refocus on Maksim. "Can we go home?"

"Let me tell the doctor you're awake."

He hesitates then gently kisses me. He quietly admits, "You scared me."

I smile. "I'm okay. At least, I think. I won't have anything long term from this, will I?"

"I can help answer that," a man's voice says.

I glance at the door. An older man with a bald head, maybe in his sixties, comes closer. He smiles. "I'm Dr. Granger. How are you feeling?"

"My arm's sore when I move it."

"We can increase the pain meds."

He addresses Maksim. "Mind if I examine my patient?"

Maksim rises and steps back.

"We'll go to the waiting room," Anna says, and everyone but Maksim follows her.

He circles the bed so he's on the other side of me.

"You're lucky. Your wound is shallow, and you got medical attention quickly. I suspect you won't have long-term issues, but you'll want to keep a close eye on things."

I release a big breath. "Okay. What kind of things?"

"Sometimes patients can have a permanent neurological injury from hypoxic encephalopathy or respiratory paralysis or cardiac arrest. Amputations sometimes occur as well."

"What?" I cry out and look at Maksim.

His face hardens, and his eyes turn icy.

The doctor pats my hand. "I don't think you'll have to worry about any of these issues. But I'll put down what to watch out for on your discharge papers."

"All right. Can I go home now?"

"We should be able to get you out of here soon. But expect pain and swelling for at least three weeks, possibly up to nine months."

"Nine months?" Maksim seethes.

The doctor jerks back.

"Maksim," I quietly say and try to take his hand, but my arm hurts again, and I wince.

"Let me increase your I.V. drip." The doctor fidgets with it, and I get a surge of warmth in my veins.

"Whoo!" I laugh.

The doctor grins. "You're probably going to get tired. Or in rare cases, the opposite will happen, and you won't be able to sleep."

I yawn and start to drift off as the doctor and Maksim talk. When I wake up, I'm in Maksim's bed. My arm is throbbing, and my mouth is dry.

It's dark, except for the glow of the fireplace. The shades cover the windows. I glance next to me, and the bed is made.

What time is it?

Where is Maksim?

I slowly get up and go out to the main room.

"Get it done, Obrecht. I'm getting impatient. He tried to kill her. My krasotka could have long-term damage." Maksim paces the room and runs his hand in his hair then stops and stares out at the lit-up buildings.

I should tell him I'm here, but for some reason, I don't. Instead, I lean against the doorframe. I'm not hidden. If Maksim turns, he will see me, but I don't voluntarily tell him I'm here.

"I want him taken to the garage, stripped, and hung by his toes. The thugs who were with him in the club, I want them there, too."

My heart races. I get dizzy and grab onto the wall to steady myself.

Maksim turns. "Get it done," he barks, hangs up, and rushes to my side.

"My krasotka. You should be resting."

"What day is it?"

"Saturday."

"I've been asleep since Friday night?"

"Yes. Come sit down." He leads me to the couch and pulls me onto his lap. "How is your arm?"

I curl up, keeping my bad arm away from him. "It's throbbing."

He kisses my head. "You have a few more hours until your next pain pill. Let me take you back to bed."

"No. Let me stay with you."

He sighs. "I'm sorry I didn't protect you."

I tilt my head. "You couldn't have done anything."

"I shouldn't have allowed you to open that box. It should never have even gotten in here."

"Maksim, don't do this. It's my fault I'm on Wes's radar. I was the one who went to the Cat's Meow. I let him take me in his VIP room."

Maksim's face hardens, and he focuses on the ceiling. "You are mine to protect. This isn't your fault."

"Please, let's not play the blame game." I rest my head back on his shoulder. Several minutes pass, and he strokes my hair. I ask, "What is the garage?"

He freezes.

I straddle him so he can't hide from me. "Tell me."

His blue eyes turn to ice. The rise and fall of his chest increases. "It's a building my brothers and I own."

How much do I ask him?

I clear my throat. My mouth is so dry, my throat hurts when I speak. My heart beats faster. "You kill men there?"

"Yes."

I nod. "Where is it?"

"I will never tell you. You do not need to know this. It is for your protection."

I can't argue with him. What would be the reason I would ever need to know? "Okay."

He holds my face. "He will pay for what he did to you, my krasotka. I will watch him take his last breath. And his thugs will not receive my mercy, either."

We stay silent for several moments. The old me would never believe I could sit on a man's lap and not feel scared or guilty or that it was wrong to kill someone. But I'm not the same woman I used to be. Everything has changed. The switch flipped in me. All I care about is that Maksim does whatever he's going to without getting hurt.

I swallow hard. "Do I need to worry about your safety?"

Relief crosses his face. "No."

"You were worried I was judging you? Or would tell you not to?"

"Sometimes, your silence makes my thoughts spiral."

"Listen to me closely, Maksim."

He raises his eyebrows.

"The only thing I care about is you. I trust you completely. So whatever you feel is necessary, do. I will never stand in your way."

"Thank you for—"

I put my finger over his lips. "But you are a calculated man. Do not act with your heart on this. Use your head. I cannot stand to lose you in any way." My stomach growls.

"Let me make you some food, my krasotka."

"Promise me first. I want to know you'll not let your feelings for me affect your ability to deal with this as you normally would."

He tucks my hair behind my ear then locks eyes with mine. "I'm a ruthless man. I promise you, I will deal with Wes Petrov and his thugs by tapping into every piece of me the devil owns."

33

Maksim

IN THE MIDDLE OF THE NIGHT, MY PHONE RINGS. I PICK IT UP quickly so I don't wake Aspen then get out of bed and go into the bathroom. "Obrecht."

"They're here."

Oxygen slowly fills my lungs, and my bear comes out of hibernation. I crack my neck. "All of them?"

"Yes."

"Was it discreet?"

Obrecht's voice lowers. "Are you trying to insult me?"

"Point taken. Don't leave. I'll be there shortly." I hang up and call Boris.

"Maksim," he answers.

"Did I wake you?"

He snorts. "Nope."

"We need to meet Obrecht at the garage."

Boris takes a deep, controlled inhale. "You going to let me have some fun?"

"Sure. I'll give you one."

"Good. I won't hold it against you for pulling me out of my warm bed."

Nora groans.

Boris says something muffled to her.

"If Nora's awake, can she come over and stay with Aspen? She's asleep, and I don't want her here by herself."

"Sure. You call the others yet?"

"No."

"Call Dmitri. I'll phone Sergey."

"Thanks." As soon as I hang up, I ring Dmitri.

"Hello?" Anna answers.

"Sorry to wake you."

Concern laces her voice. "Maksim, you okay?"

"Yes. Is Dmitri awake?"

"No, but I'm assuming you need me to wake him?"

"Please."

"Hold on."

I wait for several minutes. I go to the doorway and glance back at my bed. My krasotka is still sleeping.

Dmitri clears his voice. "Maksim."

I go back into the bathroom. "We need to meet Obrecht at the garage."

"How many?"

"Five."

"The others know?"

"Boris was calling Sergey. Nora is coming to stay with Aspen."

"Hold on," Dmitri replies. Then his muffled voice says, "Anna, I have to go out. Nora is going to stay with Aspen. I think you should go there. I don't know how long we'll be."

They murmur, and Dmitri comes back on the line. "I'm going to drop Anna off."

"All right."

I get changed and write Aspen a letter while I'm waiting for the others to arrive.

My Krasotka,

I'll be home as soon as I can, but it might not be for several days. Please do not worry. Nora and Anna are staying, but invite your friends over to help pass the time if you want.

Love,

Maksim

I SET THE LETTER ON MY PILLOW AND KISS HER FOREHEAD. SHE stirs but doesn't open her eyes. I creep out of the room and shut the door.

Boris and Nora arrive first. He takes her bag to one of the guest rooms and comes back out right as Dmitri and Anna arrive.

Anna hugs me. "Aspen still asleep?"

"Yes. Her pain meds make her tired. Her pills are on the counter, and I've been keeping a chart when I gave her them in case this came up."

Anna's lips twitch. "Aww. Aren't you sweet? I always knew you were a softy though."

"Funny."

She yawns. "Okay. I'm going to bed. Be careful. All of you."

Dmitri picks up her suitcase and follows her down the hall.

Sergey steps into the penthouse. He's dressed in all black like the rest of us. "Why do I feel this will be almost as good as slicing Zamir?"

"Wes is mine."

Sergey's eyes darken. "They're still Petrovs."

"I hate we have to pin this on Rossi's men. I'd love nothing more than to see Zamir's face when he finds out his beloved son is dead, and it was at the hands of the Ivanovs."

I point in Boris's face. "Zamir cannot know this was us. Not yet. We must pin this on the Rossis."

Boris licks his lips, and his face hardens. "Yet is the key word I'm going to hang on to. When the time is right, and I finally end Zamir's life, he will know the wrath we have brought down on his family."

"Just like how he destroyed ours," Sergey mutters.

"We are not destroyed. Don't ever give Zamir that," Dmitri says, entering the room.

"Let's go," I order.

We leave. Adrian drives us to the garage. We all go inside and meet Obrecht.

He sits at the desk, his feet on the table, tapping the pads of his long fingers together. His dress shirt has several buttons unfastened. A black suit coat is thrown on the side of the desk, and his gun is next to it.

"Brother," Adrian says, and they pat each other on the back. Obrecht is four years older than Adrian. Our fathers were brothers.

"New tattoo?" Obrecht asks and points to an abstract design on Adrian's arm.

"Few days ago."

"Slick."

Adrian nods. "How did you get them here?"

"Don't ask. I gotta tell you, though, Zamir didn't pass his brains on to Wes."

"Why? What happened?" I ask.

"Took me a day to convince his thug I just got off a plane from the motherland. Told him his grandfather sent me. Within an hour his boy led him straight into my trap."

"You're shitting me?" I mutter.

Obrecht arrogantly shakes his head. He rubs his five-o'clock shadow, and his dark eyes focus on me. "You know the balance is going to be way off."

"We'll just have to fix it," Boris responds.

"The Rossis will have significantly more leverage. And Zamir will go hard recruiting."

"We will deal with it. I will not let that piece of shit get away with what he did to my krasotka. And those other thugs will pay for touching her friends as well."

Adrian snorts. "Apparently they don't know how to abide by 'no' either."

Sergey's eyes turn to slits. "What happened?"

"Skylar said she told the bastard who's lap she was on to let her go before we got in the room. He responded by shoving his hand up her shirt."

Obrecht holds his hands in the air. "I wasn't suggesting we let them go. I'm just stating the facts."

"Enough of the chitchat," I say. The visual I have in my head of the snake biting Aspen's arm and her lifeless body in my arms drives every ounce of rage I have within me. I open the door and step into the back room.

Wes, his three thugs who were with him, and the bodyguard Adrian had by the throat, all hang in the air naked, upside down.

Their faces are red from the blood rushing to their heads, and two of them already pissed themselves.

I put on my gloves, take my knife out, and walk up to Wes.

"You mother-fucking, Ivanov," he spouts in Russian.

I'm tempted to spit on him, but then my DNA would be on him. Instead, I kick him in the face with my boot.

He screams, and blood spurts everywhere. I'm positive I broke his nose and possibly his cheekbone.

"Should I slice your balls first?" I run my blade over his scrotum, tearing at the skin so blood wells to the surface. The thing about that area of the body is, once you draw blood, it never seems to stop. As Zamir taught me, controlling the depth of your blade so you only nick the skin is important for drawn-out torture sessions.

"Argh!" he cries out.

I drag my knife down his torso, cutting him open but only slightly, leaving a trail of blood. I crouch down in front of his face. "You think snakes are bad? Hmm?"

He spits more Russian out, calling me all kinds of names.

I don't flinch and press the flat part of my blade over his eye. "They say snakes come from the devil. But the man who cuts the devil in two is no man. He's Satan himself. That's me. I grabbed your snake with my bare hand and chopped it in two. The serpent *you* sent to destroy *my* krasotka."

Piss dribbles down his body and mixes with the blood. He winces, I'm assuming from the sting of his urine on his open skin. He attempts a few more insults, but they come out weak.

"*Your father* created me. Every lesson he ever taught, I will demonstrate on you. I'm going to torture you as long as I can then I'm going to stretch it out some more. You'll be begging me to kill you. Before I am through, rats will feed on you in your final moments. Dogs will chew on your bones. And I will watch every moment, listening to you scream."

The room fills with the men shouting in Russian. I step back and turn to my brothers, Adrian, and Obrecht. Boris hands me a shot of vodka. I hold it high in the air. "We have waited patiently to seek revenge on the Petrovs. This is the beginning of the end."

"Nostrovia," they all say, hold their glasses in the air, then drink their shots.

"Nostrovia," I repeat, enjoying the burn of the liquid as it slides down my throat.

I return to Wes. His chest shakes. I crouch down. "And the entire time, you can think of my krasotka. You had no right to her. She would never have been yours. You should have known a woman of her caliber was too good for you."

He attempts to spit at me, but it barely flies out of his mouth.

I promised my krasotka I would use every piece of the devil within me. She wanted me not to make decisions tonight with my heart. But everything about this involves my heart. It's to avenge what Wes did to her. It's for what Zamir put my family through. It's to acknowledge everything the Petrovs represent and how they make their mark on the world.

I lean into his ear. "My krasotka told me to be extra ruthless with you."

34

Aspen

I wake up Sunday morning and read Maksim's note. It leaves me unsettled, but I try to trust in his words. I get changed, put on a brave face, and go out to the kitchen.

Anna and Nora are making breakfast. They both stop and assess me, as if waiting to see if I'm going to lose it.

"Coffee?" Anna asks.

"Sure."

Nora takes a waffle off the iron. "Are you a picky eater?"

"No."

She smiles. "Great. Have a seat. Everything is ready, and your medication says you should take it with food."

I grab a platter with eggs, bacon, and potatoes on it and set it on the table.

"I feel like I'm at a restaurant right now."

Nora laughs and hands me my pills. "Boris burns so many calories a day from his workouts and boxing regimen, he's pretty much always hungry. My brothers, but especially Killian, are the same way, so I'm used to it. I'm the only girl so..." She holds her hands in the air and shrugs.

"Well, thanks for cooking." I load up my plate and take a sip of coffee.

Anna and Nora continue to stare at me.

"I'm trying not to ask you anything right now since you're both waiting for me to freak out."

Anna shakes her head. "No. I'm glad you're not. But are you okay? The first time Dmitri...well, the first time he was gone..." She glances at Nora.

"It was a different situation. They are at the garage and in full control of this one. We have nothing to worry about," Nora states.

My insides flip. I take another sip of coffee. "Both of you know when things happen then? The details and such?"

"Yes and no. I trust Dmitri to tell me what I need to know. Some things aren't important for him to disclose, or it could hurt me," Anna says.

"Same," Nora follows.

"And neither of you are freaking out right now because?"

"They're at the garage. No one gets in or out unless they want them to," Nora states.

"Do you know where it's at?"

"No," Anna says at the same time Nora says, "Yes."

Anna and I gape at her.

She looks away.

"How do you know where it's at?" Anna asks.

Nora blows out a breath of air and closes her eyes.

"Nora?"

"I've been there."

"When?"

She stays quiet.

Something about it makes me shudder.

Anna's voice grows firmer. "Nora, why would Boris take you there?"

She shuts her eyes again. "Please drop it. I shouldn't have said anything. I... I assumed you knew where it was."

"No. Dmitri said it's in my best interest I don't know the location."

"Maksim told me that, too."

A tear falls down Nora's cheek, and she quickly wipes it away. "Please. Don't tell Dmitri or Maksim I know where it is, then."

Would Boris keep something from his brothers?

Why was she there?

Anna hugs her. "Okay. Don't worry. We won't say anything, will we, Aspen?"

"No."

Nora sniffles and wipes her eye. "Thanks."

Uncomfortable silence fills the room. I drink my coffee, staring out the window. "I'm sorry. I have to ask. So why aren't we worried?"

Nora sits up straighter. "Oh. Sorry. The garage is the best place for them in this situation. It's when they aren't there, and they don't control the environment, that we worry."

"Do they go often?" I ask.

"No," Anna says.

"Not to the garage," Nora adds.

"Or to other places," Anna assures me.

Nora looks the other way.

What is she hiding?

I don't ask her. "Okay. Thank you for talking to me about this."

"Anytime you want to talk about this, call me. It's hard. You can't talk to your other friends about it, can you?" Anna says.

"No. What do you tell your friends when they ask questions?"

Nora grunts. "My friends all know I'm an O'Malley. There are no questions. It's just assumed I'm involved with dangerous things."

"But you aren't?" I blurt out, and my face reddens. "Sorry... I didn't—"

"It's okay. Part of my family is into...well, let's say some nasty things. My brothers are supposed to stay out of it."

"Supposed to?"

Nora drinks her water. "That's all I want to say about it."

"Okay."

Anna clears her throat. "My brother has his assumptions. Dmitri had it out with him and set him straight. And I made it clear to Chase if he made me choose, I wouldn't pick him, I would choose Dmitri. So he doesn't talk to me about it anymore. He and Dmitri have become close. I skirt around things with my friends."

"I did that with mine," I admit.

"They aren't dumb. But they don't know the facts, either," Anna says.

"You mean, what Zamir did to them as children?"

Disgust fills Anna's face. She nods.

Nora's eyes glisten, and she blinks and stares out the window. Her voice wavers. "I knew all of them before Zamir ever dug his claws into them."

Anna puts her hand on Nora's back.

Nora turns back to us and bravely smiles. "Anna said you want to redecorate the penthouse?"

"I wouldn't say that exactly."

She furrows her brows. "No?"

I point at the black couch. "Maksim asked me to move in. I told Maksim I wanted the couch that his ex was lying half-naked on"—I nod to Anna—"the night of your wedding, by the way..."

She gapes.

"And the bed she's been in replaced. That's it. He's the one who thought we should change everything up so it's fresh and only us."

"I think that's sweet," Anna says.

I can't help but smile. "It is. I already love his house though. So I'm not sure what to do. I told him we could buy the exact same pieces, I just wanted to know she hadn't touched them."

"I don't blame you. I never understood what Maksim saw in her," Nora says.

"Me, either, but I only met her a few times. She didn't talk much," Anna says.

"At least she didn't act annoyed with him every time he talked or moved an inch the way the French Prima Donna does." Nora angrily shakes her head.

I groan. "You're not an Eloise fan, either?"

"I told Boris the next time she acts like she's better than Sergey, I'm going to tell her where to go."

"Why is he with her?" I ask.

"I don't know. But he needs to dump her ass and find someone else."

He kissed Kora.

"Wait, I do have a question."

Nora raises her eyebrows.

"Maksim made it sound like they aren't exclusive?"

"They aren't," Anna says.

"He still needs to throw her ass to the curb," Nora says.

"Agreed. So, do you want to talk about some design ideas?" Anna asks.

"Sure. What else are we going to do?"

"Nothing. We're on lockdown whenever the Ivanov wrath is being dished out," Nora says.

"What?" I ask.

Anna's eyes widen. "They want to make sure we're safe. We stay put."

"Oh. Okay." I take another deep breath.

"But everything is fine. Should we look at some things? I can pull some websites up?"

"Sure," I tell her.

The day goes slow. I try not to think about Maksim, but I can't stop worrying. When nighttime comes, and he still isn't home, I cave. "Where is he?"

"She did so well," Nora says to Anna, her lips twitching.

Anna puts her arm around me. "They are okay. It's the garage. We need to be patient. It's likely they won't be home tonight."

"Really?"

"Yes."

I stay calm, and when it turns dark, I take my medicine and fall asleep. Monday morning arrives, and the bed next to me is still empty and perfectly made. Tears form in my eyes, but I push my face into my pillow.

I need to be strong. Maksim is doing this, and it's my fault.

Since I'm still in pain and on lots of medication, I call in to work sick. Plus, Anna and Nora said we're on lockdown.

The more time that passes, the more I start to freak out. I pace the penthouse with my insides churning. "Where are they?"

I pick up my phone, but Anna takes it. "You can't call him."

"Why? If they're in control of the environment, why can't I?"

"You just can't."

I go to bed when it's after midnight. I haven't taken a pain pill all day, so I pop one in my mouth and fall asleep.

The comforting scent of bergamot and cardamom flares in my nostrils. Maksim's strong arms slide under me.

"Mmm." I snuggle into his warm flesh, sliding my hand into his chest hair. "I love you," I whisper.

"I love you, too, krasotka. So much," his deep voice murmurs in my ear.

"You feel so real."

He chuckles. "I am real."

I freeze and open my eyes. I slowly look up and hold his face in my hands. "Are you really here? You're done?"

He kisses me. "Yes."

Tears fall. "I'm sorry. I was so worried. It's been so long."

He pulls me on top of him. "Shh. Everything is going to be okay now."

"Did...did you..."

"He's gone. We will never speak his name again."

I nod and cry some more. "Okay."

He wraps his arms around me and strokes my hair.

I inhale deeply. "You smell so good."

"You were asleep. I showered."

I hold his cheek again. "And you...you're okay?"

"As long as I have you, my krasotka."

"You do. As long as you want me, you have me."

He kisses me. Every ounce of need and desire he has for me is in it.

In return, I give him all of me. Every piece that desperately craves him. Every morsel of my soul that only feels alive with him. I give him any and every part I can.

He's the only man who has ever truly loved me. He'll fight, and kill, and even die for me. I would never have thought those three things would be the definition of true love, but how can it not be?

I slide upon him and stare into his icy-blue eyes. "I'm glad what happened in Vegas didn't stay in Vegas."

His lips twitch. "I made a mistake."

My chest tightens. "What do you mean?"

"I shouldn't have asked you to move in."

"Wh..." I slide off him and lay on my back. A lump forms in my throat. "Oh. Um..."

He rolls on top of me and strokes my hair. "I want you to marry me."

"What?"

"I don't want you to only move in. I want to marry you. Everything that's mine, I want to be yours. I don't want to see Albright after your name. I want to see Ivanov. Mrs. Maksim Ivanov. I want everyone to know you belong to me, and I belong to you." He slides a ring on my finger.

I can barely see it, but he could give me a gummy ring and I'd be happy.

I blink, but the tears escape anyway. "Are you really asking me?"

His finger traces my lips. "Yes. There's nothing I want more."

I nod and whisper, "Me, too."

"Is that a yes?"

"Yes."

He smiles, and his eyes twinkle. In his deep, Russian accent, he says, "Good. Now use your sexy little body and show me how much you love me."

EPILOGUE

MC

Maksim

One Month Later

ASPEN'S EYES GLISTEN. "I CAN'T BELIEVE MY DAD KNEW WHO I was again. He even remembered your name after I introduced you. It was a half hour later."

"Yes. He seems to be happy, too?"

She puts her hand on my cheek. "Yes. I can never thank you enough. The difference in only three weeks is incredible. The new home is really helping him."

I kiss her then say, "No more thank-yous. It's your father. And I enjoy our visits. Especially the look on your face when he asks if you want a fried bologna sandwich."

Aspen groans but wears a huge grin. And her happiness is my top priority.

The car stops. I point out the window. "Anna's here."

We get out of the car and exchange greetings with Anna. Her face lights up. "Are you ready?"

"Yes. I'm so excited," Aspen admits.

I lead Aspen and Anna into the building and up to the roof. It's not built out yet, but the purpose is to look at the space and view.

"What do you think, my krasotka?"

Aspen looks around the rooftop. "I think it's perfect."

"You do?"

Her eyes shine. "Yes. This is incredible! Anna, how did you think of this?"

Anna smiles. "When I was designing it, I thought it was an amazing view. I couldn't stop thinking about it. If my wedding hadn't been in the winter, I would have done it. It's awesome and a unique location."

"Absolutely." Aspen turns to me. "And we can do this here?"

I chuckle. "If this is what you want, this is what you will have." Anna designed a rooftop garden we will soon be implementing on a building we just finished. The view overlooks Lake Michigan, and the night view is just as impressive. Glass surrounds the roof, providing shelter from the wind. Anna already has a design she showed Aspen based on what they discussed.

Aspen looks around. "This is perfect."

Anna claps. "Awesome. I can work with the wedding planner to coordinate everything."

My krasotka beams. "Thanks."

Anna hugs Aspen. "I've gotta run. But I'll call you later."

"Great. Thank you again."

"No problem."

I kiss Anna on the cheek and hug her. "Thank you."

She winks. "Of course." She leaves.

I lead Aspen to the edge of the roof. I stand behind her and put my arms around her waist. I point to a section in the far north corner. "See those buildings? Past the green billboard?"

"Yes."

"My father helped build them."

She looks up in surprise. "Your dad was in construction?"

"Among other things. Every time we passed those buildings, he proudly reminded us he built them."

She leans back into my chest, gazing at the rundown structures. "I'm glad you have some good memories of your childhood."

"I was twenty-two when everything changed. My childhood was full of good memories. We struggled for money, but our home was full of love. Boris and Dmitri were older, so they have better memories. Sergey, well, his are mixed," I admit, feeling guilty about my brother having his childhood ripped away.

Aspen hooks her hands on my thighs. She tilts her head and continues to take in the view.

I put my hands over hers. "This always reminds me of our first night in Vegas."

"Mmm." She tilts her head up. "It was a pretty good night, huh?"

I wiggle my eyebrows. "One of the best." I lean down and kiss her.

She spins and slides her hands into my hair, kissing me back.

My phone rings. I groan. "Sorry. It's Boris. He's at the job site." We only had Sam do one day of cleanup so we weren't in violation of our city contract. Then we moved him to the north lot Sergey suggested. We started the project to keep our men working. Today, they are back on the old city lot, cleaning it out.

"Go ahead." Aspen smiles, lighting up my world.

I keep her pulled close to me. "Boris."

His voice is agitated. "We have a problem."

"What is it?"

"Maksim..."

"Boris, what's wrong?"

"You need to get over here."

"I'm on my way. Tell me what is going on."

"There're bodies."

"Bodies?" I take Aspen's hand and walk toward the stairs.

"Everywhere. All over the city lot. They had to stop digging. The detectives need to talk to all of us. I explained we just bought the property."

"Shit. This is going to hold up our development. How long are the police estimating it will take to remove the remains?"

The line goes silent.

"Are you still there?"

"Maksim, they're Russian bodies. Their bones are branded."

My blood turns cold. I stop mid-step.

"Maksim—"

"Boris, I'm on my way. Stay off the phone." I hang up.

"What's wrong?" Aspen asks.

Once a year, Boris pays his debt.

"He always has me brand their bones while they are still alive." Boris's voice after one of his annual "debt payoffs" with Zamir fills my mind.

"They dug up bodies on the city lot. I think it's Zamir's graveyard. We need to go."

Horror fills Aspen's face. "Maksim—"

"I don't know the details yet. Let's try not to jump to conclusions." I put my hand on her back and lead her through the building. When we get in the car, I pull her onto my lap, holding her close.

I finally have everything I've ever wanted in my life. I cannot lose any of my brothers.

We pull up to the job site and Boris slides into the car. Out of all of us, Boris is the calm one. He never looks worried. But right now, he is agitated.

"I need to know," I say.

He glances at Aspen then me. "These bodies have been planted. Zamir is trying to set me up."

"We always cover our tracks so nothing is ever traceable."

Boris swallows hard. "What if it is?"

The hairs on my arms stand up. "Why would it be?"

"I don't know, Maksim. If he's trying to set us up, don't you think they would be traceable?"

The ruthless beast in me claws at my gut, wanting to kill Zamir. It's no different from the feeling I've had whenever I think of Zamir. But this time, killing Zamir may not solve our problems.

I reach forward and hold my brother's cheeks. "We don't assume anything. Let's take this a step at a time. Now is not the time to lose your ability to stay calm and use your head."

Boris takes a deep breath and nods, but I've never seen the worry in his eyes like right now.

I hope you loved Ruthless Stranger! Want to read Ruthless Stranger 1.5 for free? Flip now!

RUTHLESS STRANGER 1.5 - FREE!

Can't get enough of Maksim and Aspen? Want to see what her friends have in store for her on her wedding day? Download the super steamy bonus scene for one more mind-blowing chapter! Click here!

If you're on a paperback go to: https://dl. bookfunnel.com/6sgighwpqx

If you have any issues downloading this, please contact pa4maggie@gmail.com.

Come back when you're done to find out what's happening with Boris and Nora in Broken Fighter, book two in Mafia Wars!

He's my brother's best friend, a Russian killer, and boxer with no ties to the O'Malley crime family—my family.

I've loved and studied him forever. I witnessed him change when I was only thirteen. He doesn't know I'm aware he kills, or how I notice once a year he gets a call and disappears.

For years we fight our attraction. One night, we succumb to our desire.

Every touch he gives me is electric. Each moment deepens our addiction.

If it were only us, life would be perfect.

Unfortunately, our union creates targets on our backs from multiple crime families. It puts our loved ones at greater risk.

Wars from each of our enemies now plague the O'Malleys and Ivanovs.

Every time the annual call comes to pay off his debt, he crumbles further. I'm not sure how much more either of us can take.

He's my broken fighter...

READ BROKEN FIGHTER - FREE ON KINDLE UNLIMITED

BORIS

BROKEN FIGHTER PROLOGUE

Boris Ivanov

THE FIRST TIME I MADE A DEAL WITH THE DEVIL, IT WAS TO save my mother. In the end, it didn't matter. Satan still won.

The second time, I tried to buy my brothers' and my freedom. All the agreement did was create a mirage about our lives, who we were deep down, and who still owns us.

After that chain of events, you would think my conscience would have disappeared. That all reason not to take whatever or whoever I wanted would no longer exist.

But the voice in my head still told me not to make her mine. From the first time I saw her as anything but my best friend Killian's sister, that voice has screamed at me to stay far away from her.

But how do you stay away from the girl you've always known? The one whose face you can't escape all day, who seems to be the only person on earth who can look into your soul? The one who never denies what you're capable of but still doesn't run?

We had a conversation once. I caught her in a weak moment. She drank too much at her older brother Sean's funeral. Killian and his other brothers were too distraught to notice she went off. I followed her, worried. She told me she could see the killer in my eyes and not from the boxing ring. "You've killed men. I saw the change in you years ago. You were seventeen."

I stood in shock, then tried to cover it up. "You don't know what you're talking about. You're drunk."

She sadly laughed, and through tears, said, "I'm an O'Malley. I see all the males in my family morph from boys to men and what that means. And no matter what you do, Boris Ivanov, I see you. The real you."

To this day, I'm unsure why I did what I did next. Touching her opened Pandora's box. It was a dip into the well of pleasure I craved but couldn't have. I tucked her silky red hair behind her ear and possessively cupped her porcelain cheeks, as if she were mine, wiping her tears with my thumbs. "Then you should want to stay away from me."

More tears fell as her green eyes pierced mine. "Why?"

"You know why."

"I've tried. You keep coming in to see me." It was an intoxicated admission. She wouldn't have ever said it if she weren't. But there it was, out in the open. I wasn't imagining things. She wanted me as much as I was dying to have her. And she knew I wasn't only coming to see Killian.

If she hadn't been drunk, I wouldn't have stopped myself. The craving I had for her deepened with the unhidden truth. I would have put my mouth over her hot, juicy one and tasted everything I had been obsessing over.

I was still fighting the lust within me when the sound of the metal door shutting, followed by my brother clearing his throat, pulled me out of my dilemma. I released her and spun.

"Killian's looking for you," Dmitri said. I avoided his "what the hell are you doing expression" and went inside. But the damage was done. I had gotten too close to everything I had banned myself from having. I told myself to stay away from her. I couldn't even last twenty-four hours. The next day, I went straight back to Nora's pub, pretending to look for Killian, knowing he wouldn't be there but she would.

Time did nothing to quench our attraction. Anything with her was taboo in too many ways. Our families shouldn't mix, besides Killian and my friendship. It doesn't matter if she and her brothers try to stay out of the O'Malley crime family business. It's in their blood. No matter how hard they try to escape it, I see what's coming.

And while my brothers may think our legitimate businesses don't make us a crime family, how different is what we do compared to the mob? Zamir Petrov may rule the Russian mafia, but we're the Ivanovs. No one, except Zamir, messes with us, or there are consequences.

But the hands of fate shouldn't mix an Irish angel and a Russian killer. So I told myself over and over to stay away from her.

It did no good.

Almost every night, I went to her pub to meet up with Killian. He might as well have been another brother to me. While I played the charade I was there to hang out with him, both Nora and I knew the truth. Never once did I miss the faint blush when she saw me. Or her quiet, breathy gasps when I touched her when no one else was looking. God help me when I caught her green eyes sneaking a glance my way.

I'm an expert at torturing men, but Nora could have had a black belt in tormenting me. We were in a constant state of purgatory, and I couldn't climb out. Every morning, I'd wake up and tell myself today is the day to forget about her. Then I'd go right back into the Garden of Eden, where she might as well have been holding the apple to my mouth.

I never bit into it. I somehow found the strength not to press my lips on her creamy white skin or lush mouth I'd imagined doing every inappropriate thing possible with.

But Nora watched me. Closer than I ever realized. The one night a year and days after it I always stayed away from her and everyone else was for a reason.

Patience is a gift I've always used to my advantage. If you can't trust yourself to stay in control, you shouldn't step in front of temptation, especially one you've obsessed over for years.

Nora O'Malley found my weak spot, took my restraint, and broke it in two. She's a virus that won't leave my body, no matter how much she or I attempted to distance ourselves.

Sometimes, what you think you're doing for the right reasons, leads to consequences you never imagined. I shouldn't have ever allowed her to try and stay away from me after that night. The moment Cormac Byrne stepped foot in her pub and set his eyes on her, I saw it. I took him outside and warned him she was off-limits. Nora and I might not have been able to be with each other, but nothing about Cormac was good enough to even be near her.

Men like him never listen, though. His eyes revealed everything I needed to know. Why Killian and his brothers never saw it, I don't understand. They should have. Their blood boils with rage the way mine does. Men have taken their last breath under their hands. So why they encouraged Cormac to be with Nora and never saw what I did still baffles me.

The only reason I see is he's Irish. Or I should say he was.

One thing you should never do is look the devil in the eye and try to take what's his. If Satan tells you something, you listen. Any attempt to overthrow him better be ironclad. Cormac was too arrogant to understand this.

I'd always lived by this rule until recently. My brothers and I started a war between the two largest crime families. There were many reasons to do it. But taking down Zamir Petrov, the man who made me into the sinner I am, might not have been the best idea I ever had.

Bad things happen when you lose patience and act with emotions. Nora O'Malley makes my head spin so fast I struggle to breathe most days. Mixing it with the hatred I have for Zamir might be my downfall.

Every man I've ever killed on Zamir's orders, he made me brand while they were still alive. Not their skin, but their bones. A symbol of Satanism, a five-pointed star with a circle around it. I never told my brothers. The less they know about what happens when Zamir calls on me his one time a year, the better.

419

Now, there's no hiding it. All the proof of my skills is in the city lot my brothers and I bought. I didn't know. A dated newspaper from several months ago is in a plastic bag. It's from my last kill. And it's proof Zamir planted them. He's intentionally sending me a message.

There's only three reasons Zamir would bury those bones for the land cleanup crew to find. First, he wants to change the deal on our debt and pull my brothers and me back into his control.

Or, he could know we killed his son, Wes.

But the last possibility might mean I made the biggest mistake of my life. It could be far worse than living the rest of our lives under his dictatorship.

The only other explanation is he knows we started the war. One thing Zamir doesn't have is a heart. Greed rules his soul. Messing with his empire was a risk we knew going in, but one I don't want to see the consequences of.

No matter which reason it is, everyone my brothers and I love is in more danger than ever before. No one and no form of sadistic punishment is off-limits to Zamir. My gut says the first person he would go after is Nora. She's also carrying my child. The things he would do to her burn in my mind all day long.

I need to kill him before he's able to get to her. But the problem with Zamir is he's a ghost. He appears and vanishes when he chooses.

As much as I've tried to not let the devil consume me, I'm going to have to. The only way to overpower evil is to pour more gasoline on the fire. Zamir taught me that.

But how do you become more sadistic than the devil himself without harming the person you love the most? Can you really keep everything good in your life when you morph into everything you despise?

Chills dig into my bones. I gaze over at Nora, curled up in my arms, sleeping peacefully, and I can't help wonder if part of Zamir's plan is to not only destroy my brothers and me, but torture us in a different way. If I tap into the monster existing within me, the one I've never fully let loose, how will it be possible for Nora to still love me?

READ BROKEN FIGHTER - FREE ON KINDLE UNLIMITED

ALL IN BOXSET

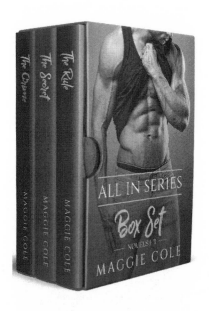

Three page-turning, interconnected stand-alone romance novels with HEA's!! Get ready to fall in love with the characters. Billionaires. Professional athletes. New York City. Twist, turns, and danger lurking everywhere. The only option for these couples is to go ALL IN...with a little help from their friends. EXTRA STEAM INCLUDED!

Grab it now! READ FREE IN KINDLE UNLIMITED!

CAN I ASK YOU A HUGE FAVOR?

Would you be willing to leave me a review?

I would be forever grateful as one positive review on Amazon is like buying the book a hundred times! Reader support is the lifeblood for Indie authors and provides us the feedback we need to give readers what they want in future stories!

Your positive review means the world to me! So thank you from the bottom of my heart!

CLICK TO REVIEW

MORE BY MAGGIE COLE

Mafia Wars - A Dark Mafia Series (Series Five)

Wondering where Dmitri and Anna's story is? Mafia Wars is a spinoff from the last book in the It's Complicated series, Wrapped In Perfection.

Ruthless Stranger (Maksim's Story) - Book One

Broken Fighter (Boris's Story) - Book Two

Cruel Enforcer (Sergey's Story) - Book Three

Vicious Protector (Adrian's Story) - Book Four

Savage Tracker (Obrecht's Story) - Book Five

Behind Closed Doors (Series Four - Former Military Now International Rescue Alpha Studs)

Depths of Destruction - Book One

Marks of Rebellion - Book Two

Haze of Obedience - Book Three

Cavern of Silence - Book Four

Stains of Desire - Book Five

Risks of Temptation - Book Six

Together We Stand Series (Series Three - Family Saga)

Kiss of Redemption- Book One

Sins of Justice - Book Two

Acts of Manipulation - Book Three

Web of Betrayal - Book Four

Masks of Devotion - Book Five

Roots of Vengeance - Book Six

It's Complicated Series (Series Two - Chicago Billionaires)

Crossing the Line - Book One

Don't Forget Me - Book Two

Committed to You - Book Three

More Than Paper - Book Four

Sins of the Father - Book Five

Wrapped In Perfection - Book Six

All In Series (Series One - New York Billionaires)

The Rule - Book One

The Secret - Book Two

The Crime - Book Three

The Lie - Book Four

The Trap - Book Five

The Gamble - Book Six

STAND ALONE NOVELLA

JUDGE ME NOT - A Billionaire Single Mom Christmas Novella

ABOUT THE AUTHOR

Amazon Bestselling Author

Maggie Cole is committed to bringing her readers alphalicious book boyfriends. She's been called the "literary master of steamy romance." Her books are full of raw emotion, suspense, and will always keep you wanting more. She is a masterful storyteller of contemporary romance and loves writing about broken people who rise above the ashes.

She lives in Florida with her husband, son, and dog. She loves sunshine, wine, and hanging out with friends.

Her current series were written in the order below:

- All In (Stand alones with entwined characters)

- It's Complicated (Stand alones with entwined characters)
- Together We Stand (Brooks Family Saga - read in order)
- Behind Closed Doors (Read in order)
- Mafia Wars (Ivanovs and O'Malleys)

Maggie Cole's Newsletter
Sign up here!

Hang Out with Maggie in Her Reader Group
Maggie Cole's Romance Addicts

Follow for Giveaways
Facebook Maggie Cole

Instagram
@maggiecoleauthor

Complete Works on Amazon
Follow Maggie's Amazon Author Page

Book Trailers
Follow Maggie on YouTube

Are you a Blogger and want to join my ARC team?
Signup now!

Feedback or suggestions?
Email: authormaggiecole@gmail.com

Made in the USA
Middletown, DE
25 May 2021

40366470R00257